THE THIEF'S ANGEL

CAROLINE LEE

COPYRIGHT

Copyright © 2020, Caroline Lee
Caroline@CarolineLeeRomance.com

ALL RIGHTS RESERVED. This book contains material protected under International and Federal Copyright Laws and Treaties. Any unauthorized reprint or use of this material is prohibited. No part of this book may be reproduced or transmitted in any form or by any means, electronic or mechanical, including photocopying, recording, or by any information storage and retrieval system without express written permission from the author.

First edition: 2020

This work is made available in e-book format by Amazon Kindle at www.amazon.com

Printing/manufacturing information for this book may be found on the last page

Cover: EDHGraphics

~

For the brains of the operation, the team's nerds, who delight in the never-ending acquisition of knowledge.

~

Because...
Omnia dicta fortiora si dicta Latina.

~

PROLOGUE

"Do ye really think he's guilty?"

Lady Rosalind Forbes had been staring out the window of the small solar, but her friend's whispered question jerked her out of her contemplation.

When she turned, Court was watching her with such anguish, such *confusion* in her eyes, Rosa didn't have to ask who she meant.

There was only one man she *could* mean.

Cam—Cameron Fraser—was the man who had raised Court, treating her the way a cherished older brother might.

He was also the one Rosa had damned.

She dropped her gaze to her hands clasped in front of her and gave her friend her shoulder.

"Aye," she said simply, allowing her own sorrow to seep into her voice, "there's nae other logical explanation."

Cameron Fraser was guilty of treason.

Rosa *knew* her mind worked differently, and she could see the forgotten details.

Nay.

Nay, she couldn't actually *see* them, could she?

But *Deus enim per singular*: God is in the details.

She had the ability to understand things not everyone else could; and the details, the clues, all added up to point to a Fraser of high standing.

It wasn't Ross Fraser; Court had vouched for him.

And Mellie's investigation proved Laird Lachlan Fraser was likewise innocent.

That only left Lachlan's younger brother, who'd been missing for years.

Cam.

Court cursed and smacked her open palm with her bow. "I'm going back out to look for him."

Rosa nodded and risked a glance at her heartsick friend. "That is likely wise."

All three of their team had been out looking for the man since he'd saved Mellie's life. Now that they knew he was here in Scone, and that he was the mastermind of the plot against the King and Queen, they were determined to hunt him down.

As her fellow Angel turned to leave the small room, Rosa reached out and placed a hand on her arm. "Court—"

Courtney had never been overly emotional, but her eyes were angry when she switched her gaze to Rosa.

Dropping her hand away, Rosa sighed. "I'm sorry," she whispered. "I didnae mean to hurt ye."

"Oh, Rosalind," Court said in a low voice. Then she sighed and reached forward, wrapping Rosa in a strong hug. "I'm no' angered at ye. I'm angered at *him* for doing something so *stupid*. I thought he had honor."

There was nothing Rosa could do except hug her friend in return and pray, when they caught, tried, and executed Cameron Fraser, her friend wouldn't be too devastated.

"I'm going to find him," Court stated again, as she pulled

away, her expression determined. "I'm going to find him and beat his arse."

There was the Court she knew.

Rosa's lips twitched as she nodded. "Aye, and I'll help."

Gesturing at the low-cut gown Mellie had found for Rosa, Court frowned. "Are ye going out looking like that?"

With a sigh, Rosa tried to pull the neckline up higher. "Ye ken Mellie's sense of humor. She thinks dressing me as a whore is hilarious."

If she were honest with herself, Rosa didn't mind the disguises too much.

She might not act the whore, but it was a boon when it came to getting close to men. They underestimated her because she was so small.

Her dark skin often drew some attention, but as far as her being dangerous—since she didn't look strong enough to squash a bug—she was often dismissed.

But she *was* strong enough to squash a bug—and larger creatures too—and Rosa had learned to accept the boon of her suspects' underestimation.

Court nodded firmly. "Funny it may be, but remember to use yer weapon if ye get into trouble."

Instinctively, Rosa touched the place on her inner wrist where her steel lengths rested, ready to protect herself. When Court saw her movement, she nodded once more, in approval this time.

"Good hunting to ye, Rosalind."

There was no joy in this search.

Rosa sighed. "Good hunting, my friend," she repeated grimly.

The Angels had their mission.

CHAPTER 1

Scone, 1320

The touch was so slight, most men wouldn't have noticed the wee hand darting into their purses as they paused among the foot traffic waiting to cross the street.

Cam wasn't most men.

With a wry grin, his hand darted around and clasped tightly onto the wrist of the young pickpocket, dragging the small body up and forward. "There's naught for ye in there."

The child—only a few years younger than Cam himself had been when he'd started picking pockets—began to struggle and curse. Cam retaliated by lifting the dirty urchin higher.

"Ye're a lass?" her dark hair hung in straggly hanks around her face, and the filthy tunic she was wearing might've been a dress.

"What of it?"

Her foot lashed out, catching him in his knee, but he didn't release her. Instead, glancing about, he dragged her to the shadows of the warehouse they stood beside mainly to get her out of the way of the dockworkers and fishmongers, who were pushing their heavy carts up and down the street.

The wharfs along the River Tay were a busy place, and dangerous for a man who didn't know how to keep his money close and his wits about him.

Reaching relative safety, he yanked the urchin before him again, forcing her up on her tiptoes as he studied her: Cheeks sunken with hunger, hair and clothes smelling and appearing as though they hadn't been washed since Hogmanay…but her eyes weren't quite sharp enough, bitter enough. Here was a lass who hadn't always had to steal for her food.

But there was desperation in those eyes right now as her struggles grew frantic, and Cam understood. She had no way of knowing if he planned on hurting her in retaliation or turning her over to the watchman…or worse.

His jaw tightened. He knew all about the *or worse* options a child this young could encounter.

"What's yer name?" he barked.

Her chin came up mulishly. "What's it to ye?"

He shook her slightly. "I'm going to let ye go, lass, but not afore I teach ye a lesson."

Her dark eyes widened in terror at his words, and he stifled a sigh, realizing how it must've sounded.

While she was busy being distracted, he reached under his tunic and groped for the hidden second purse which hung from his belt, and pulled out a coin.

"Tess," she blurted, and he nodded encouragingly, easing his hold on her just enough she could stand comfortably, but without letting her go.

"Well, Tess, I have a lesson for ye." He held up the gold

coin between the last two knuckles of his first fingers, the gleam catching in the sun, even here in the shadows.

She sucked in a breath, her eyes following the coin, and he knew she'd likely never had a prize this valuable.

"If I give ye this, what will ye do with it?" She darted a glance at him, and he saw the hesitation in her eyes, as she tried to guess the answer he sought. "Will ye give it to yer thief-master? Allow someone to take it off ye?"

Her jaw stuck out mulishly, and her shoulders hunched in on themselves. "I'll bring it to me mam. She's the one who needs it. No one else would ever ken about it." Her angry eyes flicked to his once more, then away, peering into the shadows as if looking for danger. "But I'll no' whore for it, if'n that's what ye're wanting."

If it *was* what he wanted, there was little a scraggly ten-year-old could do to stop him. With a sigh, he released her, and she darted back. But as he'd expected, she didn't go far. Not with the promise of that gold coin sparkling between them.

"Tess, if ye're caught again, by a man so much larger than ye, kick him in the bollocks. Then, if he doesnae release ye, when he's bent over, aim for his nose. A man with sense will drop whatever he's holding to keep from suffocating on his own blood."

Frowning, she shifted her weight, obviously torn between running off and humoring him. "Why would ye tell me that?"

"Because I told ye I'd teach ye a lesson."

With a flick of his wrist, the coin disappeared, the sleight of hand causing her expression to fall. But then he clapped his hands together, and just as quickly, the coin reappeared between the fingers of his other hand.

She scowled.

He grinned.

"And yer lesson, Tess, is that there are some prizes worth

fighting for. If ye have a plan for this coin, don' let anyone take it off ye, aye?"

Her little tongue darted across her dirty lips as she kept her eyes on the gold. "Aye," she whispered.

"And if someone bigger than ye tries to take it—or yer body, which is verra much worth fighting for—ye kick him in the bollocks and scream like hell. Ye understand?"

Her eyes had gone wide, drifting back to his face. Mutely, she nodded.

When he flipped her the coin, she grabbed it out of midair and bolted away from the docks.

Cam watched her go, his thumbs hooked in his belt, and wondered if he'd just caused more harm than good.

Did her mother really need the coin, or would the lassie turn it over to some ham-fisted master thief?

Someone like me?

With a sigh, he turned back along his original path and continued weaving his way through the sailors and merchants, all smelling of fish or tar, and money. The gold coin he'd given Tess would be easy enough to replace—not all men kept their purses hidden—and the sword he carried on his hip would deter any trouble.

Seeing an apple-seller kicking at the front wheel of his cart, Cam snatched a ripe fruit from the back and waited a few paces before biting into it.

There'd been a time when he'd been uncomfortable in a city like Scone, uncomfortable around this press of humanity and noise. He'd been raised a laird's son, one who liked to hunt and fish and ride. When he'd left, he'd managed to find a new home among the bandits—a group called the Red Hand—who occupied a stretch of woodland.

And then he'd become their master, collecting their takes, and distributing goods and favors. He'd sat in the center of his web and had done his best to lead his men with a firm hand, solid wisdom, and honor.

Even though they *were* a bunch of thieves.

With a smirk, he took another bite of the tart apple, his amblings taking him farther from the waterfront. *His* men knew he wouldn't tolerate rape, and any man who raised a hand to a child would have that hand removed. Whoever Tess's master was, he hoped the man treated the lassie with the same respect, or she'd be forced to learn some harsh lessons.

The same lessons Court had had to learn.

Suddenly, the fruit didn't taste quite so pleasant, and he tossed it away with a muttered curse.

Court.

The lassie he'd met when she'd been younger than Tess. The lassie he'd helped raise. The lassie he'd come to love as a sister.

The lassie he'd sent away when she'd started causing difficulty among his men.

The guilt still ate at him and explained why he'd learned to live so effortlessly in Scone. He had semi-respectable lodgings and connections, despite the way he gained his coin, and spent his days searching for information on her.

And he'd come close to finding her.

"Gangway! Move it!"

The cry came from behind him, and he stepped aside, even as he twisted his head to see the haggard-looking man standing on a brewer's cart slap the reins hard against his horse's flank. "Outta the way!"

Deciding he didn't need another confrontation, Cam ducked into an alley and watched the heavily laden cart trundle on to its destination. With a start, he realized he'd wandered into the better part of the city, and the palace wasn't all that far away.

He propped his arse against the rough boards of the shop behind him, rested his booted foot against a crate, and scrubbed a hand over his face.

Court.

She was in there, in that palace, somewhere. That's all he'd learned, all he had to show for the year he'd been there trying to find her.

When he'd discovered her whereabouts, he'd been thrilled to know she wasn't dead...but now it seemed as though she may well have been, as the distance between them felt almost as far away as Heaven would be.

Had she found another thief-master?

One who cared about her as much as he had?

Was she safe, or had she ended up dancing for the hangman, as she'd come so close to doing at least once before?

Ye'll never get yer filthy claws into her again, ye Red Hand scum!

The woman's whispered threat—accompanied by a knife at his throat—haunted him still.

Weeks ago, he'd caught a few of his men stealing, instead of keeping watch as he'd commanded, and when he'd intervened, their victim had seemed strangely familiar to him. Cam had asked the man for help finding Court, and the unseen female assailant had whispered those words to him from behind.

Of course, the man had then knocked him unconscious moments later, but Cam had been elated to discover proof Court was still alive. Alive, and obviously safe among loyal friends.

Movement at the head of the alley caught his attention, and he watched with some interest as a slight figure slipped around the corner into the shadows. When she saw him, she hesitated, then stepped closer.

Another pickpocket?

Nay, this lass held herself close—her arms around her middle, and her chin tucked against her chest—and was peeking up at him from beneath lowered lashes. She was skinny and dark, her gown unlaced to show too much skin, and her skirts cut high enough to catch a man's interest.

A whore then, and not a particularly successful one, judging by her hesitation. She looked as if she expected him to lash out at her, and he decided it was likely she had learned about a man's temper the hard way.

This is what Tess would grow up to be if she didn't learn to fight back.

The dismal thought, so soon after his other depressing musings, had Cam sighing in pity.

"Ye're new at this?" he asked the whore.

She started, her chin jerking up in what might've been a nod, before she huddled against herself once more and shuffled closer.

He sighed again. "Come here."

'Tis just my day for charity projects, I guess.

When she paused, he reached out and caught her elbow, gently tugging her closer. But he'd surprised her, and she stumbled into his arms. With a grunt, Cam caught her arms and settled her into the space between his legs, propping his arse against the wall behind him once more.

"Now then, let's see ye," he murmured.

When she didn't move, he tucked one finger under her chin and lifted her face…then sucked in a breath.

Saints above, but she's lovely!

The lass had the small, delicate build of a songbird or a fragile flower. Her skin was dark, her eyes darker still, and her black hair hung long and straight in a braid down her back. She watched him with those dark eyes wide, with something showing which wasn't quite fear in her expression.

Uncertainty?

Nay, she'd never attract customers like this.

Reaching over her shoulder, he pulled her braid forward, lying it across her chest. "Men like to imagine ye in bed, lass. They're no' going to pay money for someone all laced up, prim and proper." Dropping his fingertip, he traced the upper swells of her breast. "Ye've made a good start here, but ye must loosen yer hair if ye want to catch our attention."

The way she jerked at his touch, and the noise she made told him she wasn't yet comfortable in her new profession. Mayhap he could teach her to pick pockets instead.

Nay, ye cannae save them all.

"What's yer name, lass?"

Dark eyes flicked up to his, then settled on his chin.

"Rosa," she whispered in a feather-light voice.

"Rosa," he breathed reverently, dragging his fingertip lower, at the point where her shift parted to reveal the shadows between her breasts. The name fit her; a delicate petal amid the harshness of the world. "Loosen yer hair."

At his command, she took a deep breath and lifted her hands to her braid; her fingers fumbling with the leather tie. She didn't meet his eyes as she made short work of combing out her hair, then pulling it forward, as if using it to cover her breasts.

He clucked his tongue, brushed her hands out of the way, and reached for her locks himself. They felt smooth as water as her hair cascaded against his palm and smelled faintly of roses.

That, more than the knowledge this woman was for sale, sent a jolt of desire straight to his cock.

"No' many whores smell as good as ye, Rosa," he murmured, shifting so she was further bracketed between his legs. "But ye need to learn to be bolder. Look me in the eyes."

Dark lashes fluttered, but she did as he commanded,

lifting her gaze from his chin to his eyes. He saw indecision in her expression and offered her a quick grin. "Now tell me ye want me."

Her eyes grew wide. "Mi—milord?"

"Nay, donae call me that," he commanded, with a shake of his head. It'd been many years since the title had applied to him. "But calling a man *sir* will make his ego swell, along with his cock. Try it."

Something flashed in Rosa's dark eyes, as if his words had changed something important inside her. Her shoulders straightened, and her chin rose. "Aye, *sir*."

His lips twitched. "Excellent. Now, ye have me pressed against a wall, see? That puts ye in charge of the situation. Ye ken I have coin, because ye've seen my purse. Ye must make me believe ye want me. So what will ye do now?"

Before she had a chance to answer, Cam brushed her skin with his fingertips once more, liking the little shudder she gave. Had she been more experienced, he might've thought it feigned, but not *this* rose.

His lips curling further, he dragged his hand across her chest, his palm settling around one breast and squeezed, just slightly.

She gasped and jerked away, before swaying back toward him. His smile grew as he brushed one thumb against the bud of her nipple, hard beneath the wool of her kirtle, and she gave a little moan. Her tits were as small as the rest of her but filled his palm nicely.

Inside the trewes he wore, his cock jumped to attention.

What will ye do now?

The question hung between them, a challenge unanswered.

Until he dragged his thumb across her nipple again, and she moaned louder, then threw her arms around his neck and dragged his lips down to hers.

She looked like a rose, acted like a virgin, but she kissed like a woman who knew *exactly* what she wanted.

With a groan of his own, Cam surrendered to his surge of desire and wrapped his arms around her back, pulling her flush against him. His stiff cock, pressing against the leather of his trewes, rubbed against her belly. He knew she was standing on her toes to kiss him like this, and he shifted one hand down to her arse to lift her.

The little whimper she made against his mouth was enough to undo him, especially when her tongue tentatively probed at his lips. As he opened them and rewarded her boldness with a tender sortie of his own, he shifted so his leg supported more of her weight, allowing his hand freedom to caress her arse, then her side and tit once more.

The fingers of one of her hands curled in the overlong hair at the back of his neck, while her other hand played with his collar, then his neck itself.

When her tentative touch spread across his chest, he groaned against her lips and forced himself to pull away with a gasp.

Saints above!

He'd *never* kissed a whore with such enthusiasm before. And had never come so close to losing himself in his trewes either.

While she still panted, her dark eyes glazed with desire, he grabbed her hand still splayed across his chest and pulled it lower. When he cupped her palm around his stiff and desperate cock, she sucked in a breath and met his gaze, her eyes wide with surprise.

And somehow, he managed to get even *harder*.

"How much, lass?" he croaked in a harsh whisper. "Ye feel this? I was wrong about ye no' doing enough to entice a man; I'm damn near bursting. How much do ye want to wrap yer pretty lips around my cock? Or let me fuck ye up against the wall?"

Her lips parted; her breasts heaving with each frantic breath. When her tongue darted out to swipe across her lower lip, he *knew* she was calculating in her head, trying to figure out how much he could afford.

With the weight of gold in his hidden purse, he could meet nigh any amount she quoted him, and *would*, if it meant the chance to spend himself between her thighs!

She was going to say *aye*; he knew it!

But then she blinked, and that *something* in her eyes changed once again. She pushed against him, and only because it surprised him, he let her go so quickly, she stumbled backward.

Still breathing heavily, she lifted her fingertips to her lips, her dark eyes wide as she stared at him with that unidentifiable look.

Desire?

Shame?

Anger?

He shook his head, reaching for her. "Lass—" he began, but she darted out of his reach.

At the mouth of the alleyway, she paused in her flight and turned to glance back at him, pulling the shoulder of her gown back into place as she did.

He opened his mouth to—

What?

Call her back?

Apologize?

But before he could decide, she ducked her head and was gone, lost in the mass of humanity passing their private little oasis.

"*Shite.*"

Cam's head fell back against the wall behind him, and he

winced at the thud it made. Or mayhap he was wincing at his idiocy. He'd been rejected by whores a time or two—usually with a regretful smile on their part—so why in damnation did *this* make his bollocks ache so fierce?

With a sigh, he scrubbed his hand over his face and muttered, "Shite!" again. With his cock so hard, walking was going to be uncomfortable, and for the first time in a long while, he wished for his plaid.

Lachlan would have a plaid to borrow. A Fraser one at that.

The voice whispering inside his head had him frowning, even as he sank down on the crate and rested his elbows on his knees. He wanted to curse again, but wasn't sure if he'd be cursing himself, or the fates.

Lachlan.

As of only this past week, he'd finally learned the name of the man who'd confronted him in that alley all those weeks ago, and the reason why he looked so familiar.

He hadn't thought of the Frasers in years; it was easier that way. When he'd met the stranger with the eerie gray eyes, Cam hadn't once thought of his brother. But after the fight he'd helped win—the fight between his men, who'd been hired by another's coin, and Lachlan—Cam had done his best *not* to think of his brother.

'Twas the reason he was wandering through the worst parts of Scone, offering lessons and coin to pickpockets and whores alike.

But even now, with his cock throbbing and his ego smarting, Cam couldn't put the memory of those eyes—the same color he himself shared with his mother—behind him.

His brother Lachlan was here in Scone...and was the new laird of the Frasers.

And suddenly, Cam knew, if Lachlan was in Scone, he wanted to be far away from here. Just for a little while. Just until he could make sense of the jumble of emotions which had slammed back into him at hearing his brother's name.

Just until he knew if the Frasers were in good hands with Lachlan as their laird.

Just until he knew his responsibility to them was truly over.

Just until he could learn if Court needed his help.

Dropping his forehead into his hands, Cam whispered another curse.

Running again.

He had always run; it was what he did. When life got hard, he simply found a new life. Here in Scone, he'd been trying to fix his wrongs. But it was clear he couldn't manage to do that right now.

He needed to get away from here, and there was only one place he knew he would find the answers he was seeking: *An Torr.*

Home.

God help him.

CHAPTER 2

*W*as it possible her lips *still* tingled?
Her lips and...*other* areas?

Rosa sat on the window seat in the solar of the Queen of Scotland, staring out over Scone and the sea of humanity. But it was only on one man her thoughts were consumed with.

A man with piercing gray eyes and long blond hair and a smile which could melt steel. And when he issued his commands, his voice had done something deep inside her.

Of course, she hadn't spent the last five years with Mellie Lamond for *naught*. Simply knowing her teammate had been an education in itself, but Mellie had also given Rosa all sorts of pointers on *desire* and *lust* and words like *cock* and *bollocks*.

So she might be innocent, aye, but not *that* innocent.

And she knew *exactly* what she'd been feeling after allowing Cameron Fraser to kiss her senseless in the alleyway the day before.

Of course, if she were honest with herself, *she* was the one who had initiated that kiss. But the way he had been fondling her breast, the way he had been *looking* at her, the way he'd spoken to her as if she was much more worldly than she really was…well, it had all made her feel valuable.

Which was a problem these days.

"What do you think, Rosa?" Queen Elizabeth asked.

Her head jerked up, swinging around too quickly to seem innocent, and she didn't bother hiding her wince.

"About what?" she asked, trying to remember what they'd been speaking of.

Her fellow Angel, Court, made a noise which sounded suspiciously like a grunt, but the Queen narrowed her eyes.

"About the recent attempt on Robert's life."

Ah, yes.

Rosa closed her eyes, working her way back through the conversation going on while she'd been so distracted. It was a particular talent of hers—her memory—and would come in useful today.

Thank the Virgin.

"Is His Majesty certain the attack is related to the assassination attempt on ye?" She couldn't recall the details, but she could pretend. "Could it have been a disgruntled subject?"

Throwing up her hands, the Queen moved toward her desk. "*Anything* is possible, but who else would be behind the attempt, other than a disgruntled subject?"

"Good point," Court murmured.

"But surely he's faced threats like this afore?" Rosa shifted in her seat, irritated with herself because she still couldn't focus. "There's naught to say—"

It was Court who interrupted her, with a frown, saying, "Rosa, Andrew of Lovat *outright admitted* before we killed him, that the Queen's death would only be beneficial if Robert died as well. If a group of conspirators, noble or otherwise, wanted to put a Comyn back on the throne as Andrew had bragged, then they need Robert out of the way.

And they need to ensure Elizabeth doesn't bear any post-humous heirs."

"'Twould be inconvenient," Queen Elizabeth muttered, with a roll of her eyes as she settled herself behind her desk.

"Aye," Rosa admitted with a sigh. "I suppose we need to treat each threat against Robert as connected to the threat against Elizabeth."

Why was that so hard for her to concede?

Well, that was simple: she didn't *want* there to be more threats against either of the monarchs. She wanted this entire thing to be a hoax, and she wanted Cameron Fraser to be innocent.

But Cameron—or Cam, as Court had once known him as —*had* to be guilty. He was the only one left with any sort of connection his Uncle Andrew had spoken of, although even Rosa couldn't reason the estranged Fraser's motive.

'Twas why she and her team had been out looking for the man yesterday.

Only, *she'd* found him.

And so much more.

Focus!

She turned to face the Queen fully, doing her best to forget the feel of his fingers on her bare skin. "Have there been any more attempts? Or any new evidence about the murder?"

When Elizabeth looked to Court, the gruff Angel took over the briefing. "Naught more about Gillepatric's death. Ross and I examined the chamber, and it seems as though he'd been knifed by someone who kenned him."

"Nae signs of struggle?" Rosa murmured.

"None. Although he was dressed in a robe, as if meeting someone…intimately. He'd been dead for a while, by the time Mellie dragged Lachlan into the palace and told us Gillepatric had paid to have them killed." Her hand tightened around her ever-present bow as she shifted away from the wall. "Seems the Red Hand nae longer takes orders from Cam. He would never have allowed murder-for-hire when he was—"

Desperate to change the subject to *anything* besides they're main suspect, Rosa blurted, "And nae one has seen aught suspicious in the palace?"

Court glanced questioningly at the Queen, who sighed. "With Charlotte abed with the babe, our communication channels are in disarray, are they not?" She shook her head as she reached for a scroll on her desk. "Liam and his guard did intercept another intruder the night before the attack on Melisandre and Lachlan."

Court stepped forward and snatched up the scroll, then opened it and began reading. Her eyes moved slowly, having come into the skill of reading only within the last five years, at their leader Charlotte's insistence. Finally, with a muttered curse, she tossed it to Rosa and pierced the Queen with a glare.

"Ross mentioned naught of this, but he wouldnae have been on duty that eve. The intruder was killed too early to have been Gillepatric's murderer."

The Queen folded her hands on her lap and raised a brow at Court's accusatory tone, as if to state she wasn't at fault. As Court muttered a curse and looked away, Rosa lifted the scroll and pretended to read it.

"Rosa?"

At the Queen's prompting, the youngest Angel forced a smile and gave the judgment she knew her Monarch was looking for. "If we assume this attempt was related to the first, but not to Gillepatric's murder, then whoever is behind the entire scheme hasn't given up."

"And it *could* be related to the murder," Court pointed out as she folded her arms, "but 'twould mean another assailant.

'Tis why Ross isn't letting the Queen so much as bathe without a guard."

"Luckily, my Angels count as guards," the Queen murmured with a wry grin.

Rosa frowned down at the parchment she held open in her lap. The words blurred across the background, frustrating her. No matter how many times she pulled out one of her precious books, the verdict didn't improve: her eyesight was failing her.

And as soon as her fellow Angels—and the *Queen!*—discovered her decline, she'd become useless to them. Her spot on the team was guaranteed by her wits, her ability to understand the greater picture and her remarkable memory. Her entire life, she'd been able to remember things she'd read, almost perfectly.

But now, how could she hope to have a place on the team, when she couldn't read to *remember* anything?

"Rosa? Ye're no' still reading the report?"

At Court's prompt, Rosa jerked up to meet the concerned gaze of her teammate.

"Just thinking," Rosa lied with a bright smile. "With Liam tending to Charlotte and his son—as it should be!—who is in command of the Queen's Guard?"

"It should be Murdoch or Tearlach," Court offered with a shrug, "but since Ross's return, I think they're all deferring to him."

"'Tis good to have him back, eh, Courtney?" the Queen teased with a smile.

And—miracle of miracles!—the gruff Angel's lips twitched upward as well. "Aye, Yer Majesty. 'Tis."

Both Elizabeth and Rosa burst into chuckles at the rare sight, and Court rolled her eyes.

"Well, for the love of the saints, have Ross tell the rest of the Guard that, if there are any more assailants, they're to be taken *alive*. I'd like to question them," Rosa said.

Court's quick nod made Rosa appreciate how well her teammates knew of her talents. There weren't many places where a woman like her could be valued for her intellect, but here at the Queen's side, she'd found women just like her. Well, not *just like* her, but women with interesting talents of their own and were putting them to use.

Court had been raised as a thief by the Red Hand, but after some time spent in the gaol and preparing for her death by the hangman's noose, the Queen had saved her and offered her a place among the Angels. She was their leader on missions, because she had an understanding of their enemies the others lacked, and also because she was so deadly with her bow. She was the team's strength.

Melisandre was their heart. She was a seductress, aye, but more than that, she *understood* people. She understood how others felt and worked to give them what they wanted. For the five years she'd been an Angel, she'd been the one to, not only keep the peace, but work to *help* others.

If Court was the Angels' strength, and Mellie their heart, then Rosa was their mind. Her skills with weaponry weren't as advanced as her friends' skills were, but she could think her way through any problem, and that particular talent had proved to serve them well many times.

But soon, she'd be significantly less useful, and where would that leave the Angels?

With a sad smile, Rosa acknowledged Mellie would be leaving them before long as well. In Laird Lachlan Fraser, who they'd assumed had been behind the assassination attempt until just recently, she'd found a man—a *good* man—who valued Mellie for her heart. She'd always be an Angel of course, but soon, she'd also become Lady Fraser and would be needed at An Torr.

The knock on the door startled them all, but when Mellie slipped in with a smile, they relaxed. She was one of the few who could enter the Queen's solar without an invitation.

"Well? What news do you have?" Elizabeth asked.

"The man is *exhausting!*" Mellie said with a gasp, as she slumped into one of the chairs. Somehow, she managed to make even *that* look seductive.

The Queen rolled her eyes. "I know Lachlan isn't ready for *that*."

Mellie winked, then sighed. "Nay, much to my disappointment. But he's driving me mad checking on his mother and demanding to be let out of bed to hunt for his brother. I vow, the man doesnae ken how to rest."

"Lucky ye," murmured Court.

"Aye," Mellie drawled with a wink, "I will be."

Rosa interrupted their banter. "How *is* Lady Fraser?"

Mellie shrugged. "Ye were the last one to visit her this morn. Her attendants say she's resting well enough, although when she does wake, she speaks of her son."

"Cameron?" the Queen asked. "Or Lachlan?"

"*Cam*," Court corrected.

It was Mellie who straightened and frowned at their friend. "Court, I ken ye remember Cam fondly, but Andrew Fraser told us his clan is behind the attempts. And he spent all those years with Cam, aye? Lachlan is innocent, so Cameron *must* be the culprit."

Court scowled. "I'll believe it when I hear him confess."

"Have you had any luck tracking him down?" Queen Elizabeth asked.

Court shook her head. "Ross has men searching the city. And while he's on duty, the Angels split up to look for him as well."

"Lachlan damn near split his stitches trying to join us," Mellie added.

Their Queen rolled her eyes. "The man just escaped death in that attack, and he's ready to throw himself back into danger already?"

"An attack paid for by Gillepatric," Mellie reminded her.

"A *Fraser*," Elizabeth snapped back, "who is now dead due to an unknown hand."

"An attack which was thwarted by *Cam*," Court pointed out, "who saved Lachlan *and* Mellie's life. Why would he do that if he'd paid Gillepatric to have his own men turn against him?"

Queen Elizabeth frowned. "'Tis a puzzle."

Rosa nodded, something unknown holding her tongue. Aye, the Angels *had* gone looking for Cameron yesterday, but *she'd* actually found him.

She'd come here today with the intent of telling her teammates about her encounter in the alley with their prime suspect. Well, not *everything* about it, though Mellie would likely be able to infer enough so Rosa would have to put up with her teasing for weeks after.

Unconsciously, Rosa lifted her fingertips to her lips, the parchment still clutched in her other hand. She *swore* she could still feel his lips against hers.

Could still taste him.

Could still feel the heat which had pooled between her thighs at his touch.

Could still see his smile.

Aye, she'd planned on telling the Angels *most* of what had happened yesterday, but now, when it was time to do so, she simply couldn't.

Because Court was right: Cameron Fraser *was* their most likely suspect, but only if they took Andrew Fraser at his word. If he'd been lying or manipulating them through what he'd told Ross and Court, then Cameron *wasn't* a likely suspect, because he wouldn't have arranged an intermediary to pay his own men to attack his brother.

Unless the attack had nothing to do with the plot against the Crown?

Mayhap it had been some sort of vendetta against Lachlan?

Rosa frowned, her fingertips drumming against her lips as she jumped from one possibility to the next.

If Cameron was guilty, what would his motives be for either plot?

She couldn't see how someone in his position would benefit from a Comyn on the throne, unless he was merely a pawn in a much larger conspiracy.

The attack against his brother made more sense coming from a jealous and ambitious man, intent on taking the position of laird for himself.

But Cameron had done nothing to indicate he was that sort of man, based on what she knew of him. To hear Lachlan and Mellie tell it, he hadn't been home in close to fifteen years, which was *not* the activity of a man anxious to take control of the clan.

Her eyes widened as something else occurred to her.

Mellie had been the target.

Assuming her position as a Queen's Angel was unknown to most, why in the world would someone hire an assassin to kill *Mellie*?

Lachlan, aye, mayhap...but his betrothed?

"What are ye thinking, Rosa?" Mellie called out, and when Rosa blinked and looked across the room, the golden-haired Angel was eyeing her in speculation. "Ye only look like that when yer mind is putting it all together."

Wincing, Rosa dropped her hand from her lips and shook her head apologetically. "Nay, no' everything. But the two attacks..."

Court raised a brow. "Aye?"

"I've been viewing them as separate attacks. An assassination attempt—or two—against the Queen, and an ambush to kill Mellie. But I only just realized their similarities." Tucking the scroll under her leg to read later—when she *would* find a way—Rosa lifted her fingers and began ticking off points. "Both violent acts were perpetrated by members of the Red Hand, which means our culprit has some connection to that group. Both were attacks paid for by another source, according to Andrew Fraser at least." He'd claimed the Frasers had paid for the assassination, but she didn't bother reminding her team of that. "And both were attacks against the *wives*."

"What?" Mellie asked with a frown.

"Well"—Rosa waved dismissively at her friend—"*betrothed*, in yer case. My deductions, and Andrew's confession, both point to a likelihood that targeting Elizabeth is just a step to removing King Robert from power, aye? Because if she dies before him, assuming his death follows quickly, then there's no chance of a male heir." She waited until she saw their nods, even though the Queen's was reluctant, before continuing, "So what if Mellie was targeted for the same reason?"

Court stepped away from the wall and rolled her shoulders, then shot a glance at Mellie. "So she couldnae bear Lachlan a son?"

The way her knuckles tightened around the bow she'd picked up told Rosa she hated the idea of their friend in danger.

Rosa shrugged. "Mayhap someone"—she couldn't say Cameron's name—"plans to harm Lachlan. Or mayhap they just donae approve of Mellie as his mate. Or mayhap they donae want him to have an heir."

Mellie shifted forward in her chair as she clasped her hands in front of her and frowned. "Lachlan is verra much in love with his daughter. She's no' his heir, but he might've lived happily with just her in his life."

"So mayhap 'twas his betrothal to *you* which caused this person to jump to action?" Elizabeth murmured. "Once betrothed, there was a real threat of you bearing him a son. I am sorry, dear Melisandre."

When Mellie smiled wryly, it almost hid the fear in her eyes. "Don' be. I wouldnae change this for the world," she assured her, with a wink.

Rosa sighed and pinched the bridge of her nose, a habit which was useless as always. "I donae ken. I am sorry, these are just theories."

Planting her hands on her desk, Elizabeth stood. "'Tis more than we had a moment ago. I plan to visit with Charlotte and wee Roger this afternoon and will share Rosa's theories."

Rosa swallowed her relief; afraid it would show on her face.

Why *was* she relieved the Queen was dropping the subject of Cameron, and what the Angels had or had not found on their search?

She should've volunteered the information immediately.

But if she did, if she reported exactly how she'd followed him, and where she'd confronted him—only to have the confrontation turn entirely to his favor—then the guards would be able to track him down. Drag him to the dungeon. Interrogate him.

The man she'd met yesterday would resist, and they'd destroy him before he'd give the answers they needed.

But if *she* could find him again, if *she* could be the one to question him…?

Mayhap it was just hubris, but she believed she could unravel this knot.

And seeing him again mayhap meant *touching* him again.

Nay!

Nay, he was still their most likely culprit, and the *only* reason she would seek him out would be to get answers. And then she'd turn his location over to the guards.

"Yer Majesty, one more thing."

Mellie's hesitant words dragged Rosa's attention back to her friends. The Queen was preparing to exit, and since Court was on guard duty, she was standing at the ready. They both turned to the third Angel, who lifted her thumbnail to her teeth to chew on it, the way she always did when she was nervous.

"What is it, Mellie?" Rosa asked quietly.

" 'Tis Simone," Mellie said around her finger.

Lachlan's six-year-old natural daughter sounded as if she were both a hellion and a joy, according to what Mellie had described. He'd requested her presence for their wedding, which would be held in Scone.

"Aye?" Rosa prompted.

Blowing out a sigh, Mellie dropped her hand and slumped back in her chair. "We want her here, but with the threats against Lachlan—and me—and the possibility his own brother is behind everything"—she shook her head—"I cannae trust just anyone to go after her."

"And you cannot go to An Torr to fetch her because you need to watch over Lachlan," Queen Elizabeth guessed.

"I *could*," Mellie admitted, "but Lachlan doesnae want me out of his sight for too long. I had a hard enough time convincing him to stay abed while I went out on the search. With the Queen's Guard working double-shifts because of Charlotte's confinement and Liam's distraction, I donae ken…"

Court shrugged. "Rosalind can go." When all eyes swung toward her, she shrugged. "Ross and I are splitting guard duty for Elizabeth, and Mellie's busy with Lachlan. Rosa has the wits to fetch Simone, even without a large group of mounted men."

Mellie looked unconvinced. "She could *lead* a large group of mounted men."

With a sigh, Rosa accepted her new mission. As much as she wanted to be the one here in Scone looking for Cameron, her duty to her teammates came first. "Aye, but we'd only garner attention. But a lone nun, traveling with an acolyte to her Abbey, wouldnae be suspicious. I'll carry a disguise and have her trunks sent after."

Mellie held her gaze for a long moment, and Rosa could see the hesitation there. Her friend loved Simone as her own, and the thought of her unprotected was difficult to swallow. But Rosa merely lifted her chin and allowed her confidence to show.

Mayhap she couldnae *read* anymore, but she still had her wits. And while she wasnae as accomplished with a bow or blade as Court and Mellie were, she still had two sharp tricks up her sleeve.

She was an *Angel* after all.

It was the Queen who asked, "You are certain you can do this, Rosalind? Travel to An Torr alone and gather the lass? What if you run into difficulty?"

Rosa's lips twitched. "*Aut viam inveniam aut faciam.*"

Scowling, Court growled, "I *hate* it when ye speak in tongues."

The Queen, the most educated of them all, besides Rosa, lifted a brow regally. "If there is not a way, you will make one? Is that not attributed to someone famous?"

Rosa's bow was more than a little mocking. "Indeed. *I* just said it."

The other three women burst into chuckles, and when Rosa met Mellie's eyes, the other woman was smiling.

"Aright, dear friend. I trust ye with Lachlan's heart. The

part that doesnae belong to me, I mean. Should aught befall Simone..."

"She will arrive here whole and hearty in plenty of time for yer wedding to her da," Rosa promised.

And in plenty of time for Rosa to return in her search for the lassie's wayward uncle.

Who may or may not be guilty of treason.

It was Court who offered her hand, palm down. "Angels?"

Mellie stood and joined her by the door, grasping Court's forearm. "Angels."

Rosa hurried across the room, quick to wrap her fingers around Mellie's forearm, and felt Court's grip shift to hers, until they stood in an unbroken triangle.

The triangle was the strongest shape in architecture. It was what made their team so strong.

"Angels," Rosa whispered, wondering how much longer they'd all be together.

Without her talents, would she become useless to her team and relegated to a nunnery?

What would she do there, without her books?

Court's grip tightened on her arm, and she met the other woman's hard gaze. "Ye can do this, Rosa."

"Aye," Rosa agreed. "I can." She could still do this much, at least. "I make a good nun," she teased, reminding them of past disguises and missions.

With a grin, Mellie rolled her eyes. "Now we just need to get ye to stop *living* like one. A man between yer legs is one of—"

"I *knew* we could not have an entire briefing without the subject of sex coming up," the Queen interrupted from behind them.

As they broke apart, Mellie winked. "Yer Majesty, *coming up* is exactly what sex is all about—"

"Shut it," Court growled, but not before they could all see her lips twitching.

The Queen swept past them out the door, and Court followed. She glanced over her shoulder once, and Rosa saw certainty and *trust* in her gaze.

When Mellie pulled her into a quick hug, before hurrying out the door as well, Rosa felt her trust as well.

Aye, they trusted Rosa to fetch wee Simone, safe and sound.

But they'd also trusted her to hunt for Cameron and look what had happened! She'd found the man, and because of a few kisses and a few moments of ecstasy, she'd betrayed their trust.

With a groan, she sank into the chair Mellie had so recently vacated and dropped her head into her palms.

What had she done?

CHAPTER 3

*C*am's eyes followed the piece of painted wood bobbing in the waters of Loch Ness, enjoying the way his mind could just...*turn off* when he was fishing. Oh, there was strategy and an art to fishing, but there was also relaxation and peace.

And for now, he was watching the way a fat trout nosed suspiciously at the chunk of cheese dangling from his hook, and Cam realized he didn't care one way or the other if the fish took the bait. If it did, he'd have his luncheon early. If it didn't, he'd find an inn to sup at later.

Resting his shoulders against the large branch behind him, he let out a sigh and tipped his head back, enjoying the sun on his face as it filtered through the leaves.

This had been his favorite spot before he'd left An Torr fifteen years ago. Sometime in the past, a tall oak had fallen over, likely in one of their fierce summer storms. But instead of dying, the tree had adapted to its new location—and closer water source—by sending branches upward instead of outward. Ten-year-old Cameron had discovered the peaceful solitude a godsend during that time, and the trout who made their homes in the shadows of the branches were a pleasant bonus.

The fact the tree still remained, still offered a safe fishing perch and a place to breathe deeply, had been a welcome surprise.

He'd arrived in the village near An Torr that morning on foot to attract less attention. It had changed so much in the fifteen years he'd been gone, and he wasn't sure if he appreciated that fact or not.

On one hand, it made it easier to deal with the memories to think of this place as *different*...but on the other, he'd been holding onto his resentment for a long while, and having the place change so much was a bit deflating.

Wandering among the people, he felt like a stranger. He only recognized two people—Gorn, the smith, who seemed just as strong as the day Cameron had left, and Auld Peg, the blind fishwife. But neither they, nor anyone else, gave him a second glance. He'd kept his mantle pulled over his hair and his gaze down as he'd bought the cheese for today's bait.

And now he could sit and breathe and think about what he'd learned.

It seemed that Lachlan was a good laird, and wasn't *that* interesting?

"Who are ye?"

The petulant voice had him twisting around so fast, he almost fell from his perch. Throwing out a hand to brace himself, he gripped the pole in his other and glared at the wee sprite who stood on the shore with her hands on her hips.

"Shh! Ye'll scare the fish."

The lassie rolled her eyes and stomped her foot. "They're *my* fish, and ye're in *my* favorite fishing spot."

Cam didn't bother to hide the way his eyebrows rose at

her declaration, and he realized she had a pole gripped in one hand. "Ye've come here to fish then?"

She took a deep breath as she rolled her eyes. "Owen says Da says I can fish from the shore as much as I like, and he kens I'm here, and if I don' come back by mid-afternoon, he'll tell my nurse Ella I've been naughty, and then I'll get my arse paddled, but I don't think I will, even though Ella *is* a bore and doesnae think a lady ought to fish."

Nurse? Lady? Cam cocked his head at her, studying her pale hair and eyes. "Should ladies fish?"

The lassie shrugged. "If no', then I donae want to be a lady."

Cam's lips tugged upward at the honest answer. "Well, I like this spot fine, but ye can share it with me."

"*Ye* can share it with *me*, I suppose." She peered through the leaves at his perch. "Do ye think the tree will hold us both?"

His smile grew. "I'm auld, no' fat. Do *ye* think ye could manage the climb, being a *lady* and all?"

The curse she muttered was anything but ladylike, and he chuckled under his breath as she hiked up her skirts and scrambled up the angled tree trunk, her pole and bundle tucked into the crook of her arm.

When she reached his spot, he helped her step carefully over him, and watched with a hooded gaze as she settled herself against the next branch.

Contrary to her fear, the tree didn't dip any farther toward the water.

While he pretended to be interested in the trout—which her arrival definitely *had* scared off—he watched her as she prepared her line. He noticed her pale blonde hair and the smattering of freckles across her cheeks and nose. While she concentrated, her tongue poked out from between her lips.

She was a beauty, alright, and full of fire. Cam didn't have much experience with children—even the ones who'd found their way to the Red Hand had lost their innocence long ago—but decided he didn't mind this one so much.

"What are ye using?" she asked, nodding to where his cork bobbed serenely on the surface, the branches forming a little haven of calm among the waves.

"For bait?" He kept his voice low. "Cheese. Learned that trick a long time ago."

"Cheese?" She snorted as she baited her hook. "*Everyone* kens trout love worms the best. My grandmother says the fish I catch are almost as plump as the ones my uncle caught, and I use worms."

Cam nodded solemnly. "Sounds like high praise, but I don' like catching worms."

With a practiced flick, she tossed her line into the water beside his, then turned a pitying expression his way. "I understand. No' everyone is as brave as me." Before he could smile at her assumption, she leaned forward and dropped her voice, as if imparting a secret. "The trick is to get the cook to pull them out of his garden when he's out cutting herbs and drop them in Simone's worm barrel. That's me. I'm Simone."

Her eyes were gray.

She was still leaning toward him, staring intently, waiting for a response...and Cam's mouth had gone dry.

Her eyes were gray, and she was a lady. She had a nurse and a cook and had a bucket for her worms in the garden.

A horrible suspicion began to unfold in his mind.

Finally, he cleared his throat and dragged his gaze back to the water below. "Pleased to meet ye, Simone. I'm Cam."

"That's a nice name. Do ye have a clan? Ye're dressed like an Englishman—no plaid."

He cut his eyes toward her once more, intrigued by her energy and friendliness, despite himself. "Do ye ken much about Englishmen?" he asked, side-stepping the question.

"My Uncle James died at Loudon Hill fighting the English bastards," she said cheerfully, joggling her pole as she shifted forward to peer into the water. "Do ye think the trout will come back?"

He shrugged. "Sometimes the best part of fishing isnae *catching* the fish, but sitting and enjoying the peace and quiet."

"Quiet?" Snorting derisively, she leaned back once more. "Ye're obviously no' as good a fisher as I am. The best part of fishing *is* catching the fish. And making Grandmother pleased with me."

The way she added that last part, Cam didn't have any trouble imagining what this grandmother of hers must be like. Cold and hard to please.

Like Mother.

The suspicion was jumping up and down right now, waving eagerly to get his attention. He sighed, accepting he would have to ask.

"Who's yer parents, Simone?"

Her smile blossomed as her chin jerked up. "Da is Laird Fraser now," she said proudly. "He says he wasnae supposed to be, but he'll do the best damn job he can. Only he told me I'm no' supposed to remember he said the word damn."

Lachlan's daughter.

Cam swallowed, not sure why having his suspicions confirmed did such odd things to his insides. He was pleased his brother had started a family, especially since he seemed to not be following in their father or Hamish's footsteps.

But the way Cam's stomach knotted, he wondered if he was…jealous?

Lachlan was only a few years older than him and had been a good older brother. He'd been too old to be targeted by Hamish, but had been kind to Cam—*Cameron*—when they were lads.

When Cam had run, he hadn't thought of Lachlan any more than he'd thought of James or Mother or Hamish. Oh, he'd heard when Father had died, and Hamish had become laird. He'd said a little prayer for the Frasers then. And although he'd kept himself and the Red Hand out of the war against the English, he'd known when James had fallen, as well as when Hamish had died in that "accident" and Lachlan had taken over.

Aye, Cam's information network had kept him apprised of most of the goings-on at An Torr, but he hadn't really thought of these people as the *family* he'd once had.

Who now had family of their own, apparently.

He cleared his throat. "And yer mother?"

Simone blew a raspberry as she turned her attention back to her pole. "I donae ken her. She left when I was naught but a wee babe because she didnae love me enough."

What a horrible thing to teach a bairn!

"Ye mean she died?"

"Nay," she said, with a shake of her head. "She went back to her da, who married her off to some other unlucky bastard, Da says. Only I'm no' supposed to remember the word *bastard* either. But it's a fun word, is it no'? That's what I am, ye ken."

"A bastard?" Cam murmured, his lips twitching.

"Aye," she said cheerfully, shifting forward to peer into the water once more. "Da wasnae married to my mother, but he's going to be married *soon*. Mellie's a nice lady—she took me fishing and saved my life, ye ken—and I'm glad she'll be my mother. Look! There's a fat one!"

Her finger jabbed toward the shadows, but Cam didn't bother following her gaze. He was too busy picking through that muddle of information she'd managed to offload in one breath.

Mellie must be the lass who'd been at Lachlan's side last

week in the battle. The one who Rhys and Johnnie and the rest of them were supposed to *murder*.

Cam had lived the last fifteen years as a thief, and he had a slightly different view of right and wrong than he supposed his brother might. When he'd seen the commotion in that Scone square, he might've passed by, assuming the brawl was none of his business...until he realized who the assailants were.

The remnants of the Red Hand men he'd brought with him to Scone to hunt down Court.

And when he overheard Lachlan accuse those honorless bastards of taking money to kill a lass—the curvy, golden-haired beauty who'd been wielding a knife beside him—then Cam knew he couldn't *not* get involved.

And a good thing he had, or his own brother might not have survived, and Mellie would surely be long dead at the hands of his men. But instead, they were now both safe in Scone, with Lachlan recovering from his wound. Cam had ensured every single Red Hand member left in Scone was dead.

"Don' ye want to hear about how Mellie saved my life?"

Jerking his attention away from the ripples below, Cam eyed the lassie—his niece. She obviously didn't understand the appeal of *silence* while fishing, but he couldn't be irritated. She was a breath of fresh air to someone like him.

"Aye, tell me."

And so Simone launched into a convoluted tale of a storm, and the trout she'd caught, and how Mellie had rowed them to shore and found them shelter. Cam nodded and hummed whenever Simone paused to draw breath—which wasn't often—but her ramblings allowed his mind to wander.

Simone clearly loved Lachlan, and from what he'd seen last week, Mellie did as well. She'd not only protected his brother's back with her own blade, but he'd seen genuine anguish on her face when she saw his wound. The way she'd clutched him to her told Cam she was devoted to Lachlan.

And Cam was surprised to realize what that said about his brother. Lachlan must be a good man to inspire such love. And he only had to walk through An Torr this morning to understand the Fraser was a good laird as well; one who cared about his people's peace and prosperity.

The Frasers of Lovat deserved that.

And after the life Lachlan must've had at An Torr after Cam left, he surely deserved some happiness and love, and Cam was glad he'd gotten it.

One thought led to another, and when Simone finished her story—although it was hard to tell sometimes—he nudged the conversation where he wanted it to go.

"And yer grandmother?" he asked casually, as he reached out and snagged his line, tugging it upward to check on the bait. "What did she say about yer adventure?"

"*Bollocks!*"

Cam started, but the lassie's curse didn't seem directed at his question, because she suddenly began pulling in her line.

"Look!" she cried, jerking her chin down, "something took my bait!"

Cam thought it more likely the poor worm had gotten waterlogged and floated off, because the fish were hiding so deep after her loud description of her experience.

But Cam just hummed politely and began to untie his line, deciding he was done for the day.

While bent over her hook, trying to jam another worm on with her small fingers, Simone answered his question. "Grandmother wasnae here during the storm. Gillepatric—that's Da's advisor, only he's Grandmother's friend more than Da's—took her to Scone 'cause she wanted to go visiting. Da said we don' have to tell her."

Finished, she straightened, peering at her hook and bait critically.

Gillepatric.

Cam remembered one of his father's advisors by that name, but naught else about the man. But last week, during that battle in the square, Johnnie had said they'd been paid by a Gillepatric Fraser.

Why in damnation would Lachlan's advisor want his future wife dead?

Well, Simone wouldn't know, but there was plenty more he could learn from her.

"So yer grandmother wouldnae approve, eh?" Cam prompted casually.

The lassie made a rude noise in the back of her throat and tossed the hook and line into the water. "Grandmother doesnae approve of *anything* I do. Except she likes the fish I catch, I guess—almost as good as my Uncle Cameron's, she says. Da says I cannae call her a mean witch, but sometimes she is."

His hands curling into fists around his line, Cam nodded in sympathy.

Mother had always been…*difficult*. She'd lived in her own little world, and Cam had always wondered if she was half-mad. Mayhap 'twas the only way to survive being married to a brute like Michael Fraser for so long. She'd treated her sons reasonably well—Cam, as her youngest, had always seemed her favorite—but she'd been blind to their faults.

Like Cam's tendency to bend the rules to suit his desires. Or James' habit of hitting lasses. Or Hamish's choice of sexual partner, willing or no'.

And when Cam had worked up the bollocks to tell his parents about Hamish's depravity, they hadn't believed him. Mother had told him *her* son *couldn't* do something like that and had sent Cam to bed without supper.

He'd started making plans that very night to leave.

Aye, he wasn't surprised to learn Mother was still difficult.

So why was he just a little disappointed he wasn't going to be able to see her on his return to An Torr?

He dropped his line into his lap and scrubbed his hand across his face.

God's Teeth, but emotions were odd!

"Simone?" The call came from the distance. "Simone! Where in damnation are ye, lassie?"

Simone jerked upright, her feet scrambling beneath her to get purchase, while she swung her head toward the call.

Instinctive, Cam reached out to steady her. "Whoa—"

He was too late.

With a little shriek and arms flailing, she toppled off the trunk into the loch.

Muttering a curse, Cam dropped his homemade pole and line into the water and lurched forward. The water was shallow enough she had already popped up to the surface by the time he wrapped his legs around the tree, braced his shoulders, and reached his free hand down toward her.

Her hair was plastered to her, a wet curtain in her face. But she looked up when he called, "Here, lassie," and grinned.

And as her hand locked around his forearm, and he anchored himself to pull her up once more, he was grinning as well.

In only a few heartbeats, she was straddling the tree trunk in front of him, sopping wet and peering down at the water below. "I lost my pole."

"I did too." He shrugged. "But ye made enough commotion with the splashing around, there's likely nae fish left."

Using both of her hands to push her water-logged hair out of her face, she grinned up at him. "Aye, I scared 'em all out to the monster. She'll thank me for lunch!"

Cam rolled his eyes as he shifted his weight back along the trunk for safety. "Ye've heard those auld stories of the monster?"

"Aye!" she chirped enthusiastically. "Grandmother told me all about her. Said she'd feed *me* to the monster if I didnae eat my vegetables, but I donae like vegetables as much as brown bread and pies."

"Me too," muttered Cam as he reached the wider point of the tree and was able to tuck his feet under him to stand.

She wasn't far behind. "Ye like pies better than vegetables? Or yer grandmother told ye she'd have the monster punish ye too?"

"Both." Except it hadn't been his grandmother. And threatening to feed him to the monster wasn't the worst Mother had done.

He twisted, offering his hand to her as she picked her way along the trunk, holding one of the upright branches with one crooked elbow.

"Who was calling ye?" he asked.

As if on cue, her name came from the distance once more. "Simone? Are ye fishing again?"

"Aye!" she called back, letting go of the branch to cup her hand around her mouth. "In my spot!"

Hiding his grin at her enthusiasm, and the way she toddled precariously without any thought to her safety, Cam reached for her. He grabbed her under her arms and held her away from him as he picked his way along the trunk to the shoreline.

"I'll no' get ye *too* wet," Simone told him, giggling along the way.

"Ye'll get me plenty wet, ye wee water sprite."

When they reached land, she cocked her head to one side. "If I'm a water sprite, I want to ride the monster."

They'd reached safety, but still he held her. "Aye, lassie, ye could do that. Yer da would miss ye though."

Her solemn nod was accompanied with a too-piercing gray gaze. "I like ye, Cam."

"I like ye too," he admitted in a hoarse whisper.

God's Teeth, why was it so hard to make himself put her down?

Because she reminded him of Tessa and all the other lassies he'd helped over the years?

Or just one in particular?

Court had been Simone's age when she'd been sold to the Red Hand, and Cam had taken her under his protection. And whether she knew it or not, she was *still* under his protection, at least until he could ensure himself she was safe.

Had the lass with Lachlan—*Mellie*, he reminded himself—been the one to whisper in his ear before Lachlan had knocked him unconscious?

If so, mayhap this wee niece of his was the answer to finding Court.

"Simone!"

The call came from much closer, a man's voice, sounding angry.

Dropping the wet lassie, Cam whirled to place himself between her and the threat and eyeing the tree where he'd propped his sword before the fishing excursion. As the man came closer, he remembered where he was, and whispered a quiet curse as he tugged his mantle up to hide his face in its shadows.

But apparently, he needn't have bothered, because Simone darted out from around him to meet the newcomer.

"Owen! I fell in!"

The big, harried-looking man halted, eyeing her up and down. "I can see that. Did ye think to catch the trout with yer hands?"

"Nay, silly," she giggled. "I slipped. But Cam fished me out." She pointed over her shoulder. "He's my new friend."

The man—Owen?—hummed and took his time examining Cam, who had hunched over to look less of a threat. When Owen's gaze flicked to the sword and back, Cam hid his wince.

"Strangers are welcome on Fraser land, as long as ye look to cause nae trouble, *Cam*."

Tugging at the mantle's hood, a show of respect as well as to hide his face further, Cam did his best to appear unmemorable. "Just looking for a spot of fishing, milord."

Owen grunted. "I'm nae laird. Which is good, else I'd tan *this* one's arse for no' being with her nurse when I went looking for her."

Giggling again, Simone grabbed for the big man's hand. "Owen's Da's commander. He's in charge while Da is chasing after Mellie to make her his wife. Owen says Da's happier with Mellie around, although I donae ken why he winks and laughs after he says that. Owen says Da says—"

"Owen says ye're too smart for yer own good, lassie," the big man growled.

Simone sighed good-naturedly. "Aye, Da says that too."

"Come on." Owen tugged at the girl. "Yer father's sent an escort to take ye to Scone to be there for his wedding. I donae ken why he didnae send a whole regiment, but likely he kens more than I do. She says ye'll be safe with her."

As the Fraser commander led the lass back toward An Torr, Simone twisted to wave at Cam. "Goodbye! Thanks for talking to me and saving me!"

And Cam's lips tugged upward as he lifted his hand in return. "Goodbye, Simone," he whispered.

But Owen's words bothered him. Lachlan had sent an escort, and the commander was obviously worried it wasn't enough.

And who was the *she* he'd referenced?

Surely not Mellie, or he would've called her by name.

In a moment, Cam's next move was decided.

He'd come here to An Torr to get away, but in doing so, he'd met a niece he hadn't known existed, and had also had a realization about his goal in finding Court.

Lachlan—or at least, his betrothed—could be the key he needed to track down the lass he thought of as his little sister.

But more than that, he realized how much he could allow himself to care for Simone.

She couldn't come to harm, and wouldn't, as long as he had a single breath left in his body.

Decided, he strode for his sword, scooping it up and strapping it on in one move.

He'd head south, just far enough so the horse he planned on stealing wouldn't be tied to An Torr. From there, he'd be able to track Simone's party in order to ensure she met no danger while on her trip.

Once she was safe in Scone, he'd figure out how to make contact with Lachlan once more and ask for his help in finding Court.

After all, Lachlan owed him. Disregarding that punch to the jaw, Cam had saved his life last week and had fished his daughter out of the loch today. Aye, surely that warranted some information.

So to his surprise, as his long strides took him away from An Torr and toward the next step in his plan, Cam was smiling. He was heading back to Scone, and he would ensure Simone's safety, find Lachlan, and track down Court once he arrived.

And after he knew both Simone and Court were safe, he'd go find a tavern and buy an entire cask of whisky to drown these odd emotions wreaking havoc in his chest. Then he'd find a whore and bury himself between her legs until he forgot what it was to *feel.*

Mayhap he'd be able to track down that delicate flower, Rosa, again. Mayhap he could offer her his protection. 'Twould keep her sweetness safe and give him sole access to her tempting body any time he needed it. She'd welcome his coin as much as any other man's, he was certain.

He felt his cock stir and took a deep breath.

Aye, he had a plan, and he always worked better with plans.

Simone, Lachlan, Court.

Then, drinking, whoring and forgetting.

What could go wrong?

CHAPTER 4

Rosalind resisted the urge to sigh in frustration as she faced the two men before her. "*Because* we will attract far less attention if ye allow me to escort her, as yer laird commands." She gestured to the parchment in the hands of the older one, An Torr's seneschal, Martin. "Ye've read his letter."

Martin turned to the younger, burly man, who was An Torr's commander. "She is right, Owen. Laird Fraser claims Sister Rosa is capable of no' only escorting Simone to Scone on her own, but clever enough to come up with a ruse to fool any enemies."

Owen, who was in charge while Lachlan was in Scone, frowned. "And does he say what kind of enemies he's expecting?"

Rosa hid her wince behind a serene, nun-like expression as the two men argued. Within moments of meeting Owen, she'd decided not to mention the attack on Lachlan and Mellie. The man looked warlike enough—and seemed as if he cared about Simone enough—that he wouldn't allow the lass to go off alone if he knew the danger, no matter his laird's commands.

Finally, Owen threw up his hands. "*Fine*. I'll go fetch the lassie. She's likely fishing in the loch this morn." He jabbed a finger at Rosa. "*Ye* tell Martin everything ye need for this ruse of yers to ensure Simone is safe. I'll no' have Lachlan claiming I allowed his daughter to come to harm."

Rosa nodded demurely and waited for the big man to storm out, before turning to Martin with a smile. "Are ye willing to help, Sir Steward?"

The older man bobbed his head eagerly. "Tell me what I can do, Sister."

Taking a deep breath, she aligned her thoughts, then began to lay out her plan and reasons. "Simone willnae be in Scone for too long, but she will need baggage. A trunk, at least. Lach—I mean, Laird Fraser said his betrothed Millie will likely have need of some luggage as well, and he believed her maid, Brigit, is still here?"

When Martin nodded, she took it to mean all was as she'd planned.

"I would like ye to have Simone's trunk loaded with Mellie's trunk, along with Brigit, and mayhap even Simone's nurse, if she's available, and sent off to Scone right away. Before Simone and I leave."

"Why all that, Sister?"

" 'Tisnae all. I want ye to assign as many men as ye can to guard it, and I want a lassie to go along with them. Mayhap a daughter of one of the guards? Gossip travels faster than wildfire in the Highlands, and I want everyone to ken a baggage wagon left An Torr, heavily guarded, with a lassie. *If there is any danger to be met, she'd be well-guarded, aye?*"

This time, Martin's nod was thoughtful. "Aye... Gaspar has a daughter about Simone's age, and I'm sure he'd be keen to take her. Owen is in command of the men, but I could request he be sent as part of the guards."

"So ye accept my ruse?" she asked, her hands gripped tightly together in front of her.

" 'Tis a good plan. If there is danger, 'twill come to the baggage wagon and guards. Nae one would guess a nun traveling with a wee charge could be anything other than what they seem, if everyone assumes Simone is with her trunks."

Rosa exhaled on a pleased nod, glad the seneschal not only understood, but approved.

He gave a little bow. "If ye'll excuse me, Sister, I'll set Brigit and Simone's nurse to packing as quickly as possible."

With nothing better to do after the seneschal had scurried off, Rosa sank down onto one of the trestle table benches with a grateful sigh. It had been a hard ride from Scone, although she traded her horse for a mule before arriving in An Torr.

On the way back, she'd pick up her horse again. True, a nun and a bairn on a horse might attract slightly more attention than they would on a mule, but she'd be damned if she would wait the extra time a plodding mule would take to return them to Scone.

She wanted this mission over so she could go back to searching for Cameron Fraser.

Search for the man whose memory still made her thighs clench in anticipation.

"Are ye hungry, Sister?"

The question startled her back to the moment before she could slip away to her memories of *his* touch, and she turned to find a round, cheerful man holding an offering of bread, cheese and ale on a wooden plate.

Grateful, she took it with a smile. "Aye, and my thanks."

"Nae need, Sister," the man said with a smile as he backed away. "Just offer me a prayer here and there!"

She murmured her agreement before bending over her meal.

Deus meus!

These people thought she really was a nun, and her prayers were worth something. Half the time, Rosa was so absorbed in her studies, she forgot to say her prayers at all.

Or at least, she *used* to be that way. Soon, she'd be unable to study anything. There'd be naught left to do then *but* pray.

As she lifted the bread, the movement caused her bundle to shift. Under her scapular, she'd strapped a few necessities, her weapon, and one of her precious books, which she now pushed back into position. Nun she might be, but there were some things she refused to do without. And even if she couldn't actually read *Lanval*, it brought her comfort to hold the hand-written verse in the evenings and pull the words from her memory.

As she ate, she watched the bustle around her and was impressed. Her father's home was run the same way, thanks to her aunt. Mother had always been too focused on her books and scrolls—the same as Father—to care about running the keep. But Mother's sister had kept Rosa's childhood home in order and had made it a pleasant place to grow up.

From what little she'd heard about Lachlan's childhood, she suspected An Torr hadn't always been a pleasant place to live. But obviously Lachlan was a good laird, who cared for his people, and who was cared for in return.

But what of his brother?

Had Cameron enjoyed his childhood here?

Had he played here in the great hall?

Rosa didn't have to close her eyes to imagine a little blond-haired, gray-eyed lad running wild across these rushes, getting into mischief and fun with his brothers.

Had he eaten here at this very table?

What had made him leave?

Shaking her head, Rosa admitted the truth; she was becoming alarmingly obsessed with that man.

Who could blame me after that kiss?

Nay, it had been more than a kiss. She might be a virgin, but she was no innocent. *No one* could spend five years with Mellie without learning a thing or three about sex, and Rosa had recognized the feelings Cameron Fraser had unintentionally caused.

No' quite unintentional. He thought ye a whore and experienced, he did.

He'd expected her to *want* what he was offering, and to her surprise, she *did*.

And as soon as she got back to Scone, she'd hunt him down and get—

What?

Nay!

She dropped the bread to her plate and shook herself.

Nay, she'd return to Scone, hunt down Cameron Fraser, and get the answers she needed to solve this whole convoluted mess. If he was guilty of treason, she'd discover the truth and punish him.

Aye. Aye, she felt better with a plan.

"Here she is," came the exasperated voice behind her.

Rosa turned to see Owen holding the hand of a little girl with long, pale hair and freckles. She was peering at Rosa's disguise with trepidation, and she was soaking wet.

When Owen nudged her, the lassie dropped into an awkward curtsey.

"Greetings, Sister Rosa. I'm Simone Fraser," she all but whispered.

Oh dear.

Knowing this mission wouldn't succeed until Simone trusted her, Rosa turned on the bench so she was at eye level with the girl. "Hello, Simone," she said with a gentle and welcoming smile. "Yer father sent me to fetch ye back to Scone for his wedding. He'd like ye near him during the ceremony. Would ye like that?"

The girl let go of Owen's hand, who rolled his eyes and hurried off in another direction—likely to arrange her baggage's escort—and edged closer.

"Do ye ken Mellie?" she asked.

"I do. Mellie and I have been close friends for five years now. She told me ye're a smart little lassie, and she also told me all about yer adventure on the loch a few weeks back." Rosa made a show of peering at Simone's wet clothes. "But it looks as if ye've had another fishing adventure."

Sure enough, the girl broke into a sheepish grin as she brushed her hand down her soaked kirtle. "I went for a swim. No' on purpose."

Chuckling, Rosa stood, offering Simone her hand. "Well, in order for ye to travel safely to Scone with me, I need ye to wear a disguise. Why don' we get ye out of that wet dress, and I'll tell ye all about it?"

"A disguise?" Simone sounded intrigued as she placed her hand in Rosa's and allowed the woman to lead her toward the stairs. "Do ye ken much about disguises?"

Rosa was chuckling as they headed toward the lassie's chambers. "More than ye might expect. I'll tell ye about my current disguise, if ye can keep a secret…"

～

The rest of the day was chaotic, but Rosa stood with Simone—who was now dressed as a lad, with her braid tucked up under a tam and her knobby knees peeking out from under a Fraser plaid—and waved as the wagon loaded with her trunks of gowns passed out of An Torr's gates.

Brigit turned to wave cheerfully back, but Simone's nurse had opted to remain behind.

" 'Tis just as well," Simone said matter-of-factly to Rosa, having lost all her shyness. "Da says I donae need a nurse, but a mother."

"Well…" Rosa tweaked the lassie's nose. "Let us make haste in getting ye to Scone in time to greet yer new mother, aye?"

"Aye!"

Rosa had spent the last five years as an Angel. She'd been on scores of missions, some boring and some dangerous. She'd ridden across the length and breadth of Scotland and knew how to attract attention or hide from it.

But she'd never had a more enthusiastic—or *noisy*—travel companion as Simone Fraser.

It was hard to remain on alert with Simone's constant questions, but by the second morning of their travel, the lassie sat perched behind Rosa on the mare, and Rosa had grown accustomed to the lassie's unending prattle and could answer her, while still peering diligently about.

"How do ye ken we're going the right way?"

Rosa nodded to the path ahead of them. "Because the road only goes two directions; south to Scone and north toward Inverness. We're no' going north."

"But how do ye *ken*?"

"Because of the sun. 'Tis on our left, see? Since it rises in the east, I ken we're going south now."

"And how do ye ken *that*?"

Rosa resisted the urge to pinch the bridge of her nose, but she did let out a little sigh. "Because I read and listen and *learn* things. Ye should try it."

"Aye," the little girl chirped happily. "Da says I can repeat back almost anything naughty I hear."

Pressing her lips together to hold in her chuckle, Rosa nodded. " 'Tis a valuable skill."

"I think spies need to ken how to do that. Mayhap I could be a spy when I grow up! I already ken all about disguises, don' I, Rosa?"

Spies?

Deus in caelo, the lassie was closer to the mark than Rosa wanted to admit.

Instead of answering Simone, Rosa forced a serene expression and nodded politely to a man tugging his handcart in the opposite direction. When he called her *Sister*, she called out a greeting in return, then urged her horse onward.

Her calculations had been correct; traveling as a nun and a lad had afforded them, not only protection, but invisibility. No one would guess the nun was one of the Queen's ladies, and the lad the daughter of a powerful laird.

They'd passed the wagon with Simone's baggage early that first day—with Brigit waving cheekily from where she sat beside Gaspar's daughter—and had been making good time since. There'd been no sign of danger, but that didn't mean Rosa could let down her guard.

"Why is yer skin so dark, Rosa?"

"Hmm?" she replied absent-mindedly.

"Yer face and hands are dark, and I saw yer legs when ye were taking a piss this morning. They're dark too."

Rolling her eyes at the lassie's candor, Rosa patted the knobby knee beside her. "Ladies donae speak of pissing."

"Why no'? They have to piss, do they no'?"

Deus meus, mayhap she wasn't cut out for children.

"Aye, everyone pisses," Rosa explained slowly, "but 'tisnae polite to speak of it." She could feel the little girl taking a breath to argue, so she hurried to say, "Just promise no' to speak of pissing to anyone at court except yer father, Mellie, me or—or Brigit. Aright?"

The little hairs on the back of Rosa's neck wavered from the force of Simone's put-upon sigh.

"*Fine.* But why is yer skin so dark?"

Glancing down at the back of her own hand, Rosa shrugged. "My grandfather was a Moor."

"A *what*? Ye mean like where the heather grows?"

Rosa chuckled. "Nay. Moor is also the name for a person who comes from North Africa—a land far to the south, where 'tis much hotter. People who live there have much darker skin than most Scots or Norsemen."

Simone was quiet for a long moment, then asked hesitantly, "Is that where ye're from?"

"Nay, but my grandfather—my mother's father—was verra wealthy in his own land, and he used that wealth to travel all over the world. He collected priceless scrolls and books from Arabia and further east, and then traveled north. He met the Norsemen in Kiev on the Dnieper River and followed them home, then went on to Scotland. He met my grandmother in Aberdeen."

Behind her, Simone sighed. "And he stopped traveling?"

Chuckling, Rosa shook her head. "Nay, no' completely. Grandmother's father was a laird, ye ken, and he wanted her to stay close. So part of the year they lived with him, and part of the year they traveled to my grandfather's home and other places. My mother was raised with the most wonderful library, and she and my father taught their children to value learning."

"Tell me about some of the places they went!"

It was an easy enough request, and Rosa was able to easily split her attention between the story and the path ahead of them. Just because there hadn't been any danger yet, didn't mean there wouldn't be.

The morning turned into afternoon, and Rosa realized she wasn't going to reach Kingussie as she'd hoped. That had been her destination, but wee Simone was tiring easily and complaining often. The girl had tried her best, but Rosa couldn't expect her to sit on a horse *all* day without some respite, so she began to check for possible campsites.

The sun was almost setting when Rosa found a copse of trees tucked against a small stream, far enough from the road for some privacy and safety. Simone praised her for the find as she nearly fell from the horse, and even Rosa's legs were a bit stiff.

Still, it was short work to make a fire and prepare the girl's bedding from the small bundle the horse carried, which also contained a single dress fine enough for Simone to wear when they arrived at court and Rosa's book. After they'd supped and performed their ablutions, Rosa sat beside the fire with the book open on her lap and read to Simone.

Well, she didn't *read* exactly. 'Twas too dark for that, though all the light in the world couldn't help Rosa anymore. But she spoke the tale of Lanval and his beautiful fairy lover from memory, and soon, Simone's questions blessedly stopped as her eyes closed and the stars came out.

It was the following morning as they were breaking camp, and Rosa was explaining her actions as she went in order to stall Simone's constant commentary, when the hairs on her arms stood up.

She froze mid-sentence, wondering what had alerted her. Something had changed in the last minute, and in the back of her mind, she'd been paying attention, *gratias Deo*.

She suddenly realized what was different: there was no birdsong.

Slowly, she rotated until she was facing the copse of trees which stood between them and the road. Someone—a quiet someone—could be hiding, watching them.

"Simone," she whispered hoarsely, "get behind me."

"Why?"

"*Do it.*"

Something in her tone must've convinced the girl not to dally, because she did as Rosa commanded.

Carefully, her eyes on the trees, Rosa shook out her arms and took a deep breath, while preparing herself for what was to come.

Et cessabit.

Be calm.

Her grandfather had taught her that when he'd given her the sticks and taught her how to use them.

Now, she balanced lightly on the heels of her feet and slid one of the steel spikes out of its sheath along her forearm. It was not a blade, but a solid piece of metal eight inches long. It would block a dirk but could also be used to attack.

She'd killed men with it.

"Rosa?" Simone whispered behind her.

"*Shh.*" Rosa's gaze flicked from one shadow to the next, wondering where the danger lurked and cursing herself for her inattention. "When I tell ye to, run for the horse and ride like hell north again. Ye remember how to find the way north?"

As she reached between her legs to pull up her habit and tuck it into her belt, she heard the lassie whimper.

"Keep the sun on my right. I'm afraid, Rosa."

"I ken it, lassie. I need ye to trust me."

Rosa prayed her request wouldn't mean the death of the sweet girl.

There was no movement from the woods. Cautiously, Rosa slid one foot forward, waiting until she knew the path was clear before committing her weight. As she did it again, she pulled her other stick free.

Armed with both of her weapons, she took a deep breath. "Show yerself!"

The words seemed to echo around the small clearing. When a flock of crows took wing, the noise and movement startled Rosa so much, she flinched away.

When she looked back, a man was stepping from the shadows, leading a horse. When she saw the sword at his hip, Rosa raised her sticks.

"Get ready, Simone," she murmured. She would stand between their attacker and the girl, giving her time to reach safety.

The man's steps were easy and carefree, and his long legs were encased in leather trewes, which supported a trim torso and wide shoulders. When he reached his hand up to push his hood away from his face, she saw he had blond hair.

But it was the way he moved—as if he were in complete control and had all the time in the world—which made her eyes open wide.

"*Shite.*"

And then he smiled.

She knew she was in trouble.

Whirling, she faced Simone as she attempted to shove her sticks back into their forearm sheaths with shaking hands. At a distance, her eyesight was perfect, and she would know that smile anywhere.

Cameron Fraser had somehow found her.

"Rosa?" Simone whispered, craning her neck in order to get a glimpse of the man. "Should I run?"

Running was appealing, but Rosa knew there'd be no way to get them both on the horse and outrun him. Better to face the problem.

Once her spikes finally snapped into place, she straightened her shoulders. "Nay," she said, taking another deep breath. "I don' think he'll harm us."

"Why? Because—" The lassie must've finally seen who was approaching, because her eyes grew wide. To Rosa's surprise, she squealed in delight! "Cam!" she yelled, then ducked around Rosa and began to run toward the man.

Rosa found herself whirling once more and was just in time to see Simone throw herself against Cameron's legs.

Cam?

How in damnation did *Simone* know who *Cameron* was?

In the time it took Rosa to regain her wits, Simone had the man by the hand and was tugging him along behind her. "Faster, faster! I want ye to meet her! She's the one taking me to my da!"

His deep rumble—the voice which still did things to her insides—drifted ahead of him. "Yer da trusted a *nun* to escort ye to Scone?"

How in *damnation* did he ken so much?

"Rosa's no' a nun, silly!" Simone was giggling. "I'm no' a lad either. Did ye see my plaid? I've never worn it afore; ye can see my knees!"

Cameron's gaze had jerked upward when Simone had said her name, and she saw the moment his gaze landed on her face and realized who she was.

Then he was before her, his gray eyes more than a little surprised, and his lips parted.

His lips.

Deus in caelo!

She twisted away, taking four stumbling steps to the side, before she could force herself to face him—and those lips of his—once more. Not because she was having trouble seeing his features so close, but because she couldn't trust herself not to do something stupid.

Something involving his lips.

He was still watching her, and Simone was still chattering away about her disguise, but Cameron was clearly not listening. Nay, his gaze skimmed almost frantically over Rosa's features.

Interrupting the lassie, he asked Rosa, "I don' suppose ye have a twin sister named Rosa as well?"

Mutely, she shook her head, and he winced.

"*Shite.*" He scrubbed a hand over his face.

"Shite!" repeated Simone with a giggle. "Rosa said that too. She's in disguise, ye ken. A nun wouldnae say 'shite,' but I can now. Shite, shite, shite!"

"Simone!" snapped Rosa. "That's enough. Do no' use that word."

"Aye," the lassie said happily, dropping Cameron's hand. "I ken plenty of words I don' repeat."

From between his fingers, he glanced down at the girl. "We both ken that's no' true."

Simone's giggle burbled out. "*Mostly.*"

"Simone," Rosa said with a sigh, "go pet the horse."

"Can I talk to him? Tell him about our trip? I think his back is bony. Do ye think that too? Mayhap if I ask, he'll grow some cushion for me. Do ye think so?"

Rosa cataloged the questions. "Aye. Aye. That's interesting. Nay. Unlikely."

Satisfied, the girl darted off toward the horse, and Rosa was left alone with *him*.

Cameron blew out a breath and stepped forward, dragging a hand through his light hair so it was left adorably disheveled. "Ye're no' a nun, according to Simone?"

She lifted her chin. "Don' look so hopeful. I'm no' a whore either."

One of his brows rose, along with the corner of his lips, giving him a wry sort of grin. " 'Tis good, because ye werenae verra skilled at it."

She saw the lie in his gray eyes and matched his smirk with one of her own. "When I want to be a nun, I'm the best damn nun in the Highlands. When I want to be a whore, ye'll never meet one better."

The laugh which burst out of him quickly turned into a groan, and he scrubbed the same hand over his features again. When he emerged, he looked more than a little chagrined.

"I've been thinking of ye, Rosa."

She lifted a brow in challenge. "Is that why ye followed me? Why are ye here?"

"*Ye?*" He shook his head. "Nay, I've been following Simone. I met her two days ago at An Torr and needed to make sure she arrived in Scone safely. But I wasted half a day trailing that baggage wagon afore I realized I'd been fooled."

Rosa hid her reaction to his casual confession that her ruse had worked, and he sighed.

"Took me the rest of the day to backtrack and snoop around, just to discover she *had* left. So then I rode ahead of the damned wagon, frantic I might've lost her." He shrugged. "Then I saw yer camp."

He'd *met* Simone at An Torr?

Rosa's mind spun as she walked through the possibilities.

Had he been at An Torr to meet with someone?

For what purpose? Discovering Cameron's return to Fraser lands was damning evidence. The plot against the Crown—organized by a Fraser, according to Andrew of Lovat's testimony—could be linked to An Torr. Cameron's absence for so long spoke in his favor, but now that she knew he'd returned, she wasn't sure what that meant. Returning once meant he could've returned before.

'Tis his home! He's allowed to visit home, is he no'?

"Rosa?"

Her gaze jerked back to his, and she blew out a breath. "Listen, Cameron, ye cannae—"

A startled gasp burst out of her when he dropped his

horse's reins and grabbed her by the shoulders. As he jerked her close, his eyes bore into hers. She didn't even have time to flick her wrists to dislodge her spikes.

"Ye ken my name. How do ye ken who I am?"

His fingers were digging into her upper arms, and he was too close to easily make out his features. But his warmth and his scent—horse and leather and wind and pine—made her throat dry.

She stared up at him, struck mute by his nearness, and doing her best to control her body's reaction to him.

He shook her slightly. *"How do ye ken me?"*

Her tongue darted across her lips. "Ye kissed me," she reminded him in a whisper.

They were close enough to kiss again, but from what she could see, his expression was much too angry for such intimacies. He gave her another little shake.

"I never told ye my name. How do ye ken that? Why do ye call me Cameron?"

Gather yerself, lass.

This wasn't the first time she'd been held by a man, and as an Angel, she doubted it would be her last. She knew how to break his hold on her...

But did she want to?

Aye. Simone's safety comes first.

So she blew out a breath, snapped her forearms up between them, and swept them to each side, breaking his hold as she stepped backward. She kept her hands up, balled into fists to protect herself if need be.

"Yer brother sent me to An Torr, Cameron. I ken who ye are because *he* kens it."

Now she could see the way his gaze turned uncertain, flicking between her eyes. "He does?"

And *Deus carus*, but her heart twisted at the sound of

confusion in his voice. Did he think, all this time, Lachlan had known his brother was out there?

She stepped back again but lowered her hands. "We figured it out, Cameron, after the battle where ye saved him. I am one of Mellie's closest friends."

For a long moment he watched her, as if trying to determine if she were telling him the truth or lies. Then his shoulders slumped, and he dragged his fingers through his hair again.

"He is alive?"

His first question—and he likely had dozens—was for his brother.

"Aye," she said simply. "Mellie got him to the healer in plenty of time."

"Good." His hands fell to his belt, where he hooked his thumbs, then rocked back on his heels. "And ye're taking Simone to him?"

"Aye, so she can be with him when he marries Mellie."

"And ye're no' a nun?"

Her lips twitched. "No' a nun."

His gaze dropped to her wrists, as if he could see her secret weapons. "And no' entirely unprotected, even traveling as a nun and a lad."

There wasn't anything to say, so she nodded.

"Well then." He took a breath, and his shoulders straightened as if he'd come to a decision. "I'm going with ye."

It made sense. It really did.

They were both going in the same direction and were equally concerned for the safety of the same lassie.

And having him along would allow Rosa more time to question him, to discover the truth of, not just his journey to An Torr, but his possible motivations for putting a Comyn on the throne.

Aye, it made sense to invite him to ride with them.

But as he lifted Simone up to sit behind Rosa, his hand brushed against her leg, and she had to swallow down the moan of desire just that simple touch elicited.

And she knew this journey would be her most difficult mission to date.

CHAPTER 5

She wasn't a whore.

But on the other hand, she wasn't a nun either.

So who *was* she?

As Cam rode beside the two of them, he couldn't help stealing little glances at Rosa.

Rosa.

It had been her real name she'd given him that morning in the alley, and as far as he could tell, she'd been honest about everything else as well.

Well, not honest about being a whore.

Although it *had* been Cam who'd made that assumption, but she hadn't corrected him, had she?

But she'd been honest in her reactions to him at least.

He'd seen the way she'd looked up at him when he'd grabbed her. He'd been angry, but that hadn't been fear in her eyes.

Nay. She's been remembering the kiss they'd shared. He'd bet anything on that.

The kiss he couldn't stop thinking of either.

Who *was* she?

She was beautiful, aye, but quick-witted and confident too.

Throughout the morning, he found himself searching for topics of conversation, but she tended to answer him with curt responses.

And he eventually came to realize it was because of the lass sitting behind her.

"How much longer do ye think we'll be? Can we stop for the noon meal now?"

"Still two days, if we're lucky," Rosa said with a sigh, the muscles in her jaw jumping under her wimple. "And *nay*, 'tis no' yet noon."

One bony arm snaked around her to point. "Then can I go look at that tree? 'Tis an interesting tree. I could walk there."

"Nay," Rosa snapped. "If ye did, 'twould take us three days to reach Scone."

It was clear to Cam Rosa's patience was nearing its end with Simone's questions. Clucking to his horse, he rode up beside the pair. "Would ye like the wee lassie to ride with me for a bit?"

The sharp glance Rosa sent his way was full of suspicion. "Why?"

Why?

The question took him aback.

"Why no'? She *is* my niece."

To his surprise, Simone gasped and leaned toward him, her eyes wide. "I *am*?"

He frowned, his gaze going back to Rosa. "Ye didnae tell her?"

Rosa had known who he was, and his relation to Lachlan, so why wouldn't she have told Simone?

Unless...she was ashamed of him?

Or afraid?

Was it possible she'd guessed what he'd been up to all these years?

When she didn't respond, but kept her gaze ahead, Cam shrugged and turned back to Simone. "Aye, lassie. I'm yer Uncle Cam. Yer da's younger brother."

"Uncle Cam!" the girl squealed, as she threw herself off Rosa's horse and into his arms.

'Twas a good thing he was so close by and so ready to accept her as a passenger, because he ended up with her on his lap and her arms around his neck.

Tight.

After a quick hug, Simone reared back to study him. "Ye look like me."

"I look like yer da," he corrected. "Ye look like *him*."

Her little hand cupped his cheek. "I have gray eyes too, like ye. But ye have more beard. Will I get a beard one day? I've never seen a lady with a beard. Do ladies grow beards?"

She turned in his arms and settled herself across his lap as he answered her questions the way he remembered Rosa doing. "Aye. Aye. Hopefully no'. I've seen a woman with a beard, aye."

She sucked in a gasp and demanded the story. He easily slid into the tale of one of his best footpads, a large bull of a woman named Doris, who'd seemed more like a man than woman at times.

Although he was careful not to tell Simone details about his life as the leader of the Red Hand, he answered her questions with chuckles and details and questions of his own.

And when she started nagging him to be let down, he showed her some of the sleight of hand tricks he'd learned over the years. Mostly they were good for hiding pilfered coins, as he'd shown wee Tess, but they could also be used as a way to entertain.

After the noon meal, she lifted her arms for him to pick

her up into his lap again. Once comfortable, she curled up and was soon snoring softly against his chest.

The two horses rode in blessed silence for what seemed like an eternity before Rosa glanced at him. "She trusts ye."

It was a simple statement, but Cam saw it as an opening.

She was willing to talk to him!

He found himself smiling down at the pale head in his lap. "I am glad of it. But she'll be up all night if I let her sleep too long."

The corners of Rosa's lips were drawn downwards when he looked back up, and he noticed the flash of her dark eyes under lowered lashes.

Why?

Was she confused by his words?

Or their intent?

Finally, she shook her head. "She didnae sleep well last night; 'twas too cold and the ground too hard, she'd said. She tossed and turned all night, so I believe her in need of a nap."

His smile grew, knowing Simone was cozy and comfortable right now.

Rosa must've noticed because she made a noise like a faint snort. "*Ye* can cuddle with her tonight then."

Her tongue darted out to wet her lower lip, and although he recognized the sign of nervousness, he had a hard time controlling his visceral reaction to such a suggestive, yet innocent, gesture.

"Ye are good with her, Cameron."

God's Teeth, but he liked the sound of his name on her lips!

He cleared his throat, forcing himself to focus on her words. "I-I've always liked bairns. I've—" He shook his head, wanting to hide his past from her as long as possible. "I've taught a fair number of little ones. I only want what's best for them."

"Ye mean in the—in the years ye've been gone?"

Her hesitation raised his suspicions.

She couldn't know about his past in the Red Hand, could she?

And why in damnation did it *matter* to him if this woman knew of his sins?

Why did he want to impress her?

He decided it was easier to talk about the future, so he ignored her question. "I've always wanted a few bairns of my own. To love and raise properly, ye ken?"

She hummed. "Do ye have any? Children, I mean?"

The question startled him so much, he yanked on the reins, and the horse gave a little side-step before he got it—and his breathing—back in line.

Such a bold and direct question to come from a woman!

She was obviously worldly; not a nun, …but not a whore either.

"None that I ken of," he finally answered. "I've always been careful to—" Realizing what he was about to say—something he *never* thought he'd find himself speaking of to a lady—he weakly finished with, "I've always been careful to *no'* have children."

"By spilling outside yer lover's body?"

This time, he nearly choked on his gasp. When he swung his shocked gaze toward her, Cam found she was staring straight ahead, but he also saw a suspicious dark flush work its way up past her wimple.

She knew how sex worked.

She'd met him in that alley, had listened to his crudeness, had met his kiss with a passion and courage he hadn't often encountered. And now, he had just sat here and listened to her talk about him *spilling*.

Dear God, she aroused him. Which wasn't ideal, not with a six-year-old in his lap.

"Aye," he managed to choke.

She shrugged, still staring determinably ahead. "I only ask because I've heard that doesnae always work."

"Ye—ye've *heard*?"

"My friend Charlotte just had her first bairn. I did as much research as I could when she told us she was pregnant." As she spoke of her *research*, the tension in her shoulders seemed to relax, and her words came easier. "I read what I could, but I gained *much* more information by meeting with midwives and grandmothers." When she finally glanced at him, there was a sparkle of...*something* in her eyes. "To nae one's surprise, there arenae many treatises written on the topic. The Moors have more to say on women's health, but my grandfather's library was strangely lacking such topics."

God's Teeth, but the teasing tone of her voice made him smile. He was on horseback, his niece on his lap, speaking of *childbirth* with a woman dressed as a nun.

A woman he'd very much like to kiss.

And do *more* with.

Did *she* want bairns?

Startled at the thought, Cam jerked again. To cover his blunder—and the alarm coursing through him at the realization he was imagining a *future* with a woman he knew nothing about!—he cleared his throat.

"So ye're interested in childbirth?"

Mayhap she wanted to be a midwife and was just going about it oddly.

She blew out a breath; half-sigh, half-laugh. "I'm interested in *everything*. Some people think I'm odd, but I like learning. I *have* to learn, or I feel wasted."

When he didn't immediately answer, as he was too busy marveling at the honesty in her words, she glanced at him. "Now *ye* think I'm odd."

Slowly, he confessed the truth. "Nay, I donae. I'm just...*comparing* ye to the women I ken."

"Oh, aye?" her chin went up. "Nuns and whores?"

"Nay— Well, *aye*," her admitted with a wry grin. "But my mother, for one."

"She's a sweet lady, but no' at all interested in my research, ye are correct."

Would Rosa never cease to amaze him?

"Ye ken my mother?"

When she looked over at him and noticed his confusion, her lips softened into a smile.

"She's no' at An Toor, Cameron," Rosa offered softly. "She returned to Scone a fortnight before Lachlan, with her—well, with an advisor named Gillepatric." The name seemed to carry sour connotations, judging by the way she shook her head with a sigh. "I've sat with yer mother many mornings, and she's kind to me. But she's been confused lately. She speaks of…"

When she trailed off, he nudged his horse closer. "Speaks of what?"

"Of ye," she confessed, without looking at him. But then she sighed. "Afore a sennight ago, when Lachlan returned, yer mother enjoyed speaking of yer childhood and how wonderful ye were. Now she speaks of ye as if ye are in the palace with her. It began the day Lachlan was hurt, and I believe her mind was affected as well."

"Ye think she's crazed?"

"I…donae ken," Rosa admitted. "But she *is* confused. I've heard her call ye by several names in the course of one visit. But she deserves my respect."

Cam's gaze had dropped to the lassie in his arms.

"Why?" he murmured.

His parents had lost his respect just before he'd left their home.

"Because our elders can teach us much."

Disagreeing with her, but not wanting to irritate her,

Cam merely grunted. Within a few steps, his horse had edged away from hers, and the gap between them grew physically, as well as metaphorically.

'Tis for the best.

She was a *lady*—that much was clear. Not only did she speak and carry herself like a member of the nobility, but she spoke of life in the Scone Palace as if it were commonplace. As if there weren't people—people like him—who would kill to gain access to it.

He could use Rosa to get into the palace.

Court was in Scone Palace, and *she* needed to be the woman he was focused on now.

Not the nun beside him, who kissed like a whore.

He clenched his jaw, reminding himself he did *not* need that kind of memory distracting him.

Why in damnation did ye kiss her then?

"Why did ye kiss me?"

The question from her was so unexpected, and echoed his thoughts so closely, he answered without thinking. "Because I wanted ye. I *still* want ye."

It wasn't until she breathed a shocked little, "*Oh!*" that he realized he'd said the words out loud.

With a groan, he scrubbed his hand through his hair. "Nay, I didnae mean…" Blowing out a breath, he tried to figure out how to explain it to her. "That morn, I helped a lassie, only a few years aulder than Simone here." His arm tightened protectively around his sleeping niece. "She was trying to steal my purse, and I gave her some…suggestions. "

Rosa's chin turned his way, while her eyes remained on the road ahead. "Suggestions? Like…tips on how to steal yer purse?" Before he could answer, a smile bloomed on her lips. "Just when I think ye're noble!"

He was utterly distracted by the sight of that gorgeous smile on those sexy lips. "I am no' noble."

But when the words were said, he winced.

Ye did no' want her to ken ye're a thief, did ye?

Nay, he didn't. But she also didn't seem too surprised to learn that little revelation about his past.

Just how much did she know about Cameron Fraser?

"What does the lassie—who, presumably now, is a better thief, thanks to ye—have to do with kissing me?"

Oh, aye, the original question. He rolled his neck as he tried to find the words to explain. "She needed help. I was in the helping mindset, I suppose. Then I saw *ye* and made an assumption. Why *else* would ye be in that alley, approaching me, if not because ye were a whore?"

Why was she there?

"*Mayhap* I needed help. Or mayhap I'd simply wanted to speak with a handsome man."

She thought him handsome?

"Did ye need help?"

She snorted softly, derisively. "No' the kind *ye* were offering."

He'd attempted to teach her how to entice a man, which he realized now was an offensive assumption. But he lost all thought of apologizing when her eyes cut his way and a flush darkened her cheeks.

"But I didnae mind," she whispered.

"What?"

Her shoulders straightened, and she shifted in the saddle to meet his eyes. "I *said*, I didnae need the kind of help ye were offering, Cameron Fraser, but I didnae mind it either."

Dear God, she was saying she *liked* his kiss, his touch!

He scrubbed his hand down his face once more with a low groan, trying desperately to get his desire under control.

"Why *were* ye there, Rosa?"

Her reply was too long in coming; long enough for him to move Simone into a more comfortable position, long enough for him to wonder if she was considering lying to him.

He finally found the bravery to meet Rosa's eyes, and saw she was staring at him with her head cocked to one side, as if deliberating.

Trying to decide what to say?

Finally, she shrugged slightly and turned ahead in the saddle once more. "I was looking for ye, Cameron. Lachlan had been wounded, so Mellie and—well, *we* thought 'twould be best to find ye."

"And did ye tell anyone ye found me?" he asked quietly.

And more importantly, had she told anyone about their kiss?

"Nay," she whispered, with a wince.

Why the wince?

Because she hadn't wanted to admit the truth?

Or she regretted not telling anyone she'd found him?

Or another reason entirely?

He felt compelled to softly offer, "Ye're safe with me, Rosa."

"Am I?" Her head swung back around to face him; one side of her lips pulled up wryly.

"Aye. Do ye no' feel safe?" He nodded down to the sleeping lassie in his arms. "Simone obviously trusts me; obviously feels safe with me."

Rosa shrugged. "I feel..." Slowly, her gaze switched from him to the sky as she tilted her head back slightly and pursed her lips. "I feel safe from outside threats, aye."

He realized he was seeing her brilliant mind at work. She was peering up at the sky, but she wasn't seeing it. Nay. She was assessing, *considering* her feelings.

"I feel safe from most threats a traveling woman might face, because ye carry a sword big enough to detract all but the most desperate of men. And while I also ken I can protect myself, I donae believe ye would harm me, although I reserve the right to change my mind later."

His denial was quick, certain. "I would *never* harm ye, lass."

She didn't appear to be listening, but debating out loud with herself. "There are many things I donae ken about ye, 'tis true. But I suspect there *is* a noble side of ye, and ye will no' harm me."

Cam exhaled, more pleased than he wanted to admit when he heard she trusted him.

But then she turned sorrowful eyes back to him, and he had to swallow down the urge to reach for her, to comfort her.

"What is it, lass?" he whispered.

"I feel safe from *ye*, Cameron Fraser, but myself?" She shook her head. "I donae feel safe from myself. No' when I'm around ye."

And he *swore* his heart stuttered.

Her words, her confession—said so sadly—filled him with an odd, fierce sort of elation.

She didn't trust herself around him?

'Twas as good as saying she wanted to kiss him—to *touch* him—again!

And Cam had three days traveling to Scone left to make sure it happened.

Of course, he'd forgotten the wee lassie in his lap, who chose that very moment to stir.

"Good morn, Uncle Cam!" She giggled sleepily. "I ken 'tis no' really morn, but I say that to my nurse when she wakes up from her nap. I don't like napping, but she does. Did I nap? What'd I miss?"

CHAPTER 6

*N*ay, she didn't trust herself around him, which is why Rosa did her best to distance herself from Cameron for the rest of the day.

But it was *hard*.

Not just because they were traveling together—that was the *physical* distance. Although they were both on separate horses, he was still nearby. And eventually, she found it easier to accept his help climbing in and out of the saddle, which meant she had to endure his touch.

Endure wasn't exactly the right word, was it?

It was more—

Ye're getting off topic again.

Ah, yes. Her brain had a tendency to do that.

Where was she?

Physical distance…?

Oh yes, emotional distance. Metaphysical distance, she supposed.

He's just so damn likable.

And she already liked Cameron far too much.

So that was why she limited her contact—physical *and*

emotional—for the rest of the day. She was pleased to let him bond with Simone, because the two of them really *were* adorable together, while she pondered over the things she'd learned about him.

He wanted children, and didn't *that* just make her insides go all gooey?

She'd never considered the possibility of her own children—she was perfectly happy at court using her mind for the betterment of the kingdom, *thank-ye-verra-much*.

But soon, her place in the Angels would be called into question, and where would that leave her?

Mayhap she *should* start making other plans for her future.

But nae bairns with Cameron Fraser!

Right.

Right.

Et non vis eum.

She'd been right about Simone, at least; after they'd supped on the dried meats and apples Rosa had packed into the saddle bags at An Torr, the lassie fell asleep quickly with her head pillowed in Cameron's lap.

Rosa refused to acknowledge the burn of jealousy she felt at the sight.

The next morning, she knew she was being cold to him, but he didn't seem to mind. In fact, he and Simone had some sort of bargain it seemed, to try to make her laugh. And it worked a few times.

But the way he looked at her when she laughed…well, it made her feel as if she'd swallowed moths.

She'd been around Mellie long enough to be able to name this feeling—the way her knees went all tingly, and she felt an itchy sort of warmth between her thighs. It was desire. Something she had no business feeling when it came to Cameron Fraser.

The man was a suspect in a treacherous plot against the Queen, *ita me deo juvent!*

But no matter how capable her mind was, she couldn't seem to remember that.

Or didn't *want* to.

With a wince, she pinched the bridge of her nose and admitted she was completely and utterly confused, which didn't happen often.

"Are ye aright, lass?" he asked from atop his horse, behind and to the left of her.

"I am *fine*," she snapped. Then, to remind herself, she dropped her hand, straightened her shoulders and stared ahead, as she repeated, *"I am fine."*

I am an Angel, and I have a mission.

That resolve took her until their noon meal, when they stopped to allow Simone the chance to stretch her legs. Cameron led their horses to a babbling little brook near some boulders, while Rosa walked back and forth with the six-year-old.

"Wanna see me run, Rosa? I can run *really* fast in this kilt. Do ye think Da will let me dress like this all the time? I *like* it."

Rosa's lips twitched upward. "I can imagine. I have a friend who prefers to wear men's trewes for exactly that reason—the freedom they offer."

"And her da lets her?"

Considering Court's past—and the fact the man who was currently walking back toward them was likely the closest thing the woman had to family—Rosa considered her response carefully. "I don' think her da had much to say about it one way or the other."

"Can she run as fast as I can?"

"I donae ken. Why don' ye run to the road and back a few times, and I'll see."

The lassie was off like an arrow. "Aye!" she called back over her shoulder.

Rosa watched her for a moment, calling out encouragement—thinking it possible she *was* faster than Court—before allowing herself to stretch.

She'd just bent over, wrapping her arms around her knees and pressing her nose against her legs, when she heard Cameron chuckle.

"Well, I've never seen *this* position before."

Perturbed—both at him and the flush she knew was traveling up her checks, even though he couldn't see it—she grumbled, "I'm stretching my back."

"I can see that. Ye're quite...*limber*."

She heard the innuendo in his voice, as well as his teasing. And suddenly, she wanted to *show* him. Show him she wasn't like all the women he expected her to be.

Shifting her feet apart, she planted her palms flat on the ground. Then, taking a deep breath, she leaned all her weight on her hands...and lifted her feet off the ground.

She was careful not to pull her legs above her head, knowing that would give him a look at things she didn't want him to see. But by leaning forward and lifting her legs out at a ninety-degree angle, she was able to use her shoulders as a fulcrum and balance point, ensuring her weight was distributed evenly and—

Ye willnae impress him with geometry and physics, lass.

She didn't need to, judging by the impressed way he whistled.

When she finally put her feet back on the ground, her arms were aching, and she had dirt ground into her palms; but he was grinning, and the way she wanted to grin in return made it worth it.

Didn't it?

"Ye are remarkable, Rosa," he said in a low voice, stepping

forward. "I've kenned all sorts of people—all sorts of women—and none had that sort of strength."

"No' even—" She'd been about to say *Courtney*, but she wasn't sure she wanted to reveal her friend's secrets. Instead she corrected herself, "No' even among the Red Hand? Surely ye had plenty of— Oh."

It was the way he was looking at her, the shock—and was that a hint of *fear?*—in his eyes, which made her bite off her words. She understood then.

At no point in the last two days had she told him she knew his history as well as his name.

"Aye, Cameron," she sighed. "I ken ye were the leader of the Red Hand for many years."

His gray eyes flicked between hers, as if searching for the truth. The suspicion was still there in his gaze, as he folded his arms across his chest.

"One day I hope ye'll tell me how a woman from the palace kens so much. Ye are brilliant, I'll confess, but to ken so much about *me?*"

Could she?

She held his gaze, not sure if she should admit the truth and tell him she could *never* tell him how she knew so much about him.

Apparently, her silence was enough.

With a muttered curse, he dropped his arms and turned to stalk back toward the horses.

Which is why, when the attack came, he was already facing the right direction.

Mayhap it wasn't an actual *attack*. The footpads had obviously been hiding among the boulders and had seen their opportunity to take the unattended horses.

Hollering, the four of them—riding two per horse—rode toward Cameron, seeing him as the threat. And the stupid man just ripped his sword from his scabbard, standing there in harm's way.

Simone!

Rosa whirled, her gaze seeking out the lassie, who'd stopped near some wildflowers and now rose to peer back at them, as if wondering at the excitement.

She would be safe there, at least.

By the time Rosa turned back to the threat, Cameron was swiping at one set of footpads, but they easily side-stepped the attack, the horse's eyes wild as it followed the new commands. And then they were past Cameron, and almost past Rosa.

Her fingers had already pulled one of her spikes from her arm sheath, and as time slowed, she tracked the horse's movements. As it passed her, the dirty man clinging to the rider in the rear leered down.

She wouldn't be able to reclaim the horses, but she could certainly make the thieves pay.

Time sped back up again as she loosed her spike.

The throw took the man between the shoulder blades, the steel burying deep. With a grunt, he slumped forward against his companion, and she watched, hoping he might fall off so she could retrieve her weapon.

And when he didn't—when the four of them disappeared down the road with their horses, supplies, and her spike—her shoulders slumped.

"*Shite.*"

Cameron was breathing heavily when he arrived beside her, and she wondered how much of the battle she'd missed while she'd been searching for Simone.

"Are ye aright?" he snapped, his gaze tripping over her features, as if looking for any visible wounds.

"Aye," she muttered, staring after the horses. "But I'll no' be able to replace my weapon until I reach the armory, and *then* they'll want to ken why I left it in some whoreson's back."

His grunt sounded surprised. When she glanced at him, he was busy sliding his sword back into its scabbard.

Then he looked up and met her eyes. "When ye get around to telling me how ye ken so much about me, I'd *also* like to ken why ye and the Royal Armorer are on speaking terms."

It was such a ridiculous statement—and so completely summed up her life—Rosa felt her lips curl upward. "A lady has to have her secrets, milord."

At that, he burst out laughing. And despite the fact they were stranded now, and their journey would take them many more days, Rosa's heart lifted at the sound of his joy.

~

The woman hadn't said a damn word of complaint about the horses. Rosa had simply called Simone to her, explained they would be walking to Scone, then had headed for the road.

And now they were *walking*. To *Scone*. Clear on the *other side* of the kingdom.

She hadn't even said a word blaming him for their current predicament, but she didn't have to. He blamed himself well enough.

How could he be so stupid to have left the horses unattended?

There'd been a part of his brain—the part which had been a bandit leader for years—which had recognized the boulders as a good ambush spot as he'd led the horses there.

But had he listened?

Nay.

He'd been too intent on getting back to Rosa's side. To bask in her smiles, her clever insights. Her scathing retorts.

God's Teeth, he was even enamored of the woman's insults!

And thanks to his randy cock—or mayhap his heart—he had left the horses there by the stream, where they had become easy pickings.

Ye should've kenned better, ye clot-heid.

Aye, he should've, and he vowed it wouldn't happen again.

Unfortunately, as the afternoon wore on—*walking!*—he found himself distracted by her more than once. The way she tilted her head back to catch the sun while she pondered her way through a problem. The easy way she carried herself as they strode along the road.

He remembered the strength she'd displayed while she'd been stretching just moments before the horses had been stolen, and cursed himself.

Because it was harder to walk with a cockstand than he wanted to admit.

"I'm *tired*," Simone whined, when the sun was low in the west.

Her complaint jerked him out of his self-blame, and he realized he hadn't heard the lassie's chatter for a while. The poor thing was plain worn out, judging from the slump of her shoulders and her dejected expression.

Rosa was also peering at her, but hadn't slowed their pace. "I ken, Simone," she said softly. "But Blair Atholl cannae be more than a few hours or so."

"*A few* hours?" The little girl's eyes filled with tears.

Cam moved up beside her. "I am a sorry uncle for no' noticing how brave ye were being, lassie. Want to ride on my back?"

She needed no more urging, and when he stopped, she scrambled up atop his back, her bony legs wrapped around his waist, and his hands locked under her arse as a sort of seat.

As he began walking again, he met Rosa's gaze. She was eyeing his shoulders, and although he saw the appreciative gleam there, he also saw exhaustion.

"Mayhap 'twould be safer to *no'* stay in town?" he offered gently. Not just safer, but less exhausting, if they didn't have to press on another few hours.

Mayhap she saw the unspoken reasons in his eyes, because she sighed and nodded. "Aye. Mayhap ye are right."

And when it came time to actually stop for the evening—long before Blair Atholl, but when it was too dark to walk any farther—they did little more than retreat to a thick copse of trees not far from the road.

They had no food, other than the bannock he carried in his pouch, so there was no need for a fire someone could see.

Simone curled up on her side, her head on his thigh, her uneaten cake clenched in her hand.

Rosa settled cross-legged next to her, just far enough away Cam couldn't reach for her, and did something he hadn't expected. Of course, when it came to this woman, he was coming to realize he should *expect* the unexpected.

From her scapular, she pulled out a book. There was just enough moonlight filtering through the pines to see what she held, but there couldn't be enough light for her to actually read by.

Still, she opened the book, and her fingers began running lovingly over each page, as if reading by feel. When she reached a particular spot, she inhaled, and he wondered if she was *smelling* the page.

Did books have a scent?

But instead of reading it, she lowered the book into her lap, tilted her head back, and began to speak.

. . .

"*Her body was slim, long-waisted, tall,*
Her neck was whiter than fresh snow-fall.
Grey were her eyes, white her face,
Lovely her mouth, nose in the right place,
Brown eyebrows, forehead smooth and fair,
Bright blond, crisply curling hair—
The radiant light of pure gold thread
Fades by the brightness of her head.
Deep purple-red silk is her cloak,
Which she's draped in folds all around;
On her fist she bears a hawk,
And behind her runs a greyhound.
In the whole town, great men and small,
Old men and babies, one and all
Came running just to watch this show."

It took him a few lines to realize she was quoting the book. She wasn't reading it—she had it *memorized*. Of course, if the book was important enough to carry around inside her scapular, mayhap that explained why she had it memorized.

It was long after Simone had fallen asleep—and he'd saved her oat cake for her breakfast the following morning—when Rosa stopped speaking. Night had settled completely, and the silence spread out from their little group.

Finally, Cam spoke. " 'Tis been many years since I've heard *Lanval* spoken so sweetly."

He couldn't see her surprise, but heard it when she said, "Ye recognize it? Nay, donae answer; 'tis obvious ye do. I didnae expect—"

"A thief to ken literature? Why no'? *Ars longa, vita brevis.*"

There was no bitterness in his question. He *knew* who he was, but also what he liked.

"Nay, Cameron," she said softly. "Ye are more than that."

He didn't know how to respond to her faith, so he didn't. Instead, he moved Simone from his leg and stood. "We have a long walk tomorrow, unless ye'd object to riding stolen horses."

Her reply took a moment. "I object to *Simone* kenning her uncle doesnae object to stealing horses."

It was a convoluted answer, but thoughtful. And because he wasn't surprised by it, Cam found himself chuckling as he made his way into the trees. She hadn't exactly given him permission to steal animals for them, but she hadn't said nay either.

"She makes one hell of a nun," he muttered to himself, as he pissed against the last tree, hoping the scent of humans would be enough to keep predators at bay. Just to be certain, he would sleep with his sword by his side.

Because the day had proven the predators in the area were two-legged as well as four.

Of course, there was one less now. Rosa had thrown her weapon this afternoon, and her aim was dead-on with one of the bandits.

Cam found himself grinning wryly as he made his way back to the two females who had so completely consumed his attention, but his current thoughts remained locked on Rosa.

She was intriguing.

And alluring.

And damned arousing.

And dressed as a nun, laddie.

Still, that didn't stop him from crouching down beside her as he returned to find her asleep with one arm around

Simone. Neither of them had blankets, but she was sharing her voluminous habit with the lassie.

The least he could do was help.

Drawing his sword, he laid it on the ground. He *intended* to sleep back-to-back with Rosa tonight to protect them both, while still offering her some of his heat.

But in the middle of the night, he woke to find her in his arms, her small arse tucked snuggly up against his unruly member.

If he'd been a stronger man, a more noble man, he might've released her. Might've held tight to his principles.

As he pulled her snug against him, then reached around her to cup Simone's shoulder, ensuring she was safe too, Cam felt himself smile.

'Tis a good thing I'm no' a noble man.

CHAPTER 7

Deus in caelo, but her feet hurt.

It wasn't the first time she'd had to walk this far, nay, but it was the first time in these flimsy nun's slippers. And come to think of it, the first time in a few years.

I'm no' as young as I once was.

The thought that, at two-and-twenty, she could be considered *old*, made the corners of her lips tug upward.

"Well, 'tis glad I am to see *someone* smiling."

She glanced at her companion. Cameron was once again carrying Simone, but she obviously wasn't so tired she couldn't chatter on and point out every interesting sight. His words came during one of the lassie's rare quiet moments, and Rosa completely forgot what she was going to say when she saw the twinkle in his gray eyes.

"Hmm?" was all she could manage.

That's when he grinned, just a little one; just enough to make her draw in a breath and force her eyes away from his handsome mien.

"I said, 'twas nice to see ye smiling, Rosa. Care to tell us what ye were thinking of?"

"Aye, Rosa! Tell us!" Simone chimed in.

Rosa wracked her brain for something to tell them and found salvation in a far-off sight. "I was merely noticing that small loch." She pointed. "I thought 'twould make a good resting place."

When Simone squealed and demanded to be put down, insisting she had her strength back, Cameron complied. Then he fell into step behind Rosa as they watched the lassie run ahead.

"Ye're sure ye want to stop?" he murmured.

With a sigh, she admitted the truth. "Ye might be braw, Cameron, but Simone and I cannae keep up the pace for long. I suspect I need a break as much as she does."

"Cam," he said suddenly.

She tilted her head his way, one brow raised, and he flushed—actually *flushed*—then looked away.

"I just meant, call me Cam. I havenae been *Cameron* for many years."

"Ye were *Cam* when ye were with the Red Hand." It wasn't a question. She knew it to be true.

But he nodded. "I was. And I also learned no' to push my men." He raised a brow right back at her.

So she grinned. "I'm no' yer *man*. But I'll no' argue either."

"Will ye let me *acquire* some horses for us?"

Turning her attention back to the loch—where Simone was even now stripping out of her carefully arranged plaid—Rosa shrugged nonchalantly. "The more my feet hurt, the more I'm considering compromising my ethics. Or rather, deciding Simone's ethical education isnae up to me."

His laughter followed her to the water.

. . .

It was a while later that the two of them found themselves sitting beside the loch, a little bit away from where Simone was still frolicking happily in the clear water. Rosa had removed her shoes and was resting her feet in the water as she relaxed against a boulder, and Cam sat perched beside her, a hastily constructed fishing line and pole in hand.

"Ye think ye can catch us a meal?" she asked drowsily, dropping her head back against the rock, glad for the cushion of her wimple and veil.

"I *ken* it, aye."

Her lips twitched at the arrogance of his claim. "Yer mother often speaks of yer prowess with a fishing pole."

"My niece tells me Mother oft compares Simone to me when it comes to fishing."

Rosa hummed. "Are ye watching her?"

She would, but it felt so *nice* to rest here with her eyes closed...

"Nae need," he murmured. "She swims almost as well as one of these fish."

And wouldn't Mellie be interested to hear that, after the storm she and the lassie had battled a few weeks back?

To hear Mellie tell it, their wee rowboat had almost been lost on the loch which bordered An Torr, and the "poor, wee bairn would have drown from her inability to swim at all" had Mellie not been there to save the lass.

"How about ye, Rosa?"

She hummed again, in question this time.

"Do ye swim?" he clarified. "Did yer family teach ye?"

Family...

With a faint smile, she lifted her head from the rock and opened her eyes. "Nay," she confessed. "My parents likely never learned themselves; they were far too interested in their studies. I learned from— I learned after I arrived at court."

Courtney had been the one to teach her to swim on one of their very first missions together. The older woman had thrown Rosa in a pond and yelled instructions, until Rosa managed to keep from drowning.

The memory made her heart feel a little lighter.

They were interrupted when Cam pulled in his first fish, then rebaited the line with a bug he'd found—"Simone's suggestion," he told her—but once they were settled, he pushed for details.

"So yer parents are as studious as ye?"

"More so." Just thinking of them made her heart ache to see them again. "I'm a Forbes. My father is our laird's younger brother, and thankfully, my uncle is hale and hearty, because Da would make a terrible clan leader. He's much happier in his library."

Cam grunted, twitching the line this way and that. "And yer mother?"

She pulled her legs up, digging her toes into the wet sand at the edge of the water, and smiled slightly. "My mother is... remarkable. Her father was a wealthy merchant from North Africa, a place called *Jazaʾir Banī Mazghanna*. He met my grandmother on his travels and settled in Aberdeen near her father, who was Laird Hay. They still travel extensively, but his library was likely what attracted my father to my mother."

Letting a handful of sand trickle through her fingers, she sighed. She *missed* her parents and sisters. She missed Grandfather, and his wonderous library. She knew she was doing important work for the Queen, but she regretted she was unable to sneak away to visit him far more frequently.

"So ye're all scholars? Yer parents and grandparents?"

"And my sisters," Rosa was quick to offer, then shrugged.

"My parents had five daughters and educated us all. I am the youngest. My older sisters have all married, but not before having their husbands *swear* to my father they'd educate their daughters the same as their sons."

"He sounds like a remarkable man," Cam offered. "I'd like to meet him one day."

I'd like that.

But she bit down on the words, knowing she shouldn't say them.

Couldn't say them.

If Cameron Fraser was guilty of treason, he would have no future. No chance to meet her father. No chance to be with *her*.

And here she was, lounging by the water, wasting a perfectly good opportunity to find out if he was guilty.

She wracked her brain, trying to come up with *some* way to bring up the scheme against the Crown without giving him any details.

What would make him spill his secrets without the exchange being too awkward?

Her opportunity came when he caught another fish and tossed it up on the grass, while accepting Simone's wet cheers from out in the loch. He even bowed extravagantly to the lassie, before settling back down to bait the hook again.

An opening!

"Ye look as if ye belong at court with that bow."

He stiffened at the word *court*, but then exhaled.

"Nay," he said nonchalantly, as he tossed the line in the water. "I just remember some of the manners my mother tried to teach me."

Before his life of crime.

What else could she say…?

"I do love fish, if 'tis well-prepared. The royal family's chef ensures we're all well-fed at the palace. Is the Bruce no' a wonderful king? Strong and brave and kens what's best for all of us?"

She bit her lip when he turned to her, confusion evident in the way his brows drew in.

"Aye," he agreed curtly, eyeing her and her odd questions, which seemed to come from nowhere.

In desperation, she continued, saying, "He's so much better a king than, say, John Comyn, would ye agree?"

Cam frowned and lifted his shoulders as he nodded. "Aye, ye're likely right. The man was killed after I left home, but my parents always spoke well of him. I donae remember what they said now, but I ken I didnae like to hear him praised." He glanced sidelong at her. "From what I've heard of the man, I donae think he would've had the strength to break from the English the way King Robert did."

That was...that was a remarkably accurate, insightful, and entirely *innocent* thing to say.

His father, Michael Fraser, had been a Comyn supporter for the Crown. 'Twas why it had been so easy to believe someone from his clan—specifically his brother, Lachlan—had led this murderous scheme against Robert and Elizabeth.

But Lachlan was innocent, per Mellie's investigation. As was Ross Fraser. Andrew Fraser, Cam's uncle, was dead.

Cam was the only suspect left.

But was he guilty?

With a sigh, she let her head flop back against the boulder.

What was happening to her mind?

Usually she was the sharp one; the one who could question suspects with little effort.

Here and now, she was asking questions which made her seem mad.

Of course, he likely thinks 'tis normal when it comes to me.

She groaned aloud and pinched the bridge of her nose,

wondering if she could sink into the sand from embarrassment.

"Ye ken, I met ye only two days ago?"

"Nay," she muttered, her eyes tightly closed. "We met a sennight ago."

He chuckled. "I met a gorgeous, intriguing woman I thought a *whore* a sennight ago. I met *ye* just the other morning, on the road from An Torr."

She peeked one eye open and glared at him. "So?"

"*So...*" He shrugged, his attention on his niece in the water. "I think ye're a fascinating woman. Brilliant, beautiful, and intriguing as all of Creation. The way yer mind works is a mystery to me."

"Me too, sometimes," she groaned.

He chuckled again. "And I like how honest ye are."

Honest?

Nay!

This time it was her turn to chuckle, but not happily. If only he knew...

"So the book ye carry?"

The question was an odd enough one it had her pushing herself upright, her hands clutching for the hard rectangle under her scapular. "What about it?"

"Did that come from yer grandfather's library? The one ye value so much? Do ye carry it with ye wherever ye go?"

Her grip relaxed, but then she reconsidered and pulled it from under the material. Staring down at the cover, she traced the engravings. "Whenever I'm"—*on a mission*—"away from the palace," she said instead, "I bring one of my books with me. They help me stay focused."

"By reading them?"

Her fingers caressed the leather. "No' exactly."

"Will ye read it to me now?" he asked quietly.

She didn't even have to glance at him to know he meant

what he said. Simone was still playing happily; calling out for them to watch her and splashing merrily.

Why not?

Rosa pulled her legs up, crossing them to create a resting spot for the precious book. Reverently, she opened the pages, the parchment stiff and glorious under her fingertips. She found her favorite passage and peered down at the page.

Even here, in broad daylight, she couldn't make out the words. Not this close.

If she held the book at arms-length, she could read more clearly, but even that was becoming difficult. Luckily, she didn't have to.

"*Those who love the knight Lanval
Come running to him now to tell
Him about the maiden come to court
Who will free him, please the Lord.*"

She lost herself in the words. So much so that when he interrupted her, she actually jumped.

"Yer eyes are closed." There wasn't accusation in his tone, just interest.

And she realized he was right. Her eyes *had* been closed.

Flushing, she darted a glance his way.

He was busy unhooking a third fish from his line. She'd been so immersed in the words, she hadn't noticed him catch any more. But after he tossed the thing up with the others, he wiped his palms on his leather trewes and settled back against the boulder beside her, one brow raised in challenge.

He wasn't going to drop the question.

"Aye," she finally admitted. "I—I ken the verse."

Humming, he eyed her. "That was part of the passage ye

recited last night, when the lady appears and vindicates Lanval. But I prefer the beginning, when her handmaidens bring him to her tent. 'Tis my favorite part."

He had a favorite part of *Lanval*?

Be still, my heart.

Of course, judging from his lewd wink, there was a *reason* that was his favorite part of the epic poem.

Fumbling with the book, she tried to calm her pulse as she carefully flipped through the pages.

Why did it matter if he knew the story as well as she did?

Why did it matter if they both shared an interest in books and stories, and God knew what else?

It *mattered* because no man besides her father and grandfather had *ever* acknowledged her mind…and Cam had called her brilliant. No man had ever shared these interests with her.

If she'd ever considered marrying, it would've been a man like her father; calm, scholarly and kind.

So why in damnation did *this* man—this braw, handsome *thief*—make her legs weak with desire?

Because he cared.

He cared to discover a connection with her. He cared to help tutor a whore, so she'd be successful. He *cared* to help a young pickpocket, and to raise young Courtney.

He cared, and the longer she was with him, the more she doubted her conclusion he was guilty.

The parchment crinkled in her fingers. Smoothing out the page, she began to read. Or pretend to read.

But she didn't make it two sentences, before he interrupted her. "Ye're on the wrong page."

Her gaze jerked to his, then back down to the book.

Nay, surely she wasn't?

She lifted the book, pulling it closer, then farther away, as she peered at the words she could no longer make out.

But it was his soft grunt which gained her attention once more. "Nay, my mistake. Ye were on the right page all along. But ye can no' see the words, can ye?'

In the three years since she'd noticed her ocular degeneration, *no one* had caught on. She'd been so careful, so *certain* she could fool her fellow Angels and the Queen, and here was a man she'd just met, a thief, who'd figured it out?

She considered denying it, making an excuse, but every version of that conversation she could calculate resulted in embarrassment for her.

So, shoulders slumping, she let the book drop to her lap once more. "How did ye ken?"

He didn't reply for a long while, long enough she peeked up at him. From this distance, she could see him clearly, but if he were any closer…

Finally, he shrugged. His gray eyes holding hers. " 'Twas no' obvious. Just some ways ye look at things. Yesterday, when ye were braiding Simone's hair, I saw ye tracing the shape of her head with yer hands afore ye placed her cap on, as if ye couldnae quite make out what ye were seeing. Ye donae seem to have problems with things at any distance, like where I am now."

"Aye," she whispered, shame causing her cheeks to warm as she dropped her gaze to his chin. "I can see ye fine."

"But ye have trouble seeing things up close, am I right? I noticed ye squinting earlier when ye were examining that hole in yer hem." He stretched his legs out in front of him. "Ye didnae read the book last night, but were reciting the words. Ye must have a remarkable memory."

Rather than be soothed by the compliment, Rosa felt tears pricking at her eyes. Shame and anger washed through her. A remarkable memory wasn't going to help her, not without the ability to actually *read* the words!

"Nae one else has guessed," she whispered, her eyes going

back to the beloved, useless book on her lap. "Three years it's been happening, and nae one else has guessed. Except ye."

"Mayhap none of them spend as much time watching ye as I do."

She snorted softly. It was hard for her to believe this man, this virtual stranger, knew more about her than Court or Mellie did.

However...she'd been able to hide her secret from her closest friends. Cam had just met her, and he saw things, understood things, she hadn't thought for a moment he would have.

She slanted a sidelong glance at him. "I donae ken what to do," she confessed.

He shrugged, lacing his fingers together on his lap and looking for all the world like a man completely at ease with life. "There's naught *to* do. I kenned a man who lost his vision like that, up-close. He was no' a reader like ye were, so it was nae great loss. But he compensated for it in other ways."

Curious despite her misery, Rosa lifted her chin. "Like what?"

Faster than she could react, Cam had leaned forward and snatched the book from her lap. Gasping, she lunged after it, but he was settled back against his boulder before she even had a plan.

To her surprise, he opened the book, flipping through the pages as if this was an everyday occurrence for him. Ignoring her, he muttered to himself—so quiet she couldn't make out the words—until he reached the page he wanted.

"Ah, here it is, my favorite part." He flicked a glance her way, his lips curling up into that gorgeous smile which made her insides churn. "One of the ways to compensate is to accept help, even if ye donae want to."

And then he began to read.

. . .

"*This tent was the maiden's bower:*
New-blown rose, lily-flower,
When in Spring their petals unfurl—
Lovelier than these was this girl.
She lay upon so rich a bed,
You'd pay a castle for the sheet—
In just her slip she was clothèd.
Her body was well-shaped, and sweet.
A rich mantle of white ermine,
Lined with silk, alexandrine,
Was her quilt, but she'd pushed it away,
On account of the heat; she didn't hide
Her face, neck, breast, her whole side,
All whiter than hawthorn blossom in May."

Deus in caelo!

He was lounging on the shore of a loch as if it were the most natural thing in the world, *reading a book to her.*

It had been years since anyone had read a book to her. Read *anything* to her. As soon as she could read herself, her parents had gone back to their own studies, allowing her and her sisters to choose their own material from the library.

The tears which had pricked her eyes earlier now materialized. Two fat drops slowly crawled down her cheeks, but despite them, her lips pulled upward.

He was *reading* to her.

And it was glorious.

Cam had a beautiful voice, his tone rising and falling with the verses. His pronunciation was perfect, and he even put emphasis on the words she would have.

Listening to him was soothing in a way song or food, or even *breathing*, wasn't.

Listening to him read to her was…was…*everything*!

She scooted back down against her boulder, resting her head and staring up at the sky, the words washing over her.

And in that moment, she knew she was falling in love with Cam.

CHAPTER 8

*H*e thought she was asleep.

Rosa hadn't moved once over the last four pages, but when Cam closed the book and looked over at her, she was staring up at the sky, tear tracks marking her cheeks.

He wanted to ask what was wrong, wanted to ask if he'd offended her by taking the book from her and reading it, but then she lifted her head and met his eyes.

And she was looking at him as if he were some kind of...*hero*?

Some kind of *noble* man. Someone who'd just done something wonderful.

All I did was read a book.

It'd been a while since he'd had the opportunity, he confessed to himself. The library at An Torr had been small, only containing a handful of volumes, and most of those were religious treatises. His mother had had a copy of several Lais of Marie de France, including *Lanval,* before Father had sold them, and young Cam had been enthralled by the story.

About ten years ago, while trying his hand at highway

robbery, he'd taken a wagon with some books in it, and had confiscated those as part of his share of the booty.

But imagine having an entire library of books at her fingertips…and not being able to read any of them.

"Does yer family ken? About no' being able to see up close?"

Mutely, she shook her head, then he remembered.

She'd said no one knew.

Except him.

She'd shared a secret with him.

It wasn't an explanation of her past, or why in damnation she carried weapons and dressed in disguises and was part of the palace life.

Nay, but somehow, it was better.

Leaning forward, he carefully placed the book on her lap where he'd taken it from. As he did, her hand came down to cover the book protectively and unintentionally captured his.

He gently clasped her hand and squeezed it. When she met his eyes, he nodded solemnly. "Thank ye, Rosa. For sharing with me."

The book and *yer secret*.

She blinked those lovely dark eyes, then dropped her chin and her gaze, as if suddenly unsure what to say. So he gave her hand another squeeze, reveling in the touch of her skin on his.

"Uncle Cam! Uncle Cam, look at what I can do!"

Blowing out a breath, he dragged his attention away from Rosa to the little girl he was supposed to have been watching all this time. "Aye, lassie?"

As she threw herself forward into the clear water, her little white arse flashing in the sunshine, he smiled and pulled his hand away from Rosa's. He stood, shading his eyes, until Simone came back to the surface.

"That's enough, lassie!" he called, beckoning her in. "Yer lips are turning blue."

Simone protested all the way to shore, but once on solid ground, she shivered fiercely as Cam used her plaid to dry her off. She stood, knobby knees clattering together, and her arms hugging her elbows, while her teeth chattered.

"Here," Rosa said as she handed him Simone's shirt and took the plaid from him.

It was a little complicated, trying to figure out which hole the girl's head was supposed to go through, and she was giggling by the time the shirt was on properly. Then Rosa pulled Simone down to sit in her lap while she dried the lassie's hair with the plaid.

Cam sat back on his haunches, watching the two. " 'Tis a useful piece of material, aye?"

"Lachlan would be happy to give ye one, I'm sure," Rosa murmured, not looking at him.

The thought of once more wearing the Fraser plaid had him flustered. "Nay. *Nay.* No' for me."

Little Simone piped up as Rosa plaited her damp hair. "If ye're my uncle, then ye should have a Fraser kilt."

He shook his head as he stood. "I havenae been a Fraser in many, many years," he called over his shoulder as he fetched the three trout he'd caught earlier.

But he still heard the lassie's snort. "I ken ye havenae been home in many years, but ye're still a Fraser. Can I go pick berries now, Rosa?"

"Aye, lassie," came the woman's quiet murmur. "Fill yer tam, and we'll eat them with the fish yer uncle caught."

With an excited squeal, the girl jumped up and ran for the berry bushes at the top of the hill. Rosa got up to spread the plaid on a boulder to dry, and Cam…

Well, Cam couldn't stop thinking about his niece's words. *Ye're still a Fraser.*

Was that true?

He'd turned his back on his family, his clan, years ago. He hadn't *wanted* to be a Fraser, not then.

But now...?

Now Father and Hamish were gone, and Lachlan was the laird. And he had a precious daughter Cam already loved.

And Mother was alive.

Cam wasn't sure if he could forgive her, but mayhap the chance to get to know her again...?

Shaking his head, he set to making a fire to roast the fish.

A week ago, his goal had been to find Court and make sure she was safe and doing well. Now, he was considering his mother and brother and *family*.

Considering his *future*.

And it was all thanks to this woman beside him. The one who, even now, sat quietly, staring out over the loch with a pensive expression upon her face.

Somewhere over the last few days, she'd changed his goals. She'd come into his life with her brilliant mind and her clever wit and her *unique* way of looking at the world. She'd been the push he'd needed to visit An Torr and had told him so much about his family.

There was still so much he didn't know about her, but he couldn't deny the truth: Somehow, Rosa Forbes had found a way into his heart.

As they ate—the berries were juicy and ripe, a perfect complement to the fish—Simone's eyelids began to grow heavy. Her shoulders slumped, and she asked fewer questions —a sure sign she was exhausted.

"Ye've been walking and swimming all morning," Rosa told her quietly, tugging her down to rest against her leg. "Close yer eyes for a moment."

The lassie was asleep before Cam had even finished kicking the coals apart.

He stood, hands on his hips, and watched as his niece mumbled in her sleep, then rolled over, sprawling across the grass. Her linen shirt was all tangled around her gangly limbs, and she reminded him of a shepherd's lad.

"What?" Rosa asked him, wriggling out from under the lassie and gently lowering the young girl's head to the grass.

Cam shrugged, realizing Rosa had asked why he was smiling so hugely. It was the first words she'd spoken to him since he finished reading, since he realized how much she meant to him, and mayhap *that* was why he was smiling.

Instead he jerked his chin toward Simone. " 'Tis glad I am Lachlan is raising her with so much freedom."

One of Rosa's brows twitched as she peered down at the girl. "She's no' exactly a proper lady, is she?"

Chuckling, Cam offered her his hand. "Let her sleep for a bit. We can pick some berries for later while we wait. Unless ye prefer bannock again tonight?"

She must've heard the challenge in his voice, because she was smiling when she reached up and took his hand. The warmth which spread up Cam's arm was everything he'd hoped for, everything he'd ever wanted.

Only now, he wasn't sure *what* he wanted, which path his future would follow.

Did he have the choice? Could one path lead back to An Torr? Back to his family?

Back home?

The silence followed them up the hill to the berry patch. Instead of using Simone's cap to hold them, Rosa pulled a pouch from inside her scapular and offered it instead.

They worked beside one another, avoiding the wicked, long thorns as they plucked the ripe berries.

They shared a companionable silence, but he wanted to learn more about her.

When he shifted so he could see her better, he discovered

she was frowning in concentration at a particularly thick patch of thorns, carefully maneuvering her fingers toward the berries. Her tongue stuck out between her lips.

It was purple.

When he snorted softly, she froze for a moment, then her dark eyes flicked toward him. His smile grew as he lifted a berry and popped it into his mouth, certain his own tongue was now just as stained by the berry juice as hers was.

Confronted with the evidence of her crime, Rosa pulled her hand back and straightened, her own smile growing, showing even more berry stains across her lips. "I confess I've stolen a few from our communal bag."

"*Stealing*, eh?" His smile grew even more as he dropped a few more berries into the bag. "And have ye ever stolen aught before?"

"Aye."

Her answer was too quick, too certain, to be anything other than the truth, and *that* surprised him.

"Really?" One of his brows rose. "What?"

She shrugged and turned her attention back to the berry bush. "Once, one of the Queen's letters fell into the wrong hands. It was from Robert, and Elizabeth believed the man who stole it from her would use the information in it against the Crown's best interest." Rosa spoke nonchalantly, as if this information wasn't incredible. "I devised the plan to get it back, which involved breaking into the inn where he was staying and stealing."

She kept picking berries and dropping them into the bag, while Cam stood there with his mouth hanging open.

Not only did she live in the palace, but she was on intimate terms with the *bloody Queen of Scotland*?

Rosa had just called the *Queen*—and even the *King*, for that matter!—by their given names, without a single blink or hesitation.

He *knew* she wasn't pretentious. *Knew* she wasn't the kind to be impressed by titles or name-dropping. Which meant she was *friends with the King and Queen of Scotland.*

God's Teeth, she was about as far from a thief like him as he could imagine!

But she kens the palace. She could help ye find Court.

Aye, he knew it. He knew Rosa would be a valuable asset in his mission to find his old friend. But he also knew he wouldn't be able to take advantage of her, to *use* her like that.

Not with how she'd worked her way into his heart.

He cleared his throat. "It sounds as if the Queen trusts ye."

"I am one of her—her ladies." Rosa still wasn't looking at him. "There are some plans which have a higher chance of success if implemented by a person no-one expects."

"Like ye." Like an intelligent woman who knew about disguises. "Dressed as a nun?"

She stilled; her gaze locked on the bush before her. He was able to count to five before she suddenly turned, a wide smile on her face.

Which looked false as hell.

"What about ye? What was the first thing ye stole?"

He crossed his arms before his chest and raised a brow at her. She was changing the subject, fine. He'd go along with it.

For now.

"A horse," he said succinctly. "Like we need now."

Without rising to the bait, she merely hummed, as if the information was fascinating. "Who'd ye steal it from?"

His gaze drifted away from her, across the hill, toward the angelic figure of his sleeping niece.

"My father," he murmured. "Nae one questioned me when I saddled the beast and rode away from An Torr. They all assumed I had Father's permission to go riding, and I'd be back that same evening."

"This was when ye were twelve?"

She knew so much about him, and he knew next to nothing about her.

"Aye," he grunted.

"Will ye tell me why ye left, Cam?" she asked softly.

Without looking at her, he shook his head once. "Suffice it to say, I have never regretted leaving. That first winter, I had no plan, no destination. I traded the horse for a few month's shelter in Glencoe and scrubbed tables at an inn. After the snows cleared, I headed south."

"To the Red Hand."

He sighed, his shoulders slumping.

God's Teeth, how could he be so entranced by a woman he knew nothing about, but who knew so much about him?

Scrubbing a hand over his face, he simply mumbled, "Aye."

Then he laced his fingers across the back of his head and stretched, watching the way the sun reflected off the waters of the loch.

"Aye. When I found them, 'twas not yet a year after I'd left. I was big for my age, but no' big enough to survive long on my own. I kenned I needed…*something*. I didnae realize it at the time, but that *something* was a teacher, someone to help me survive."

"By thieving."

There was no use denying it. He was a thief. It was what he was good at.

"I'd stolen to survive up until then, but I would've been caught had I tried it for longer. The man who ran the Red Hand at the time…"

Remembering the pain inflicted during his training, Cam blew out a breath.

"He was a ruthless bastard. But he was good at what he did. I learned from him, learned how to steal, learned how to pick pockets, learned how to turn stolen coin into food for the whole band. I learned how to *lead*. And when he was gone, I took over."

He'd been little more than a lad when he'd challenged for —*and won*—the chance to lead the Red Hand. It wasn't the first time he'd killed a man, even at that young age, and it hadn't been the last. But he liked to think he'd been able to mold that dirty, lawless group of men into something resembling a team.

At least until he'd given it all up to atone for a past sin.

Once in Scone, the men he'd brought with him from Kintyre had gone back to their honorless ways. They stole, raped, and killed against his orders, and he hated how easily he lost control of them among the temptations the city offered.

And then, a sennight ago, he'd killed the last of them to save the man he now knew was his brother.

All because he'd given up everything he'd built in order to find Court.

"There was...a lassie."

"A lassie?" she repeated flatly.

His hands dropped to his sides. "Aye. Courtney," he said softly. "The lads called her *English* because she spoke with an accent when she was verra young. She was sold to the Red Hand when she was Simone's age."

Staring down the hill at his niece, he couldn't imagine the terror she—or any child—would face in that situation. Court had handled it by being tougher and angrier than any of the lads, and he prayed she'd maintained that fire.

It would keep her alive.

"I protected her," he whispered. "I taught her what I kenned. She was—she was like my little sister. And then, after I became leader, I betrayed her."

Rosa was silent for so long, he glanced at her. She was staring at him, chewing on her lower lip.

It wasn't one of her signs she was thinking, nay. This was her *concerned* look.

"I'm no' a hero, Rosa," he said in a low voice, willing her to understand. "I'm a thief. I've done terrible things. And Court..." He shook his head, remembering the anguish on her face when he told her he was sending her away. "I sent her off on her own. She landed in gaol *twice*. The last I heard of her, she's alive and working in the palace. That's *all* I ken, and it's driving me mad."

"And ye want to find her?"

As always, her mind was two steps ahead of him.

"Aye. I *need* to find her to make sure she's safe and happy. To *apologize*."

He'd given up trying to understand Rosa, the way her mind could jump from one thought to the next. But whatever response he'd expected from her, it *wasn't* the one he got.

Surging toward him, she dropped the berries on the ground and threw her arms around his neck. Before he could react, she was tugging his lips down to hers.

And then he wasn't thinking about anything, because she was kissing him, and—*God Almighty*—it was everything he remembered.

And more.

With a groan, his arms snaked around her waist, lifting her up and pressing her slender frame against his larger one. Although her heavy habit was between them, hampering her movements, she managed to lift one leg and wrap it around his, pulling him closer, as her lips parted and invited his tongue in to play.

Dear God in Heaven, he couldn't recall ever feeling this way with any other woman. The desire hit so sudden and strong, he became lightheaded, all the blood rushing to his cock where it rubbed against the junction of her thighs.

She clung to him, her fingers twisting in his hair as if she were as desperate as he was, her hips undulating against his hardness in the most delicious torture.

One of his hands reached for her veil, yanking it off so he could feel her hair under his fingers. She broke away from his lips with a moan, dropping her head back to allow him access to her throat, which he happily took. His lips trailed across her skin, branding her.

Mine.

Mine!

He slowly let her slide down his body, and she eased her hold on him until both her feet were on the ground. With his other hand free now, he cupped her breast, teasing and squeezing through the rough material.

She moaned, arching against his touch, which brought her pelvis into contact with his stiff cock once more. Cam wanted to slam his eyes shut, to focus on the pleasure he was feeling at that moment, but then he'd lose the sight of Rosa, presenting herself to him like some kind of feast.

"Cam..." She moaned again, undulating against him, as her hands reached around to cup his arse. *"Please."*

His lips trailed back up her neck. He knew what she was begging for. He knew what she needed, what he could give her.

And he knew why he wouldn't give it to her.

She was offering herself to him. To *him*!

But no matter how deliriously aroused she made him, she was still one of the Queen's ladies, and he was still a common thief.

And as his lips claimed hers again, stifling both of their groans of pleasure, he knew he would have to be the one to pull apart, to step away from this—this—whatever *this* was.

But she surprised him yet again.

Rosa was the one who broke their kiss; the one who pulled away with a gasp.

And he let her go.

She was breathing heavily when she pressed her cheek against his chest, her small hands trailing up to wrap around his waist. He missed the feel of them on his arse.

It wasn't until he wrapped her in his arms and dropped his chin to her head that he realized how hard *he* was breathing. How much she had affected him. How much her touch—her *kiss*—had affected him.

Had been affecting him since that first meeting in the alley.

Was this what it was like to kiss someone he cared for?

Light as a feather, he felt her place a kiss against his chest. Then another one. He tightened his hold on her and willed his heart to stop pounding as if he'd run a race.

Wait…cared for?

Hellfire!

He was falling in *love* with a completely unsuitable woman, and despite the terror that evoked, he couldn't be happier.

Suddenly, she groaned, then turned her head so her forehead was pressed against him. He stiffened, not sure how to react.

Was she regretting their kiss?

Then she nodded, pounding her head against his chest twice, before groaning again.

"*Stupid*," she hissed.

"Rosa?" He pulled her gently away from him. "Rosa, what's wrong?"

She stared up at him; her lips swollen, her eyes dazed, and her hair in wild disarray. She looked as if she'd been thoroughly kissed, and despite his sudden worry, Cam felt a spike of primal pride.

He'd been the one to kiss her like that.

Mine!

She squeezed her dark eyes shut and wrinkled her nose. "I'm going to do something wrong. Something stupid. Something there's a high likelihood I will find myself regretting at least once in my life."

Mind racing, Cam's gaze skipped over her face, looking for clues.

Was she leaving him?

Before they even reached Scone?

Or was she talking about something different?

Did she want...did she want *him*?

And she thought that was a stupid thing?

It *was* stupid to want a man like him. But he couldn't deny he wanted her with all the aching in his heart.

And his cock, if he were being honest.

"What are ye saying, Rosa?" he asked hoarsely. When she didn't answer him, he moved his hands to her arms. "Rosa?"

Taking a deep breath, she opened her eyes.

There were no answers there, and her expression turned even more neutral.

"Go steal us some horses, Cam."

It was so unexpected, he reared back. "What in damnation?"

"The horses," she repeated. "The ones ye've been wanting to steal. I'll get the berries and wake Simone. Ye find us some horses. We'll meet further up the road to Scone."

He felt his mouth open, but no sound came out.

What was she saying?

Her hands loosened their hold on him and came around to pat his chest. But her eyes held only determination when she nodded at him.

"Go. Hurry. I would have this betrayal over and done."

CHAPTER 9

This betrayal...?

Rosa's confusing, terrifying words echoed around in Cam's head two days later, as he followed her along the palace's curtain wall.

He'd done as she'd asked that day beside the loch. They'd split up, with him finding a crofter's hut with a broken-down nag in the barn. Surprised at the way his conscience pricked, he continued to the next village, where he borrowed two horses.

Borrowed?

Ha!

His mantle's hood up to hide his face, Cam shook his head in disgust. He was a *thief*. 'Twas foolish to call it aught else. Foolish to lie to himself about who he was.

"Shh!" Rosa hissed from ahead, flattening her back along the wall and gesturing to him to do the same.

Far above, the sound of a guard's patrol passed slowly by. With them tucked against the wall like this, they'd be invisible...unless the man had reason to look straight down, alerted by, say, a noise Cam made.

This time his disappointment was silent, but he shook his head once more.

God's Teeth, he was a bloody *thief*!

He should be better at sneaking into the royal palace, shouldn't he?

Better than Lady Rosalind Forbes, at least.

But here she was, picking her way along the wall, as if she were quite used to doing things such as this. She knew the Guard's patrols, and she was leading him very confidently in one direction.

Who in damnation is this woman he'd fallen so hard for?

And how did she know how to break into the royal palace?

After he'd *stolen* the horses, it hadn't taken him long to overtake her and Simone. He scooped up the lassie to carry her, and had been impressed, yet again, by Rosa's riding ability. They traveled hard and fast, on her urging, and reached Scone last night.

There they'd split up: him to sell the horses for a profit, and her to return Simone to her father.

The lassie had hugged him tightly, instructing him to "Come find me and Da and Mellie. They're getting married soon!"

Rosa hadn't said goodbye to him and had appeared to be distracted. Probably because she had yet to tell his niece Lachlan had been wounded.

But she did finally turn to him before they actually parted. "Tomorrow morning, find me in the spot where we first met. Bring yer mantle."

It wasn't a goodbye.

It was *better*.

And now he was following her, avoiding the paths of the guards above, until the great walls turned to simple, shallow stone, and the Guard's patrols turned in another direction.

"These are the gardens," she whispered, hurrying along the uneven wall. "They used to be just herbal, for the kitchens, but Elizabeth has a fondness for nature and spends a lot of time out here. *Proxima natura.*"

There she went again, calling the Queen of Scotland by her Christian name.

He snorted softly, amazed by how nonchalantly she said such things, and she swung to a stop. With a raised brow, she seemed to ask him why he was laughing.

Offering a smile, he covered his fumble. "*Omnia dicta fortiora si dicta Latina?*"

Her suspicious look softened. "Aye," she whispered. " 'Tis well-known, speaking in Latin makes *anything* sound more profound."

Credo te amo.

I think I love you.

But he didn't say it. *Couldn't* say it. He knew nothing about this woman, not really.

Rosa stepped up beside a series of stones which looked exactly the same as the stones around it. But she lifted her hands and pressed against two different blocks at the same time, and they depressed under the pressure. Then she raised a knee and pressed against a third block, and something *clicked* inside the wall.

A door—cleverly concealed by a facing of stonework—swung inward.

She slipped inside, and he followed, stepping into a manicured woodland. Sucking in a breath, he looked around. These trees weren't mature, but had to have been planted right after Elizabeth became queen. The fallen pine needles made a soft bed between his boots and the soil beneath, as he picked his way toward the cobblestone path.

Ahead of him, Rosa was ignoring the flowerbeds carefully cultivated to look natural, or the little pond with fish and frogs croaking in the sunshine. He could believe he'd stepped into someplace magical...if he weren't so intent on figuring out *why he was here.*

"Rosa!" he hissed, grabbing her hand and swinging her around to face him. "I've been following ye all this time and am confused as hell. I will be forever grateful to ye for getting me in here to have a chance to see Court again, but I have to—"

"We're no' here to see Court."

She lifted her small chin and met his gaze with a challenge in her own, the fancy pearl netting she wore over her dark hair making her look as if she *belonged* in a place like this.

But he was too busy focusing on her words to care.

She kens who Court is!

He'd wondered—*hoped*—that was the case, but she'd never said anything.

"Ye ken her?" he asked in a rough whisper, searching her face for the truth. "Ye ken Courtney?"

She stepped out of his hold. "Aye." Her voice sounded too bland. "But she cannae ken ye're here. *Nae* one can ken ye're here."

When he stepped toward her, she backed up again, shaking her head.

"I mean it, Cam. If they found out I brought ye here..."

Betrayal.

Is this what she'd meant?

"Who, lass?" he asked, his voice hoarse with confusion and dread.

She shook her head again.

The lass is full of secrets.

"Why did ye bring me here?" He gestured around the garden. "Why did ye give me a glimpse at my goal, and now ye're saying nae?"

To his surprise, her expression softened, and she stepped forward to take his hand once more. "Because there's someone else ye need to see first. Come."

She tugged him toward the palace door and, wanting answers, he could do little else but follow.

∾

Deus in caelo, she *really* shouldn't be doing this.

Cam was a suspect against the Crown, and guards were looking for him everywhere.

So why are ye currently leading him through the guest hall of the royal palace?

Because she trusted him. She trusted him *not* to be the kind of man who would lead a coup against the Crown.

Her reasoning for wanting to be the one to find him was so she could question him, learn more about him. Things hadn't worked out the way she'd intended, but she'd gotten her chance.

And now that she *did* know him, she couldn't believe he was guilty of what they'd all suspected.

Her included.

Inferos!

The doubt and certainty warred within her, and luckily, Cam didn't ask any more questions as they strolled, as nonchalantly as they could manage, through the palace. He didn't have to; whenever she glanced at him, she could see the questions in his eyes.

The lovely gray eyes she'd seen often enough, not on Lachlan, but on his mother, Isla.

"Here we are." She took a deep breath and turned to him, her hand on a door she'd visited many times. "Are ye ready?"

His brows lowered in a glare. "Nay. Where in damnation *are* we?"

Pushing open the door, she answered over her shoulder, "Yer mother's room," and prayed he'd follow.

"Rosalind, dear, is that ye?" The call came from the aged woman who sat bent over her embroidery in the beam of sunlight by the window. When she looked up, her face broke into a smile. "I was hoping ye'd come visit me when ye returned to the palace. With Gillepatric gone, there's few people to talk to, and I was going to take myself down to the throne room to listen to the Queen's judgements today."

Stepping farther into the room, Rosa plastered a smile on her lips and snuck a glance over her shoulder. Cam was still standing in the doorway, his large hand holding the door open, and shock in his expression as he stared at his mother.

Was he angry?

Rosa had heard his declarations, his intentions, there among the berry thorns, and had *known* he was innocent.

But before she could consider her next step, she knew there was someone else who needed to know that as well.

Lady Isla Fraser had arrived at court weeks ago with her advisor, Gillepatric. According to the men who'd attacked Lachlan and Mellie, the older man had been behind their attack, offering coin for their murder. But he himself had been murdered that very day, and his killer never found.

"Well, dear?" Isla placed her sewing to one side and smiled pleasantly, gesturing Rosa toward her. "Where have ye been over the last sennight?"

Remembering the kiss, the aching feet, the sheer *joy* she'd felt while Cam had read to her, the fear and stress and laughter, Rosa wondered how she could summarize her trip.

Crossing the room and taking the woman's outstretched hand to squeeze it, Rosa smiled gently, knowing she couldn't tell her everything. "I was with yer son, Lady Isla."

The older woman scowled in response. "Lachlan? He's still intent on marrying *that woman*."

Shocked at Isla's vehemence, Rosa allowed herself to be pulled down onto the bench. "Mellie?"

"Aye. Lachlan *has* a daughter already. Why does he need to marry again? He's only setting himself up for more heartache."

Rosa tried not to show how surprised she was, but tilted her head back as she worked her way through Isla's words. Lachlan needs an heir, but Isla obviously thought Simone was good enough. But from all accounts, Isla wasn't very kind to her granddaughter, so it was surprising to hear her think the lassie a sufficient enough heir for a clan with such an unstable history.

Frowning, she pushed the problem aside, vowing to dissect the quandary later. For now, though…

She squeezed Isla's hand. "Nay, milady. I was with *Cameron.*"

He chose that opportune time to step into the room, and Rosa sucked in a breath. He looked so…*lost*. One hand was curled around the hilt of his sword, the other in a fist at his side. His jaw was tight, and she remembered the way those hard lips had felt under hers.

Then he'd been warm and welcoming. But now, facing his mother—a surprise Rosa had sprung on him—he was every inch the cold, hard warrior.

Not just a thief, but a leader of men.

"Oh, Cameron," Isla said, glancing up with a smile. " 'Tis good of ye to visit."

The comment was so bland, so nonchalant, that Cam's steps faltered. He glanced at Rosa, a frown on his lips, and she shrugged slightly.

The woman hadn't seen her son in fifteen years.

Why was she not welcoming him with open arms?

"Isla," she began gently, "this is *Cameron*. He's been gone many years, remember?"

"Of course I ken who he is." The older woman pulled her hand from Rosa's and offered it to Cam. "Welcome to Scone, lad. I've been waiting impatiently."

Awkwardly, Cam took his mother's hand.

Had expected a warm embrace?

Had he *hoped* for one?

Instead, he bowed over her hand, the way a stranger might.

And Isla beamed.

"Ye always were a sweet lad to ken when ye're mother was lonely and bring her joy. Yer father was like that too, as I recall. I've been waiting for ye to visit."

Visit?

Father?

Cam was doing a good job of hiding his confusion, but Rosa could see it...because she was feeling the same thing.

From all the stories she'd heard, Michael Fraser had *not* been the type to bring others joy.

And Isla was acting so nonchalant...was it possible she thought Cam was someone else?

Rosa caught Cam's eye and winced, just slightly, hoping to convey her theory that his mother's madness had progressed.

The older woman pushed herself to her feet. As she adjusted her sleeves, she said, "I *ken* ye'd come find me, Cameron, once ye were without yer uncle's council."

And if her previous words had surprised him, these latest had obviously shocked him to his core.

Cam actually stepped back. "Ye—ye *kenned* I was alive? All this time?"

"Of course." Isla looked up, surprised. "Well, no' at first. That's why I sent yer uncle Andrew after ye. *He* at least understood how important ye were." She shook her head a little mournfully. "My husband was useless when it came to that sort of thing. *Andrew*, on the other hand, didnae stop looking for ye until he found ye."

Cam had told Rosa more about his life with the Red Hand, and she knew that Andrew of Lovat had arrived a few years prior to Court's banishment. It had taken him that long to find Cam. But it was a surprise to learn that Isla had *sent* her brother-in-law.

"And—" Cam cleared his throat, his eyes carefully locked on his mother. "Ye ken where I've been? What I've done? All these years?"

Isla smiled up at her son as she lightly rested her hand on the sleeve of his tunic. "Aye. Andrew tells me everything." Her expression fell. "*Told.* He's..." She turned away. "He's dead now."

Cam shouldn't have any way of knowing that information, but his expression was blank and only a muscle in his jaw jumped. "How did it happen?"

"He took over the Red Hand, of course, after ye left," she went on, as if she hadn't heard him. "After ye ran off, chasing that whore of yers."

Cam's anger was immediate and palatable. He jerked out from under Isla's touch, even as Rosa sprang to her feet to defend her friend against this woman she suddenly didn't know.

She needn't have worried.

"Court isnae a whore!" Cam growled. "She was my *sister*. I protected her the way nae one protected me, and I sent her away to protect her from *Andrew*." Shaking his head, he stepped back once more. "I swore I'd find her, and my uncle was welcome to the entire damnable gang, for all I cared."

Tsking, Isla glared up at him with identical gray eyes. "That's where ye were wrong, lad. Ye *never* give up power, no' for anyone. Yer father would've taught ye that when ye were a lad, had he lived." She shook her head as she stepped up beside him. "Ye do no' ever give it up until it's *stolen* from ye."

Cam's eyes were wide, confused. "What the hell are ye speaking of, woman?" he asked hoarsely. "My father lived long after I left him—left both of ye. He refused the protection he owed his own son, and ye—"

"No' Michael Fraser, lad," she said sadly, reaching up to pat his arm once more. "Yer *real* father. Red Comyn."

CHAPTER 10

In Rosa's mind, the tangled skeins of suspicions, the threads of ideas which hadn't led anywhere, all suddenly began to unravel in the most wonderful way. The final piece of this puzzle was there, just out of her reach.

She'd known putting Isla and Cam together would give her the clue she needed to solve this mess…but she hadn't realized what it would reveal.

As the older woman patted her son's arm and swayed out of the room, Rosa watched her go in shock. Isla's lack of reaction to her son, as well as her casual revelation, had shown her to be more crazed than Rosa had suspected.

And it *had* been a revelation. She only had to glance at Cam to realize that.

The man was staring down at his palms, the same shock on his own face, though likely much more.

It was obvious he hadn't known about his parentage before this moment.

But who else did?

Isla, of course.

Andrew?

If Andrew had known Cam was Red Comyn's son—and now the last of the Comyn line—it would explain why he'd given up everything he'd known to find the Red Hand and stand beside Cam.

How many of his actions over the years had been influenced by Andrew Fraser's council?

Had it been Andrew's idea to kill the King and Queen and put Cam on the throne?

Did Cam know about—

As she watched him sink down into a chair and drop his head into his hands, Rosa bit down on her thoughts.

Nay, Cam might've been influenced by an evil man, but she didn't believe he was evil. At least, she hadn't believed that when she'd snuck him into the palace, and she couldn't believe that now.

And untangling this mess could wait. For now, Cam needed her.

Carefully, she moved to sit beside him, not touching him, as she was unsure of her welcome. "Cam?" she whispered.

His voice was muffled as it came from between his palms. "I'm...I'm a Comyn."

It hadn't been a question.

She didn't know what to say, but tried anyhow. "Ye didnae ken?"

"Nay!" When he dropped his hands, his gray eyes were bright with confusion. "How could I?" He stared out the window where his mother had been sitting. "I never thought..."

Shaking his head, he muttered a curse and pushed himself to his feet once more, as if he had too much energy to sit still. "My father always seemed to hate me. At least, that's how it felt as a child—he'd punish me for no reason and showed my brothers more favor."

"Do ye think this is why?"

He was stalking around the room, no purpose in his movements. "I...I donae ken. Did Mother tell him? Mother was unfaithful to him! *God's Teeth!*" He dragged his hands through his over-long hair. "Mother was unfaithful to him with *Red Comyn*. The man my father wanted to be *king!*"

Launching into motion once more, he shook his head. "Were they hosting him at Inverness or Dounie when it happened? Comyn wouldn't have been too old then—*God's Teeth*, that was when *Toom Tabard* was still king!"

"Cam." When he didn't seem to hear her gentle interruption, she repeated his name again. "*Cameron!*"

He whirled and pierced her with a glare. "Did ye ken this? Is that why ye brought me to visit my mother?"

Surprised, she shook her head. "Nay, I swear. I just knew that, if I wanted to think of a future with ye, I couldnae allow yer poor, sweet mother to continue thinking ye were dead."

"Sweet mother?" He muttered something unkind and turned away. "The woman didnae seem to miss me at all. She was only thinking of her own inconveniences."

Rosa had to admit he was right. She'd enjoyed her time spent with Isla, but the woman *did* seem to be growing madder by the day.

"I'm sorry, Cam," she whispered. "I thought she'd be pleased to see ye. *Deus scit*, I would miss ye if—" She cut herself off, unwilling to admit her feelings aloud, especially with him so agitated.

He was staring down at his hands again, as if seeing them for the first time. "Red Comyn is my father," he whispered.

"Aye," she began carefully, "and some might say that makes ye a verra important man."

With a snort, he curled his fingers into fists and met her eyes. "I am a thief."

"Ye are the son of a man who many wanted to be the King."

He shook his head. "I do no' want to be. I didnae ken."

Holding his gaze, Rosa stood, willing him to understand how important this was. "Cam, *swear* to me ye had nae idea."

His answer was an immediate nod. "Aye. On my honor—as a thief." His voice turned bitter on the last part, and he shook his head just slightly.

Exhaling gratefully, she knew what she had to do. "I believe ye."

On the other side of the room, one brow rose disbelievingly. "Ye'd take my word on something this important?"

He had *no* idea how important. But... "Aye. I think ye're a good man."

This time his snort was softer, as he turned away. "Ye'd be the first."

The time had come.

"Cam, I..."

She suddenly wasn't sure how to say what needed to be said. Not while looking at him, at least.

Turning toward the window, she inhaled deeply, focusing on the city of Scone spread out below her. It was one of Scotland's great accomplishments, this city, along with so many others. She'd spent five years protecting not just the Queen, but the Crown and the country.

And she prayed she wasn't about to betray them all.

"Weeks ago, there was an attack against the Queen. The assassin almost succeeded, but he was killed." For now, she'd leave Court out of this. Her friend should be the one to decide when to reveal herself. "Before he died, he said he'd been sent from the Red Hand."

There was no sound, no reaction behind her. But the silence felt *anticipatory*, as if Cam was listening.

She took another deep breath. "When—when the Queen's representative went to Kintyre and confronted the Red Hand, yer Uncle Andrew was in charge. He revealed the

Frasers of Lovat were behind the attempted coup, in order to remove the Bruce and his wife from the throne and return the Comyn line to power."

"Return the Comyns to the throne?" Cam's voice was dull. "Red Comyn and his *legitimate* son have been dead for years."

"Aye." She turned to find him staring suspiciously. "There was no indication *why* Andrew, or any of the Frasers, would believe the scheme would succeed, but before he was killed, yer uncle definitely implicated the Frasers of Lovat."

Cam crossed his arms in front of his chest, the movement pulling his tunic tight across his shoulders. "And the Frasers have a history of supporting the Comyns for the throne, so it was easy to believe."

Again, not a question, but she dipped her chin in acknowledgement. "Aye," she repeated softly. "Yer brother Lachlan was the laird, and the most likely suspect. But he was investigated"—best to leave Mellie's secret out as well—"and determined to be innocent. And then *ye* arrived back in Lachlan's life, proving ye had ties to the Red Hand."

The way his eyes darted between hers made it obvious he was trying to understand what she was saying. *Deus in caelo,* but she wished she were closer to him. She wished she could put her hand on his forearm or wrap her arms around his waist and rest her cheek against his chest.

She wanted to *feel* him. To offer him whatever comfort she could.

But if she were that close to him, she wouldn't have been able to see the confusion in his eyes slowly turning to anger.

"And I was a Fraser," he bit out. "I donae *want* to be one, but I was a Fraser son, who had led the Red Hand." He spit out the words as if they were a curse and jerked his gaze away from her. "And *ye* were the one to put it all together, were ye no'?"

There was no use denying it. "Aye," she whispered.

"*Shite*," he swore, turning completely from her and lifting his hands to yank at his hair. "Ye think I'm guilty, is that it? Ye think I was the one to plan a *coup against the Crown?*"

Whirling back around, he pierced her with another glare.

"Is that it? Ye thought, since I was a thief, I might be a traitor as well?"

Deus meus, how was she supposed to respond to the hurt and anger in his eyes?

With the truth.

"I did," she admitted, embarrassment coloring her tone.

She didn't *want* to feel embarrassed—it had been the logical conclusion at the time—and even more so now that she knew the secret of Cam's birth.

But her heart didn't want to accept *logic* at a time like this...and wasn't *that* a novel realization?

"And now?" he asked in a hoarse whisper.

Now?

Now I love ye.

But she couldn't say that. She'd just betrayed her Queen, her country, and her fellow Angels, and she wasn't even sure she'd done anything wrong.

So she lowered her head, staring at the floor between them. "Now I donae ken what to think."

With a muttered curse, he stalked for the door, and her gaze flew up.

"Where are ye going?"

"Leaving," he snapped over his shoulder. "Don' bother showing me the way out. I'm a *thief*, remember? I can find my *own* way in and out of a palace."

"Cam—" she began, but he yanked the door open and was gone.

And she suspected she'd just made a huge mistake.

Because she'd been thinking with her mind instead of her heart?

Or because she'd allowed her heart to override her mind? *Deus in caelo*, what a mess!

~

Cam wasn't thinking straight.

That was why he got turned around on his way out of his mother's chambers and was now silently cursing himself. But on the other hand, it wasn't hard to understand why.

Red Comyn's son.

All these years, and now he discovered he isn't a Fraser at all. Not really. His father—the man who'd treated him like refuse and allowed even *worse* to befall him—wasn't really his father.

'Twould explain much, he supposed.

And honestly, after fifteen years away from his family, the sting of their betrayal hurt much less now than it did then. Nay, it was Rosa's opinion which burned him now.

She thought ye a thief and a liar.

Why no' a traitor as well?

He scrubbed his hand over his face and blew out a breath.

Regardless of what had just happened, he needed to put it behind him and figure out how to get out of here.

Nay! He needed to find Court. It had been his goal for a year now, and he was finally in the place to make it happen, and he had no idea where to find her.

Rosa did, but he'd just stormed off from her like a clot-heid, because his *feelings* had been hurt.

Ahead of him in the corridor, a door opened.

No matter where his mind was, fifteen years of instincts couldn't be overridden. He flattened himself into a window nook before the person even stepped out of the chamber.

"Do ye think he'll recover fully, Healer?" came the soft question.

"Aye, lass." The healer sounded elderly. "The Fraser is a strong man. Ye saw how far he's come in a fortnight? He'll be hale and hearty by his wedding night, and I suspect that pretty betrothed of his is helping his recovery nicely."

Their chuckles faded in the distance, and Cam exhaled.

The Fraser.

Lachlan.

His brother.

He was moving toward the room before he'd fully come to a decision. When he realized what he was doing, his hand was already on the latch.

'Tis a day for revelations.

Taking a deep breath, he pushed open the door and slid inside the chamber before he could change his mind—or before anyone else could spot him in the corridor.

His brother's back was to him, the bandages the healer must've just reapplied stark against his tanned skin. Cam heard him curse quietly as the shirt he was maneuvering over his head got hung up on those bandages. The fact Lachlan couldn't lift his arm all the way didn't help either.

Cam's lips tugged upward. "Do ye need some help?"

His brother spun around, dropping halfway into a crouch to meet whatever danger he expected.

The fact that Lachlan looked even more ridiculous crouched there, with one arm tangled in the linen above his head and a scowl on his face, made Cam's smile grow.

But as his brother slowly straightened, the surprise in his gray eyes turning to wariness, and Cam's amused expression faded.

Lachlan's lips parted, as if he wanted to say something, but no sound came out.

Cam's heart began to pound in trepidation.

Would his brother accept him?

And would it matter if he didn't?

So he swallowed—his throat dry—and nodded to the bandages on Lachlan's shoulder. " 'Tis glad I am to see that healing."

It was as if his words had broken some spell. With a growl, Lachlan began to struggle with his shirt again. "It wouldnae if no' for ye. I have ye to thank for my life."

Grunting, he finally pulled the linen down over his bandages, so that his shirt hung too long over his kilt. But he didn't seem to care.

Instead of reaching for his belt, Lachlan rolled his neck, then his shoulders, all while staring at Cam.

Finally, he grunted again, as if coming to a decision. "Why are ye here?"

Why?

Cam couldn't say, because he didn't know why himself. So he shrugged, his thumbs tucked into his belt. "I wanted to ken if ye were healing. If ye'd live."

"Oh, I'll live." His brother eyed him from across the room. "Is that the only reason ye came?"

The only reason he'd snuck into a heavily guarded royal palace?

Nay, there were other reasons, and Rosa had given him even more. But now…

"What other reason would I have?" he asked warily.

Suddenly, Lachlan sighed and scrubbed a hand over his face in a gesture eerily similar to something Cam would do. "I was hoping ye'd come because ye wanted to see our mother. Because ye wanted to see *me*." He dropped his hand and pierced Cam with a glare. "I was hoping I was going to get my *brother* back."

There was anger there, but pain too. And for the first time, Cam realized how much he might've hurt Lachlan by leaving all those years ago.

"I'm sorry I've caused ye pain, Lachlan," he whispered in a hoarse voice.

Muttering a curse, his brother launched across the room toward him, and Cam braced himself for a blow. A blow he mayhap deserved.

But instead, Lachlan wrapped his arms around Cam, pulling him into an embrace. A *hug*.

When was the last time a man had hugged him?

Not since...well, not *ever*, that he could recall.

Slowly, awkwardly, Cam raised his hands and hugged his brother back.

It felt *right*.

As Lachlan pulled back, he clasped Cam's upper arms and met his eyes. "I'm sorry I wasnae able to help ye. Ye cannae ken how many times I've asked myself what I could've done. How I could've stopped Hamish—"

"Nay." Cam cut him off with a jerk of his head. "Hamish preyed on the weak, and I was the youngest. Ye were just a lad yerself and didnae have any idea what he was capable of."

With a nod, Lachlan dropped his hands and stepped back. "I am still sorry. I've missed having ye by my side all these years."

If Cam were honest with himself, he missed it too. He'd had Uncle Andrew, but the man had thrived among the cutthroats and thieves of the Red Hand. Having a brother like Lachlan mayhap would've made all the difference.

But all Cam could do was curtly nod. It was the only answer either could afford to give at that moment.

Lachlan gestured to a little sitting area near the hearth. "Will ye join me for some ale?"

Shifting his weight awkwardly, and wondering if he really should be there, Cam asked, "I'm no' interrupting ye? Someplace ye have to be?"

"Nay." His brother's answer was immediate as he crossed for the pitcher of ale. "Naught is more important to me right now than having my brother back in my life."

So with a sigh, Cam acquiesced. "Fine. As long as ye donae punch me again. Took three days for my head to stop aching."

Wincing, Lachlan handed him a mug. "I am sorry for that. I couldn't let ye harm Mellie."

"Och, brother, I was teasing ye."

When they both settled themselves into the wooden chairs, they were smiling.

"My daughter told me she'd met ye. In fact, she hasnae stopped talking of *Uncle Cam* since we got her back yesterday." Lachlan sipped his ale, staring at his brother over the rim of the mug. "She said she met ye at An Torr, fishing."

Cam shrugged as he put the ale down, untasted. "She was in my favorite spot."

"She reminds me of ye, sometimes. At least, the way I remember ye."

And there was naught to do other than grin proudly. "Aye," Cam admitted. "I thought the same."

"God help us," Lachlan muttered under his breath, which had Cam chuckling.

"She's a fine lassie. Smart and full of joy."

"Full of questions, more like," Lachlan corrected.

"Aye, she drove Rosa near distraction with them all."

Mayhap it was the way he said her name, but his brother's gaze turned speculative as he settled the mug on the table beside him. "Aye, *Rosa*." Then, entirely too nonchalantly, he offered, "Simone *also* said she saw Rosa kissing her uncle."

His brother's expression was carefully neutral, but Cam felt his hackles rise. "I'm nae a lad to be reprimanded for kissing a pretty lass. And ye're no' my father to do so."

"Fair enough." Lachlan's chin dropped. "And I cannae imagine our father caring about us, one way or the other."

Our father.

This would be the perfect time to reveal what Mother had said earlier. To tell Lachlan they didn't share a father, but Cam was the son of a traitor.

But something—some shame—held him back.

If Rosa, who'd come to know him and thought him a good man, still believed Cam's parentage gave him a reason to want the Queen dead, then what would Lachlan think?

Lachlan, who had just met him again after so many years apart?

Who knew him only as a leader of thieves now?

So they sat in silence, Lachlan staring thoughtfully back at him. Finally, his older brother shifted. "Ye were looking for Courtney, as I recall."

Cam's chin rose hopefully. "Aye?"

He remembered telling Lachlan—whom he hadn't realized was his *brother* at the time—about his quest to track down Court in the palace...just moments before his brother had landed a punch which had knocked him out cold.

"Court is close friends with Mellie and Rosa. I cannae say more—she has her secrets—but she is here, in the palace."

Curling his fingers around the arms of the chair, Cam tried to understand the tightness in his chest.

Was it because he was so close to completing his mission?

Or because Rosa had kept this information from him, as well?

She has her secrets.

Lachlan's words were accurate for Rosa as well. There was *so much* Cam didn't know about her.

But he didn't *need* to either.

"At least—" He shook his head, clearing the emotion from his throat. "Tell me, is she safe? Healthy? Happy?"

Lachlan's lips twitched. "She is. I also ken she's been out in the city looking for ye every chance she gets. When she's no' guarding the— Well, that's her business to tell, I suppose."

All the breath seemed to go out of Cam. He slumped in the chair and reached for the ale with surprisingly steady fingers.

Court was safe. *Happy*.

Did he have to see her to be sure?

Or did he trust his brother's word?

Closing his eyes, he breathed a soft prayer of thanks for her health. But at the same time, he knew he needed to see her, to apologize for sending her away. To hear her forgive him.

Or curse him, whichever the case may be.

Lachlan began to speak about Mellie, and how they'd met —a betrothal which turned out to be a charade—and the wedding they planned to have soon. "I've convinced her to wait a few days until I get my strength back."

Cam eyed his brother's shoulder. "Ye *are* healing, right?"

"Aye." Lachlan rolled his shoulder for effect. " 'Twas a clean strike, and only the blood loss was a concern. Mellie tells me ye were the one to help, after I—*passed out*."

The way he said it made Cam wonder at the rest of the story, but he just shrugged. "Those men attacking ye used to be mine. I thought I could control them when we came to the city, but…" He shook his head. "I was less of a leader than I imagined."

Mayhap Lachlan heard the bitterness in that claim, because he sat forward. "Tell me."

And so they spoke of Cam's history, and his years with the Red Hand.

Finally, Cam concluded by saying, "Rosa had this all figured out though. That woman is brilliant."

"And beautiful," Lachlan said mildly, from behind his mug. "Surely ye noticed that, as ye were kissing her?"

Mayhap it was the ale, but Cam was less defensive this time. "Aye. Beautiful and brilliant. And feisty. And witty. And full of fascinating insights." *Fascinating.* That described her well. "She's the kind who, once ye meet her, ye cannae forget her."

"Once ye meet her, she gets under yer skin and burrows next to yer heart?" Lachlan clarified.

"Aye," Cam admitted.

His brother nodded. "Ye love her then."

With a sigh, Cam put the ale down again and scrubbed his hand over his face. "Aye. I do."

"Ye havenae told her though."

Scowling, Cam dropped his hand. "How do ye ken?"

"Because if ye *had*," his brother unhelpfully pointed out, "ye wouldnae be here looking so forlorn when ye talk about her."

"What do *ye* ken of it?"

Chuckling, Lachlan took another sip. "It took almost losing Mellie for me to figure out my feelings for her. Ye're smarter than I am, apparently. But no' smart enough to tell her how ye feel."

Cam snorted. "And why would I? She's a *lady*. A confidante of the Queen." He sat forward and braced his elbows on his knees. "And I'm a thief."

A *bastard* thief.

Lachlan didn't speak, but the way he was looking at Cam before he ducked his head made Cam wonder how much he knew about the conspiracy against the Crown.

Did Lachlan believe him guilty as well?

What did it matter?

Finally, his brother asked quietly, "Does *she* think ye're a good man?"

A good man.

She'd said those words. She'd said she thought he was one.

Slowly, he lifted his head. "Aye," he admitted.

"I imagine Rosalind Forbes kens ye better than I do right now, brother," Lachlan began earnestly. "And she *does* have a brilliant mind, and Mellie trusts her implicitly. If Rosa kens ye to be a good man, then she trusts ye as well."

As Cam just stared, Lachlan shook his head with a small smile. "And if Rosa trusts ye, then ye can tell her how ye feel. Like as no', she feels the same way."

Was that possible?

Cam straightened, his gaze on the far wall.

Was it possible that somehow, someway, Rosa felt the same for him?

"There's only one way to find out," Lachlan said quietly.

But he'd stormed out. He'd left her in his anger.

She'd told him some of her secrets, and aye, he'd been bitter she'd only been *investigating* him...but the sorrow in her dark eyes told him it had become something more.

Something special?

He reached for the ale and downed it as his brother chuckled.

"Aye, love makes us feel that way. Donae run off yet though, brother." Lachlan gestured to the pitcher again. "Tell me of yer adventure. Tell me more of our years apart."

With a sigh, Cam took the coward's way out.

He'd stay. He'd get to know his brother again. And once he'd had time to think more on his feelings, he'd find Rosa.

"Aye, Laird," he teased, reaching for the pitcher. "But only if ye tell me about Simone."

As Lachlan stood, he was smiling. "My favorite topic!"

But instead of speaking, he crossed the room and stood

before a trunk. After rummaging inside, he pulled out a folded tartan.

A Fraser plaid.

When he held it out in offer, his expression was hesitant. "I was reminded when ye called me *laird*. I didnae want this position, but I am determined to make our people's future a peaceful one." He dropped his gaze to the wool between them. "I donae ken yer plans for the future, but I want ye to ken ye'll always be my brother."

A Fraser.

A place at An Torr.

Assuming he wasn't executed as a traitor.

Hesitantly, Cam stood and stepped toward his brother. Lachlan held the plaid out further.

And Cam took it. "Thank ye, brother."

Whatever the future might hold, he'd face it as a Fraser.

CHAPTER 11

*R*osa's eyes ached from weeping, which was daft. Weeping never fixed anything, and only made her feel worse. Her father had always told her logic was the only way to solve problems...but Mother had once confessed sometimes tears helped.

Not today though.

Today, no matter how long she sat there in Isla's chambers and cried, Rosa couldn't erase the memory of Cam's hurt, the way he'd looked so betrayed when she'd confessed the truth.

Then he'd stormed off, and now she was worried about him. Worried, despite knowing his skill as a thief, and his ability to navigate the palace.

Still, that didn't stop her from peering into corners and niches as she dragged her feet to Charlotte's solar, hoping she wouldn't see him hiding. Hoping he'd made it safely out into the city.

As she reached the Angel leader's room, she took a deep breath. Her eyes ached, aye, and rubbing at them hadn't helped. But it was time to issue her report, and she guessed her teammates would be inside at this time of morning, since Liam and his men would be guarding the Queen.

She was right.

As soon as she pushed open the door, Mellie looked up from where she lounged in front of the cold hearth.

"Rosa?" the buxom Angel asked, pushing herself upright. "What's wrong?"

Leave it to Mellie to notice things few others would. Court—who stood in front of the window with her omnipresent bow—probably had noted Rosa's puffy eyes, but would never think to mention them. Mellie, on the other hand, was the *heart* of their team, and the idea of losing her when she married Lachlan made Rosa feel weepy all over again.

Nay. Weeping hadn't solved anything before, and it wouldn't now.

Besides, there was no way to describe what Cam had come to mean to her, was there?

So she forced a smile. "I will be aright."

Mellie didn't look convinced, but Court gave her a hard, quick nod.

Charlotte, who was bent over her desk and cradling her infant son against her breast with her left hand, barely glanced up. " 'Tis glad I am ye're finally back, Rosa. We've needed yer mind."

Pushing down her sorrow and guilt, Rosa straightened her shoulders. It was time to do what she did best. What she could *still* do.

She was an Angel.

"What do ye need?"

With a sigh, Charlotte tossed down her stylus and sat back in her chair, shifting wee Roger slightly. "We cannae find Cameron Fraser anywhere in Scone."

"And believe me," Court cut in flatly, "we've looked."

Rosa knew how much finding Cam meant to Court, now that her fellow Angel knew the truth of Cam's actions when he'd sent her away. And now that she knew Cam, she knew how important it was to *him* to find Courtney.

But before Rosa could tell Court all this—explain why they hadn't been able to find Cam in the city—Charlotte was growling again.

"*And* there's been another attack against the King. He's coming back to Scone to get to the bottom of this, which means we'll have to give up control of the investigation if I donae get some leads *fast*."

Rosa's stomach churned, torn between guilt and loyalty. "Another attack?" she asked weakly. "What are the details? Any connection to the first one?"

Charlotte detached her son from her breast and lifted him to one shoulder to burp. "There." She nodded to a scroll atop the chaotic parchments on her desk. "The details are there." She patted the bairn's back. "Read it and tell me what ye think. Can we connect it to the Red Hand?"

And just like that, her old worries came crashing back.

Read it.

Her steps hesitant, she crossed to the desk and picked up the scroll. "Were there witnesses? Did the assassin claim to be from the Red Hand again?"

Charlotte frowned and looked ready to respond, just as Roger let out a magnificent burp, and she became distracted. "Who's Mama's brave little warrior, eh? Ye are, aye, ye are!"

Court rolled her eyes and Mellie smiled, and Rosa realized there was nothing she could do but read the infernal letter.

Except…she couldn't.

After unrolling the parchment, the words were just as blurry as any other. She straightened her elbows, hoping that by holding the words farther away, she could make out what they said, but no luck.

"Rosa?" When she turned her attention to Mellie, her friend was looking at her with pity. "Ye cannae see the words, can ye?" she asked softly.

Rosa's shoulders slumped with defeat. "How long have ye kenned it?" Mellie was by far the most caring and observant of their group. If *anyone* was going to notice Rosa's vision problems, it would be her.

Her...and Cam.

But Mellie has known her for five years, and Cam only a few days.

Yet Cam still knew her just as well.

"I've wondered a few times," Mellie confessed, crossing the room to wrap Rosa in a hug. "Ye've been trying to keep it from us, have ye no'?"

Rosa didn't have time to respond.

"What's this?" Charlotte barked, as she stood with the bairn against her shoulder. "Ye cannae see?"

With a sigh, Rosa slid from her friend's embrace to face their leader. Mellie stood beside her, one arm around her shoulders in support.

"I cannae read," Rosa said simply, tossing the scroll onto the desk. "I ken how valuable ye think me to the team, so I've been hiding the fact my vision is failing."

Court looked slightly horrified, and Charlotte was still frowning. "Ye *cannae see?*"

"I cannae see up close," Rosa corrected. "I can see ye all fine, but words are all blurry."

Mellie's hold tightened. "I'm so sorry, Rosa."

And *damnation*, but Rosa felt tears prick at her eyes in response to her friend's sympathy. "Thank ye," she choked, leaning into Mellie's embrace.

It was Court who cleared her throat. "If ye cannae read..."

"Aye," Rosa said with a quick nod. "I am useless to the team."

Mellie gasped a negative, but Charlotte snorted. When they both looked at her, the older woman was rolling her eyes. "Ye're no' *useless*, Rosa."

Straightening once more, Rosa pushed her shoulders back. "I ken why I was made an Angel, Charlotte. I am the youngest, the most sheltered. I cannae handle a weapon as well as Court, and I donae understand people the way Mellie does. I am an Angel because of my mind."

"Aye, and yer mind is still as sharp as always, right?" When Charlotte lifted one shoulder, the bairn started to fuss. "No' now, love, Mama has work to do."

With a short chuckle, Mellie pulled away from Rosa and hurried to the other side of the desk. "Come here, wee warrior, and tell Auntie Melisandre all about it." She took the bairn from Charlotte, who seemed happy to let him go. "Let yer mama explain to Rosa why she's still a valuable member of this team."

Charlotte nodded sharply as she sank down into her chair. "Aye, Rosa. Yer mind is still just as sharp, even if yer eyes arenae. We'll just have someone read to ye."

Read to ye.

The memory of Cam's soothing voice, reading from *Lanval* there beside the loch, rose up in Rosa. The warmth from that moment spread throughout her chest now, giving her strength.

She met Charlotte's eyes and saw nothing but certainty and trust there.

Yer mind is still sharp.

Aye, that was the truth. It *was* still sharp...when memories of Cam and feelings of guilt weren't distracting it.

With a tsk, Charlotte snatched up the scroll. "Here." She opened it, her eyes scanning the words. "The King was resting with his advisors on Arran when an assassin burst in on them. He was killed before he could get close, and before he could be questioned." She skipped ahead. "He was dressed rudely, with a pockmarked face. Nothing in here seems to tie him to the attempt a fortnight ago. Um... Oh, here 'tis. The Bruce suspects the accidents which have befallen his group in recent weeks might be connected, but doesnae describe them more than a reference to a bridge giving way before he reached it."

She allowed the parchment to roll back up as she looked at Rosa expectantly. "Well?"

It was the trust in her expression which warmed Rosa more than anything else, and her mind was already whirling.

She hummed as she tilted her head back to look at the ceiling—only, she wasn't really seeing it. "The assassin didnae look like a noble or a merchant, so the bandit theory seems likely. Without proof, there's naught to tie him to the previous attempt. I'd like to hear details of both before I draw conclusions. The accidents are impossible to determine, this far removed. If I could examine the sites, mayhap..."

"See?" Charlotte tossed the scroll to her messy desktop with a chuckle, which quickly turned into a sigh. "I *kenned* ye were still a valuable member of this team. But without *certainty*, this new information does naught for us. The King will still be returning, and we will have to turn the investigation over to his men."

"Aye, and we'll have scores of new suspects to worry about," Court grumbled from her place in the corner.

Mellie was bouncing the bairn. "What do ye mean?"

The curt woman looked surprised at the question. "Only that the nobility are already arriving, have ye no' noticed? The Queen's schedule is busier, with all the requested audiences. With the King back at Scone, *everyone* wants to be here for the festivities."

Charlotte muttered a curse as she slumped in her chair. "Which makes *our* job harder."

"Why?" Mellie asked.

The tangled threads in Rosa's mind were weaving together, and she held her breath while an idea formed.

"Because..." she whispered. "Because, if there *is* a scheme against the Crown, 'tis either the work of a single, crazed, or disgruntled person...or a conspiracy involving multiple nobles. If a person—a *leader*—wanted to remove Robert as the king, that person would need the support of the nobility, the lords with the most power."

"And soon we'll have scores of them staying right here in the palace," Charlotte grumbled.

The curse Mellie whispered wasn't suitable for the bairn's ears, so it was good he'd fallen asleep.

"So we need to find Cam and put an end to this before the King returns," Court said in a flat voice.

Rosa winced, knowing it still hurt Court to think the man who'd raised her might be guilty of this. She opened her mouth to tell her friend he *wasn't*, but realized she didn't know how to start her confession.

Charlotte interrupted her thoughts. "If we could just figure out what in damnation the plot against the Bruce was *for*. Why would someone—Comyn supporter or no'—want to remove the King? 'Tis no' as if Red Comyn or his son is still alive to take his place. Is there a cousin somewhere we donae ken about? A nephew?"

This was it. This was the moment Rosa had been dreading.

Moments ago, Charlotte had proved her worries completely unfounded. Her dear friend had heard of Rosa's incapacity, and still told her she was valuable.

Charlotte valued her mind and her insights.

She'd value what Rosa had learned as well.

So why did speaking the truth feel like such a betrayal?

Rosa took a deep breath. "No' a cousin, nor a nephew. But a son. An illegitimate son, but a son all the same."

"Of course," Charlotte whispered. "If there's a proven son of Red Comyn—some sort of *proof*—then the dissatisfied nobles would flock to him. Especially the ones who supported the Comyn in the first place—they'd leap at the chance to put a Comyn son on the throne."

Ever the impatient one, Court snapped, *"Who?"*

And Rosa, wincing at how it would sound, turned to her friend with sorrow in her tone. "Cam."

"Nay," Court whispered, eyes wide, at the same time Charlotte slapped her desk triumphantly.

"Aye!" their leader crowed. "Now we have him! This quandary is starting to make sense. Cameron Fraser, leader of the Red Hand, son of a would-be-king. He has the connections, the support, and the motive to—"

"Nay!" Rosa interrupted, before she could think better. "He's a good man. He—"

It wasn't until all three of her friends turned incredulous eyes on her, that she realized what she'd said, what she'd revealed. Sucking in a sharp breath, she whirled to look out the window, hoping to calm her mind.

It didn't work.

From Charlotte's solar, she could see the Queen's garden, where she'd shown Cam the secret entrance the Angels had used for years.

Who had she betrayed?

Her loyalty to the Crown?

Or loyalty to her own heart?

"Rosalind," Charlotte began in a low voice, "tell me everything."

She had to.

She owed it to the Angels.

But mayhap not *everything*.

"Cam was at An Torr," she began dully. "I didnae realize it until we were a day on the road, and he caught up with us."

"Mellie?" Charlotte snapped.

Mellie was trying to soothe the bairn, who'd woken at his mother's angry tone. "I didnae ken," she offered helplessly. "Simone arrived here too late last night for me to have seen her, and I've been with ye all morning."

Charlotte muttered something under her breath. Then, "Go on, Rosa."

Taking a deep breath, Rosa did. "He traveled with us. I learned about him. I learned *from* him." She remembered the warm sound of his voice as he read to her and closed her eyes on the guilt which threatened to overwhelm her. "I ken I thought he was the guilty one. For all the reasons ye list, Charlotte. But…" She shook her head.

"Oh, nay," Mellie breathed.

At the fear in her friend's voice, Rosa whirled around to see all three of them looking at her in shock.

Mellie patted the bairn's back. "Ye fell in love with him, did ye no'?" she whispered.

And Rosa couldn't even pretend not to understand.

"Aye," she whispered, dropping her chin in shame.

"*Shite*," Charlotte muttered, throwing herself back in her chair. "No' another one. I thought *ye* were the logical one, Rosa!"

I did as well.

When Court slammed the end of her bow into the wooden floor, all of them jumped.

"This is good news," she declared, glaring at all of them. "Cam is a good man; I've said it all along. He has the motive and the method, aye, but that does *no'* make him guilty." She met Rosa's gaze fiercely and held it. "Tell me how ye ken it, Rosa."

It was her support which gave Rosa the courage she needed. Straightening her shoulders, she nodded to her friend. When she began to speak, to tell Court of her journey with Cam—how well they worked together, how charming he was, how good he was with Simone, how unsure he was of his own worth—she felt as if she were speaking *only* to her friend.

It was Cam's hesitation, more than anything, which had convinced her of his honor. He'd spoken of his years leading the Red Hand—years she'd already known about, thanks to Court's stories—but didn't seem to understand how incredible it was that he led those men with honor. He'd focused on his failings and what he saw as his lack of worth, while all along showing her how worthy he really was.

He was kind, and thoughtful, and intelligent. Aye, he was a thief, but he was so much more than that.

"He's a good man," she finished, ending with her leaving him in the city to return Simone last night.

Court was nodding, but Mellie was watching Rosa speculatively, the look in her eyes conveying, despite Rosa leaving out the bits about the kisses and the way they made her feel, Mellie had guessed.

Charlotte was still slumped in her chair, her lips pursed, and her brows lowered. Rosa couldn't tell if she was thinking, or bitterly angry.

Finally, the older woman blew out a breath. "And how do ye ken about him being Red Comyn's bastard son?"

"Because I was there when his mother told him. Just a few hours ago. He had no idea—and in fact, was completely surprised by the revelation."

"Ye're sure?" Mellie pressed.

Nodding, Rosa held her gaze. "He had nae idea Michael

Fraser wasnae his father, no' until Lady Isla told him he was Red Comyn's bastard. I would stake everything on it."

"Ye might have to," Mellie muttered.

"Damnation!" Charlotte's palm slammed against the desk. *"Damnation!"* She pushed herself to her feet, ignoring the way the bairn squirmed in Mellie's hold. "Ye had our prime suspect in the palace *alone*, and ye *let him go*? Ye didnae alert the guards, or us? Or *anyone*?"

Eyes narrowing, the Angels' leader pointed one long finger at Rosa's nose. "We've been searching everywhere for him, for *days*, and ye just let him *stroll* in here? *How?*"

Rosa lifted her chin, praying she was doing a tolerable job of hiding her fear. She'd rarely seen Charlotte this angry, and never at *her*.

What would the woman—the leader who'd so recently assured Rosa of her value to the team—say if she found out Rosa had showed Cam their secret entrance to the gardens?

But Charlotte was clearly waiting for an answer, so Rosa forced her jaw to unclench. *"Factum fieri infectum non potest."*

"What in damnation does *that* mean?"

Rosa shrugged. " 'Tis impossible for the deed to be undone."

Scoffing, Charlotte threw up her hands. " 'Tis the *doing* of the deed which angers me."

"I needed to see them together," Rosa jumped to defend her choices, although she wisely left out the hope for a future with Cam. "His mother was a key to his past, why he left. Why he started down this path."

"The path to *treason*," Charlotte muttered, shaking her head. She glared. "And now that ye *have* seen them together?"

Rosa shrugged. "Lady Isla is crazed. Mad."

Mellie was nodding. "Lachlan has said the same. He says she's become more obsessed over the last weeks with her missing son. Now, when she speaks of Cam, 'tis as if he's in the room with her."

"Aye, and this morning, she greeted him as if she'd only just bid him farewell an hour or two ago. It hurt Cam to no' be welcomed." She saw Charlotte frown and hurried on. "She casually revealed her infidelity to Cam, telling him he was a fool to give up power to Andrew Fraser to chase after some—to chase after Court." She turned to her friend. "As Andrew told ye, Cam left the Red Hand to come to Scone looking for ye. His mother thought 'twas the sign of a weak man, and his father—the Red Comyn—would've kenned better."

Just as Court opened her mouth to reply—and Rosa couldn't ignore the flash of hope in the stoic woman's expression—Charlotte's fist slammed against the desk for a third time.

"Ye expect us to believe this?" She shook her head. "Ye expect *me* to believe he was completely surprised by this revelation? That he hasnae kenned all along who his father is—what his birthright could be? Damnation, *this* is the motive we've been looking for!"

She stomped around her desk, reaching for her son.

"I need to go check on the Queen. If our *prime suspect* is wandering around the palace still, her guard needs to be doubled."

Settling the whimpering bairn against her shoulder, Charlotte turned her glare on Rosa. "As for ye, I absolutely *forbid* ye to be alone with him again. Ye're not a fighter—"

While Rosa stood, shocked, it was Court who spoke up in her defense. "Rosalind is stronger than ye think, Charlotte. She is capable and intelligent—"

"Nay!" Their leader made a slashing motion with her free hand as she glared at Rosa. "Rosalind is an *Angel*. She follows orders."

The three Angels stood silent as Charlotte stalked out the door, grumbling.

Then, as if all the energy had been stolen with their leader's leaving, Rosa felt her knees go weak. She sank down into the chair Mellie had been in when Rosa had entered.

But as soon as Charlotte's footsteps faded, Court threw herself across the room, dropping to one knee beside Rosa.

Grabbing Rosa's hand, Court squeezed. "Look at me, Rosalind," she ordered gruffly. When Rosa complied, Court nodded firmly. "I believe ye. I'll stand by ye. Whatever yer decision is about Cam, I'll support ye."

To Rosa's surprise, her friend's words dragged a sudden flood of tears to her eyes, and she squeezed Courtney's hand in response. "Thank ye," she whispered hoarsely.

Hand in hand, Court rose to her feet and drew Rosa to hers. "What's that Latin thing ye're always saying? About fortune favoring the bold?"

Through her tears, Rosa smiled. "*Audentes fortuna iuvat.*"

Court nodded. "Aye, well...nae matter what Charlotte says, Rosalind, I have yer back. I owe ye for believing in Cam, even with the evidence against him. Sink or swim, the two of us are together."

There was a snort from Mellie, as she stepped up beside them. "Nay, the *three* of us. I'm an Angel too, for a bit longer. And Cameron will no' only be my brother-in-law, but he saved Lachlan's life. I owe him, and the least I can do is believe in his innocence when the most intelligent woman I ken says he isnae guilty."

Nodding curtly, Court shifted her grip, so her fingers wrapped around Rosa's forearm. "Angels."

Mellie grasped Court's forearm. "Angels," she repeated firmly.

By grabbing Mellie's forearm, Rosa completed the triangle. She looked at her team, the women she'd trusted with her life more than once. They were her best friends and were willing to risk one of the things they valued most—their position in the Queen's court and Charlotte's trust—because they believed in her. In her *certainty* Cam was innocent.

So she nodded, hoping Court and Mellie could feel her love for them. They were more than her friends, more than *sisters*. They were...

"Angels."

CHAPTER 12

Why in damnation were there so many people in the Queen's garden?

As the afternoon shadows lengthened, Cam crouched against one of the stone walls—certain the thick vegetation and his green tunic hid him from all casual observation—and watched the main paths.

There seemed to be dozens of people out enjoying the fresh air. During the hours he'd been waiting there, he'd seen the Queen and a retinue of her ladies, two fine nobles arguing over a woman, four priests strolling along and murmuring between themselves, and even a nurse with two young, well-dressed lassies.

But no one he recognized.

He'd come here originally with the intention of thinking, but couldn't shake his brother's words from his mind.

If Rosa trusts ye, then ye can tell her how ye feel. Like as no', she feels the same way.

Lachlan had lived a very different life than Cam, but had only just found love himself. The hours he'd spent with his brother this morning had revealed all that, and more. The

Fraser laird was a *good man*, one Cam was proud to call his brother.

Or laird.

Unconsciously, his fingers drifted to the bundle of tartan on the ground beside him. When he'd left his brother's chambers, he'd taken the plaid with him. Lachlan's gift had surprised Cam with how fiercely he cared for it.

A fortnight ago he would've said belonging to a clan—especially the Frasers of Lovat—meant nothing to him. Now, after meeting the adult version of his brother, after hearing of his plans for the future, Cam questioned his certainty.

Mayhap he'd never really *belong* with the Frasers, but his brother's offer of the plaid—offer of a *place*—had meant something more to Cam. It meant a possibility of a future.

A future with Rosa?

Like as no', she feels the same way.

If he had a clan, a place to belong, and not just a future as a wandering thief, then mayhap he could offer a place to Rosa as well. *If* she was willing to tie her future to someone like him.

If he could prove he was more than just a thief, mayhap he had a chance.

So he'd been crouching here for hours, standing and stretching only when no one was about, in the hopes she might pass by. And if not her, then Lachlan and Mellie or Simone…or even Court, although he wondered if he'd recognize her after all these years.

More voices!

He shifted slightly, peering through the rose bushes and carefully cultivated pines toward the sound, and spotted two women chatting. Ladies, judging by their garb and head coverings, who were giggling about something. One had dark hair, but as they turned away from him on the path, he saw she wasn't his Rosa.

The skin of her hands was too pale; her hips too wide to be the woman he'd been dreaming about since that searing kiss in the alleyway.

Blowing out a frustrated breath, Cam sank back against the wall, using the rough stone to scratch an itch between his shoulder blades caused by a trickle of sweat. Staking out a target was naught new to him; he'd been doing it since he was a lad, since he possessed a patience few others in the Red Hand did.

But today was different.

Today, he wasn't waiting and watching so he could *steal* something...but so he could *give* something.

And that's when he saw her.

A lithe figure, her dark hair covered in a pearl-studded net, strolled several paces behind the chattering pair. She was ignoring them, her head tilted back to catch the last of the afternoon sun, her lids lowered most of the way. Her skin, darker than average, seemed to glow in the reflected light, and she gestured her hands as if engaged in an argument.

She looked like an angel. *His* angel.

His angel was muttering to herself.

Slowly, Cam pushed himself to his feet, leaving the bundled plaid by the wall. He smiled as he watched Rosa turn off the main path, drifting along one of the smaller graveled paths which wound throughout the garden.

Her path would take her near him.

Silently, he drifted through the foliage, years of moving in the forests of Kintyre serving him well here. No one would hear him unless he wanted them to.

He waited in the shadow of a tree, knowing she'd pass by him.

As she approached, she was still muttering to herself, flipping her hands palm-up to palm-down as if debating two sides of an argument. He loved to see her like this, see her brilliant mind at work. But he had other things in mind, which needed to be discussed.

"Rosa," he hissed. When she didn't seem to hear him, he tried again, louder. "Rosa!"

Still naught, and she was close to passing him by. So he stepped out of his shadows and grabbed one of her hands, tugging her back toward the trees.

"Oh! *Cam!*" As she stumbled against him, she braced her free hand on his chest and smiled into his eyes. "I've figured it out."

His gaze locked on her lips, he murmured, "Me too."

And then he gave up fighting. He'd been wanting to do this all day—all *week*—and had thought of little else but tasting her lips again.

He leaned down and kissed her—kissed her with all the yearning and desperation he'd been feeling. He kissed her with all his fear and self-doubt. He kissed her with all his future and hope.

And she kissed him back.

And God forgive him, but he could've laid her down right then and made her his. Hell, he could've done it up against this *tree*. The way she fired his blood, the way she made him want to be a better man, the way her touch—her lips—made him want to beat on his chest and scream to the sky...

Rosa Forbes *would* be his.

But not like this.

With a gasp, he dragged his lips from hers, surprised to discover the fingers of one hand tangled in the knot of hair at the base of her neck, while the other cupped her breast through her silk gown.

Her eyes were shut, and she dropped her head back with a moan, offering herself to him. The junction of her thighs pressed against his hardness, reminding him where he so desperately wanted to be.

But *not like this.*

He would *not* take her in the palace gardens, like…like a common whore.

There was nothing *common* about Rosalind Forbes.

"Cam," she murmured, pressing her warmth against him. *"Please."*

God in Heaven, how was he supposed to remain strong against such a plea?

"Rosa, I cannae ask—"

And then he lost his capability to speak, when she grabbed the hand which was still pawing at her breast…and moved it lower.

When had she hiked up her dress?

Had he really been so befuddled by her lips, he hadn't noticed—

God's Teeth!

She was already wet for him.

Wet and smooth and oh-so-perfect.

When he slid his forefinger along her cleft, parting the folds, she whimpered, shifted her weight to one foot, and hooked her other leg behind his. Her hands gripped his shoulders, and from behind, they might've been no more than two people meeting in the dark garden…except her head was thrown back and her hips were undulating under his touch.

Inside his leather trewes, his cock strained to reach her, each movement a glorious, torturous friction which sent him closer to spilling like an eager lad.

His other hand supported her between the shoulders, and she arched toward him, mewling and gasping. His thumb found her pearl, the hidden center of her pleasure, as he slid a finger—then two—inside her.

Suddenly, she froze.

She froze, then her head jerked up with a gasp. Her wide,

dark eyes met his in the shadows, just as her muscles constricted around him.

She found her release in absolute silence, her hips bucking in minute movements against his hand, as he fought for control of his own desire.

God's Teeth, he wanted to be inside her!

And that was exactly why he wouldn't.

Why he couldn't.

As her breathing slowed, her leg unhooked from the back of his knee, sliding slowly down to support herself. Her hands slid down his arms to his backside, settling easily there.

Her cheek settled against his chest, and he knew—*knew*—he'd never felt such contentment. He hadn't even spilled his seed, and here he was basking in the afterglow.

God's Teeth, he was in trouble.

"Rosa, I love ye."

Shite.

Her head jerked up, her chin bumping against his chest, as she swung to face him so quickly.

He held his breath, torn between closing his eyes so he wouldn't have to see the pity in hers, and keeping them open to imprint every little move she made on his memory, in case this was his last chance to hold her.

He settled on a sort of squint, which is how he saw the confusion in her eyes when she finally seemed to come back to her senses.

"What?" she whispered.

Swallowing, he committed himself. "I love ye, Rosa. I ken I'm no' worth it, so ye donae need to say it back. Ye donae need to say aught. But I needed ye to ken it."

Blinking, she shook her head and pushed away from him. One hand went to her coiffure, trying to fix the damage he'd done.

Already, he was losing her.

"Cam, I—"

"Nay." Unable to help himself, he placed a finger on her lips, then replaced it with his thumb.

Not the hand which had given her such a release though. Nay, those fingers curled into a fist, as if he could save that glorious memory for himself.

He traced her lower lip with his callused digit and shook his head. "Nay, Rosa," he whispered. "Ye donae need to say it. I understand who ye are. And who I am. But I needed to say those words to ye."

And then she stepped backward, away from him. "Aye," she said with a firm nod. "And I have much to say to ye." She looked up the path, as if expecting another visitor to the garden. "But no' here and now. There are too many people in the gardens during the day."

When she met his eyes, he couldn't read the emotion there, and his chest squeezed. Something resembling both hope and terror warred within him.

She smoothed the wrinkles of her gown—wrinkles *he'd* caused—and lifted her chin. "Meet me back here tonight after moonrise. Right here. Ye understand?"

God's Teeth, but he'd botched this confession, hadn't he?

Resigned, he nodded. "Aye," he choked out. "And I am sorry."

"Oh, I hope no'."

And that's when she smiled. And God help him, her smile hit him right in the center of his heart, and the terror fled while the hope bloomed stronger inside him.

"Until later," she called softly, as she turned away, still smiling.

He watched her until she turned a corner in the path and disappeared. When he inhaled, he felt as if he hadn't truly breathed since that kiss. That kiss, which had not only taken his breath, but his very soul.

And knew it had been worth it.

~

Rosa was still smiling when she slid into the seat beside Isla Fraser for the evening meal. Because the Queen wasn't dining with the court that evening, supper would be less formal than it would have been had she been in attendance.

This meant Rosa had more time to investigate her theory.

Of course, it *could* have meant she had time to smile dreamily into space, imagining a future with Cam.

He loves me!

And that was even more amazing than what he'd done for her. The way he'd given her pleasure so freely, without thinking of his own, had seemed nigh miraculous. But what had come after...

He loves me!

The revelation had been one more in a day of revelations, but of all of them, Rosa was most excited about that one.

Cam loves me!

The knowledge should've had her humming joyfully and twirling in circles, but she was practical. As much as she wanted to daydream about a future with him, she had to ensure there'd *be* a future with him.

And the only way to do that was to prove he was innocent of the plot against the Crown.

"Good eve, Lady Isla," she murmured politely to the older woman.

"Good eve, Rosalind," Cam's mother muttered distractedly, peering around the large room at the other diners.

"Have ye seen Lord de Soules? Or the Countess of Strathearn?"

Thanks to her years reading the Queen's correspondence and studying Scotland's politics, Rosa knew the names, but she wouldn't be able to identify them by sight. So she didn't answer directly.

"Why are ye looking for them?"

It was the way Isla waved away the question which raised Rosa's suspicions. Not because the motion or the older woman's expression were particularly suspicious, but because they reminded Rosa too much of her attitude toward Cam that morning.

If the woman was mad, then this could be a sign de Soules and Strathearn were important indeed.

If Rosa's theory was correct, then it was entirely possible they were co-conspirators, intent on removing the Bruce and his wife from the throne.

And making Cam king.

But rather than pursuing that line of questioning, which was sure to make the other woman even more close-lipped, Rosa tried to imagine what Mellie would do. Mellie was the Angel with the clearest understanding of people and would surely know how to steer this conversation.

Taking a deep breath, Rosa reached for her wine and did her best. " 'Twas a blessing to see yer son Cam today, was it no'?"

Distractedly, Isla nodded. "*Cameron* was always a dear boy, at least before he left."

"Why did he leave?"

"Hmm?" The older woman blinked, as if noticing Rosa for the first time. "Oh, he had a tale to tell about his older brother, but that's what happens when one has three older brothers, I assume. They were a rough-and-tumble bunch!"

As she chuckled happily, Rosa pushed Isla's wine goblet a

little closer to her hand, hoping to loosen the woman's tongue.

"So he didnae like being on the receiving end of their violence, I suppose?" she prompted.

Success! Isla reached for the goblet.

"Something like that," she murmured cagily, as she took a sip.

Rosa carefully considered her phrasing before she spoke. "And I suppose he came to ye and his father before—"

"My husband was *no'* his father," Isla said sharply, the wine inches from her lips as her eyes narrowed. "Ye heard that this morning, dear. My Cameron's father was the great Red Comyn, the man who *should* have been king!"

Exhaling, Rosa surreptitiously peeked around her, wondering if anyone was listening. Isla might be mad, but she was edging ever closer to public treason.

"That is a...bold claim, milady," she finally murmured.

To her satisfaction, Isla took the bait, finishing the last of her wine and lowering the goblet with a haughty sneer. Her shoulders were back, her chin high, as if announcing she had nothing to be ashamed of, when she turned to Rosa.

"I have nae need to *claim boldly*, Rosalind. I possess a letter, signed with the Red Comyn's seal, thanking me for raising his son so well. Ye see, when my Cameron was five summers, John returned to visit us and met his son for the first time. He said then—and also in the letter—Cameron's resemblance to his heir was proof he was his natural son."

Her fingers still clutched around the stem of her wine goblet, Rosa cautioned her heart to stop pounding so strongly, lest she give away her intentions.

This is it.

Cam was the son of Red Comyn.

The Angels knew the plot against the Crown was in support of Red Comyn's line.

If a conspiracy existed, it would be made up of powerful lords who would require a clear plan of succession once they removed King Robert. They would demand *proof.*

And Cam's mother had the proof of her son's sire.

The threads of this investigation, which had been so tangled in her mind for the last several weeks, suddenly fell out of their Gordian knot and rewound themselves into perfect skeins.

Now it was up to Rosa to turn them into a tapestry which told the full story.

Cautiously, she offered, "If Cam—*Cameron*—has proof he is of the Comyn line, there are many who would consider him a candidate for the throne. As Robert's heir."

Isla snorted delicately, picking up her goblet once more. "Heir? There are many who think my Cameron should be king *now.*"

And there it was.

Not quite a confession, but the confirmation of Rosa's guesses.

Still, she played the idiot. "How could that be, milady? The Bruce is king *now.*"

"He is the king today, Rosalind, but will he be the king tomorrow? A sennight from now? These things are hard to foretell. Accidents happen every day. *Where* is that server? I am ready for my venison."

Accidents.

Rosa's mind skipped back to the incidents described in the King's letters to his wife. The letters Mellie had read to her because they needed Rosa to know that information. Those had been *accidents* which had nearly taken the Bruce's life.

Had they been part of the conspiracy after all?

And was that conspiracy being led by this woman seated beside Rosa?

Torn between elation at having solved the riddle, and horror at what Isla Fraser planned, Rosa pretended to search for the servant as well.

"I donae ken, milady. But I am no' as hungry as I expected. Mayhap, since he is taking so long, I'll just sup in my chambers tonight."

With a dry chuckle, the woman sipped from her goblet again. "Mayhap I'll join ye. But the wine is delicious, so I will wait a bit longer until I give up and call for a meal from the kitchens."

Rosa took her time standing and offering a proper curtsey to the older woman, keeping her breathing steady. She wanted naught to alert Isla to her suspicions.

But once she was out in the corridor, she hiked up her skirt and began to run.

Charlotte had forbidden her to be alone with Cam, and she'd already broken that edict. Cam was innocent, and her team needed to know.

She had to find Court and Mellie *now*.

CHAPTER 13

"*Cam!*"

The hissed call startled him enough to jerk away from the tree where he was crouched. "Rosa?" he murmured in a low voice.

The footsteps on the gravel path suddenly halted, and he turned his ear toward the last place he'd heard the sound. "*Rosa?*" he called again, hoping he wasn't making a mistake. Since dusk, there'd been no one out here in the gardens…except him.

Suddenly, a noise from a different direction had him whirling, and then she was there, throwing herself into his arms.

He realized the lack of footsteps had meant she'd stepped off the path, and the knowledge made him inexplicably proud.

"*God's Teeth*, lass," he murmured, "ye move like a thief!"

"Thank ye!" She giggled against his chest. "I learned from the best, ye ken."

He wrapped his arms around her waist and nuzzled at her

hair, wondering if she remembered his vow from earlier in the day. "Aye? And who was that?"

In the faint moonlight, her teeth flashed in a smile when she tilted her head up to look at him. "Courtney taught me and Mellie both. And *ye* taught Court."

He blew out a breath. "Ye *do* ken Court, then."

It wasn't a question—Lachlan had told him as much—but hearing her admit made him wonder if he would finally learn some of her secrets.

"Aye, but we have more important things to speak of. Will ye come with me?"

More important than learning her secrets?

More important than finding Court again?

Aye, the feel of her body pressed against his reminded him of what was *truly* important.

"Lass," he murmured truthfully, "I'd follow ye anywhere ye asked."

Which is how he found himself slipping through the quiet halls of the palace, avoiding the guards as if it were second nature. What surprised him was the way his beautiful flower did the same.

As she pulled him into a small room containing little more than a trunk, a bed pushed against one wall, and a shelf with more books than he'd ever seen in one place, he was smiling.

"Naught ye do should surprise me anymore, Rosa." He pulled her into his arms. "But I'm damned impressed by how *sneaky* ye are. Ye move with a grace Court never seemed to master."

She giggled and laced her fingers behind his waist. "Aye. Ye ken she was in the gaol? 'Twas because she was shite at breaking into houses. Too tall."

Shaking his head, Cam couldn't quite lose his smile. Heaven knows he'd teased Court about her height many times, but the reminder of his little sister being locked up made his heart clench. It was his fault she'd been in that damn place to begin with.

"I've looked for her for so long." He blew out a breath and dropped his chin to Rosa's head, glad for the privacy and the single candle which spread a golden light around the room. " 'Twas why I came to Scone, why I gave up the Red Hand to my uncle. I sent her away because— Well, it matters naught now." His hold on Rosa tightened. "But when I brought my men here and discovered she'd been in gaol, had been *branded*, because I wasnae there to protect her…"

"I ken," she whispered. "It hurt ye to learn that."

"How?" His voice was strangled when he pulled back enough to stare into her eyes. "*How* do ye ken it?"

The way her lips twitched upward looked almost sad.

Sympathetic?

"Because I ken ye are a good man, Cam Fraser. Because I ken what Court has told me of yer years together, and I ken what ye mean to one another."

Ye are a good man.

It was what Lachlan had asked, and hearing the words from Rosa's lips gave him a fierce sort of joy. His gaze flicked between her eyes, trying to guess at some motive for speaking them, but seeing only honesty.

"Ye mean it, Rosa?"

This time her smile bloomed like her name. "I do." She tucked her cheek against his chest once more. "I am intelligent, I ken it. And I've put everything I ken about *ye* into my mind, thought it through, and the only logical conclusion is that ye are a good man."

With a surge of fierce joy, he tightened his hold on her, wondering what he could say in response which he hadn't already said. His declaration of love earlier hadn't been reciprocated, and he didn't want to embarrass himself further.

But then she spoke, where she was still pressed against his heart. "Ye ken, today I was forbidden to see ye again? Alone, at least. I was no' going to let that stop me though. No' if ye love me as much as I love ye."

He stiffened, wondering if she was reading his mind.

Slowly, painfully, not daring to breathe, Cam untangled himself from her and pulled away, leaving his hands to rest on her upper arms.

"What did ye say?" he choked out.

She shrugged. "Charlotte thinks she can just *forbid* me to see ye, but I ken ye are a good man, and arenae guilty of the things she thinks. Aye, there's still secrets I donae ken of yers, like why ye left home in the first place, and yer mother isnae being forthcoming. But now that I ken the truth about the plot against the Crown, and now that Court and Mellie ken as well, there's nae reason I cannae be alone—"

"*Rosa!*" *God's Teeth*, but he was frantic. "Rosa, no' that. Ye said…" Blackness was creeping into his vision, and he forced himself to suck in a breath. "Ye said ye loved me."

"Oh." Her chin dropped, as if embarrassed, but dark eyes peeked up at him through her lashes. "I do. Is that aright?"

God in Heaven.

His lips crashed down on hers, showing her how very, very *aright* it was.

Her little whimper of pleasure, and the way she curled her arms around his neck, told him she agreed.

That knowledge is what sent him over the edge. She loved him, and she *wanted this*.

With a groan, he lifted her, allowing her to tighten her hold around his neck, and to kick aside her silk skirt and hook one ankle behind his knee. As he kissed her with everything he had, everything he *was*, she jerked her pelvis against him, stroking the length of his hardness through the leather of his trewes.

And then they were on the bed, him pressing her against the mattress, her hands tearing at his tunic and shirt, as frantic as he was. He couldn't seem to pull away from her lips long enough to take a breath, much less speak coherently.

But it wasn't until his hand curled around her bare breast, and he realized he'd managed to undress her as much as she'd undressed him, that he forced himself to control this—this—*lust*.

"Rosa," he gasped, pulling his lips from her skin, and pressing his forehead to her jaw. "Ah, *Rosa*."

"Please, Cam." She was tugging at his trewes. *"Please."*

"I...Rosa, stop," he begged, breathing in her perfect scent. He remembered holding her in that alley, weeks ago, and thinking he'd never smelled anything so sweet. But now... "Ye're killing me, lass."

"Please don' stop, Cam. I— *Oh!*"

When she arched against him, the junction of her thighs cradling his cock, Cam groaned again and pushed off her.

"I love ye, Rosa," he said as he stood, "which is why I *cannae* allow ye to debase yerself with a man like—"

"Like *ye*?" she snapped, pushing herself upright. "Is that what ye were going to say?"

Blowing out a breath, he moved across the room, wondering where in damnation she'd thrown his shirt. And how she'd managed to tug it off over his head so easily. He dragged his hand through his hair and tried to control his breathing.

"Cam?" She stood up, her eyes spitting dark fire. "That *was* what ye were going to say, aye? That if I lie with ye, if I give myself to ye, I'd be *debasing* myself?"

Swallowing, he curled his fingers into fists at his side to stop himself from reaching for her. She was so damned *magnificent*.

"Aye," he whispered hoarsely. "Ye ken it. Ye deserve better than me, Rosa, and—"

"Well, *fuck that*," she snapped.

And as his jaw dropped, she reached for the hem of her kirtle, grasping it and the léine in both hands, and dragged it over her head.

There she stood, wearing only her stockings, her chest heaving with the intensity of her emotion, which did all sorts of interesting things to her breasts. She lifted her chin and met his eyes defiantly, as if *daring* him to judge her.

And God help him, he couldn't. His hands, his lips, his heart, his very *being* ached to reach for her.

To make her his.

"I've done little but lie to ye since we met, Cameron Fraser," she said in a low voice, full of warning. "Ye donae ken who I am, no' really. But somehow, someway, ye claim to be in love with me."

" 'Tis more than just a claim, lass." His tongue dragged against his lower lip as he contemplated her words. "And when ye told me ye loved me?"

"That was nae lie." She took a step closer, then another, tilting her head back to meet his eyes, but not touching him. "I love ye, Cam. I believe in ye, and *I want ye*. I want ye to make love to me. I've wanted ye since that day beside the berry brambles. I've wanted ye since before then—starting with that kiss in the alley when I was only supposed to follow ye, no' speak to ye, and I *kenned* it, but that didnae stop me from following yer orders, from kissing ye, from—"

She shook her head and took a deep breath.

"It matters naught. I love ye, and I want to feel yer body against mine—*in* mine." Her dark eyes were serious, but there was a heat in them he knew wasn't just reflections of the candlelight. "I want to bring ye the pleasure ye brought me."

With a groan of surrender, Cam stopped fighting. If she was going to stand here in front of him and all but beg him to make her his, he would comply.

"Rosa," he whispered hoarsely, as he reached for her. "Oh, God…"

And then she was *his*.

~

Deus in caelo!
Deus in caelo!

Dimly, Rosa noted her inability to form coherent thoughts, but decided it didn't matter.

Deus in caelo, but the way he made her feel…!

Cam's mouth was everywhere, kissing, licking, *loving* her, and in between, whispering both words of praise and curses against her skin.

She dropped her head back and offered herself, body and soul, for him to worship.

And worship he did.

When he curled one arm around her waist and lifted her, she sighed with pleasure and wrapped her legs around him, glad to be free of her skirts, as the wet center of her being pressed against him. And when his mouth closed around one pebbled nipple, she couldn't help her gasp of pleasure, nor her desperate gyration.

He growled against her skin, and she could swear she felt it in her core.

Then she was splayed on the bed, his heavy body wriggling atop hers as he kicked off his belt and his trewes. She was nearly breathless in anticipation, the pressure building in her faster than she'd ever experienced.

One of his hands found her wetness, stroking her with a

heart-aching gentleness, which nearly sent her over the precipice.

"Cam!" she gasped.

He paused, one thick arm braced beside her head, lifting his torso over hers, with his fingers still inside her. His beautiful, haunted gray eyes stared into hers.

"Tell me again, Rosa," he commanded.

And just like that day in the alley, she couldn't contain the shiver his low voice sent through her. She was no meek lady, but there was no way she could deny his command either.

She was an *Angel*, and Angels knew how to seize what they wanted.

"I want this, Cam," she repeated slowly, dragging her palms up his side and curling them around his back, pulling him closer. "I want *ye*. I want to feel ye in me, against me."

He shuddered, but didn't give in, not yet. Instead, his tongue darted out over his lower lip. "I am no' a gentleman, Rosa. I can only offer myself, as I am. I will likely hurt ye."

She squirmed underneath him, desperate for something only he could give her, *willing* him to continue his strokes. "I'm nae dullard. I understand."

"I cannae go slow. I am a thief, used to taking what I want—"

"Oh, *Deus meus*! Cam, just fuck me already!"

The sincerity in his gaze turned to incredulity, then humor, as his lips curled upward. With a chuckle, he shook his head. "Ye make me want to be honorable, lass, but..."

When she tugged him, he allowed himself to lower, to cover her.

"Ye *are* honorable, Cam," she whispered, his lips so close to hers. " 'Tis one of the reasons I love ye. Now *please*."

"*God's Teeth*, I love ye, lass," he groaned, then withdrew his fingers from her and reached for himself.

And then he was *in* her, filling her with a tightness she

hadn't expected. There was pain, aye, but as the tightness turned to *fullness*, her thighs slowly relaxed, before falling open on either side of his hips.

He'd stilled, his breathing ragged and his eyes on hers. When she relaxed, he slowly exhaled.

"Lass?" he whispered. "I am sorry."

Then he moved just slightly, the slightest little shift, and she sucked in a breath, her eyes going wide. "I am no'. Oh, *Cam*."

His jaw was tight, even as his fingers went to her core again. "If ye look at me like that, I'll no' be able to hold myself back."

She smiled, holding him tighter. "I donae *want* ye to hold yerself back, ye clot-heid."

With a groan of surrender, he dropped his head to the pillow next to hers and moved again. Just another slight in-and-out, but the friction was delicious. She stretched her legs wider, wondering if she could take more of him, and wriggled beneath him.

"*Please*, Cam," she begged.

As he began to move, as his thumb found the little pearl of pleasure hidden in her curls, she damn near screamed.

Each thrust of his took her higher, brought her closer to the precipice she *ached* for. Oh, she might've been a virgin, but she was no fool, not when it came to her own body. She knew what she needed, what she was so desperate for, but had never felt *this* way before.

And when her pleasure built around him, she knew she'd never again experience anything so breathtakingly perfect again.

The noise she made might've been a cry, might've been a groan, but as she stared wide-eyed at the canopy above her, she realized she wasn't breathing.

Stop thinking about it, ye ninny!

So she stopped. She stopped thinking, stopped analyzing, and allowed herself to just *feel*. Just feel the pure pleasure burst over her, *feel* the white lights behind her eyelids when she squeezed them shut, *feel* the clenching, grasping sensation of wanting *all of him*.

It was Cam who bellowed as a rush of warmth spilled deep inside her.

Deus in caelo, she'd barely had time to inhale before he'd rolled to the side, taking her with him, and burying his face in the curve of her neck. They were both breathing heavily, and she found herself stroking the skin on his back, reveling in the freedom of touching him.

Finally, he muttered something against her neck.

"Hmm?" she asked, enjoying this moment too much to pull away.

"I'm sorry, " he said. He was the one who lifted his head, guilty eyes meeting hers. "I should no' have spent inside of ye."

Her eyes widened slightly, counting. After all the times she'd teased Mellie about *preventing* a pregnancy, all the times she'd joked with Queen Elizabeth about counting in order to *ensure* a pregnancy, and she hadn't even considered it before this moment.

Suddenly, she understood what Mellie had been trying to teach her, all those times she'd spoken of unbridled passion.

" 'Tis the wrong time of my cycle to worry about that," she reassured him.

And to her surprise, her first reaction hadn't been relief, but disappointment. Her eyes dipped slightly, her cheeks heating.

She was embarrassed *now*?

Better tell him the truth.

"I am surprised to find I don' mind the thought of carrying yer bairn."

When he didn't speak, she risked a peek up at him. They were still pressed together, and she could feel his heartbeat against her chest. But the look in his eyes was somewhere between yearning and acceptance.

"Cam?"

"Ye're better than that, Rosa." He rolled away from her and sat up, his legs already over the edge of the bed. "Better than to bear a bastard's bastard."

This, at least, was something she could address.

She sat up, pulling her legs under her, as the air suddenly seemed colder without his warmth, and reached for him. She rested her hand on his shoulder as he scrubbed one of his own hands over his face.

"If it *did* happen, if I *did* bear yer bairn…he wouldnae *have* to be a bastard," she offered hesitantly.

He stiffened but didn't turn. "Ye speak of marriage?"

Didn't he want to marry her?

He'd claimed he loved her.

Wasn't that usually the next step?

Everything she'd done lately had been to build a future with him.

But if he didn't want the same…

"Aye," she croaked.

"*Damnation*," he muttered, standing up.

When her hand fell away from him, she felt a hollow place open in her stomach.

He padded nude across the floor to where he'd dropped his sword belt and satchel when he'd come inside. Reaching into the bag, he pulled out a bundle of material.

When he turned to her and shook it out, she realized what it was.

"Do ye ken what this is?" he asked.

"The Fraser plaid."

He swallowed, staring down at the tartan. "Lachlan gave

it to me. He's offered me a place at An Torr. Offered me a place with my clan and my family."

If he had that, would he want a future with her?

Rosa twisted her fingers together to hide their trembling. "He kens ye're a good man, same as I do."

The little breath he let out might been a laugh. "I love ye, Rosa, and I want a future with ye. But what can I give ye now?" When he extended his hands, as if offering her the tartan, the pain in his eyes almost broke her. "Ye said yerself I'm suspected of treason. Ye said ye're no' even supposed to *be* with me, although I have no notion of who this *Charlotte* is. Ye *ken* I'm as good as dead if anyone suspected me of being here with ye."

As the silence stretched between them, Rosa's heartbeat slowed. It slowed, and a sense of certainty filled her. "Aye, Cam," she whispered, taking a deep breath, "all of that is true. But I also ken I want a future with ye. I want to be with ye, as yer wife, if ye'll have me. I will fight for ye, and I *swear* everyone will ken ye are innocent."

"How?" he cried, anguished. "*How?* Ye claim I'm a good man, but ye donae ken what I've done. Ye donae ken my secrets."

There was only one secret which mattered.

"Why did ye leave An Torr, Cam?" she whispered. "Ye were so young. 'Tis a miracle ye survived."

His nostrils flared, as if surprised. "Everything I've done, and ye want to ken *that?*" he croaked.

"I've been friends with Court for five years. I love her, and I ken she's a good person, despite what she's done to survive. From her stories of ye, I ken ye to be a thief, but ye've led yer men with honor and discipline." She shrugged, remembering the horses he'd stolen on their journey to Scone. "And besides, sometimes a bit of theft is necessary, *ad maius bonum.*"

His brow twitched. "For the greater good?"

Bonum Deus, but this man was remarkable.

"Aye." She nodded solemnly. "For the good of the throne, for the good of Scotland, I myself have stolen before."

"Ah, aye." His shoulders slumped, the plaid dropping to one hand. "The King's letter to the Queen. Ye told me."

There was so much she *hadn't* told him, and he still loved her. Holding her breath, Rosa waited. And prayed he'd make her happy.

"I'll tell ye," he said with a sigh, the plaid dragging behind him as he moved to the bed.

But once there, once she'd scooted over, he surprised her. With a few efficient movements, he reached for her, then wrapped them both in his clan colors. In moments, they were both cocooned, warm and intimate, inside his plaid.

A remarkable man, indeed, considering how long it'd been since he last wore Fraser colors.

"Cam?"

"Shh," he commanded, pushing her head down so he could rest his chin atop it. They faced each other snugly, and it didn't take her long to snake her arms around his middle and pull him even closer.

He sighed. "I might be illegitimate," he began in a low voice, "but my eldest brother was the real bastard."

Hamish.

She remembered the rumors Mellie—or rather, her clever little maid Brigit—had found at An Torr. Guessing where this confession was going, she pressed her lips together and tried to soften the ache in her heart.

"Hamish liked to prey on those younger and weaker than him." Cam's voice was empty, the lack of emotion betraying how hard this was for him to share. "He'd hurt them, *use* them in ways ye cannae imagine—"

"I understand," she cut in, pressing her cheek against his

skin. "Ye don' need to say it."

When he slowly exhaled, she joined him.

Silence stretched before he inhaled again, then whispered his confession. "He hurt *me*."

There was anguish in his voice now, and as much as she ached to hear it, she was glad he was at least reacting.

"He hurt me. *Many* times. He took me, hurt me, and I was too young to fight him."

It wasn't until she felt the wetness between them that she knew she was crying. Crying for his pain, and the betrayal by those who should've protected him.

"I told my parents. Mother didnae believe me, and my father—" When Cam shuddered, she felt it course through her as well. "Father told me to shut up and allow it, because Hamish would be my laird one day."

She'd intended to stay silent, but couldn't help the way her whisper caught on a sob. "Oh, Cam..."

He took another deep breath. "I decided then and there he'd never be *my* laird. 'Twas the dead of winter, but I stole a horse and left, kenning I'd die happy if I never had to see any of them again."

He'd told her of his survival on his own. But now... "Ye had nae wish to see yer mother again, and I forced ye to, did I no'?"

When he shifted his hold on her, somehow, she managed to end up snuggled even tighter against him.

"I cannae fault ye, Rosa. If ye hadnae, I would no' have learned of her infidelity, and the truth of my past."

"Ye think yer father kenned about ye being the Comyn's, 'twas why he treated ye so poorly?"

When Cam shrugged, it jiggled her enough to squirm her way back, then push herself up to look into his eyes. "I'm sorry for causing ye more pain, Cam."

His lips twitched sadly. "I am no' sorry, love. Ye brought

me here to the palace so we can be together."

"Aye," she breathed, her eyes caressing his features. "Ye've told me all yer secrets, have ye no'?"

He winced. "Ye ken the worst of me."

She freed one hand and lifted it to his cheek. When he turned his head to press a kiss into her palm, her heart melted.

"I ken the *best* of ye, Cameron Fraser. Ye have none of Michael Fraser's blood in ye. Ye are no' to be blamed for the sins of those who were meant to protect ye." Her voice shook with her conviction. "I love ye, and I will stand between ye and *anyone* who claims ye are no' any man's equal."

This time his half-smile was a little wry. "Ye'll fight for me, my wee flower? With those sticks of yers?"

"*Aye.*"

Lying there in her bed, wrapped against her with his brother's colors, Cam studied her. His gray eyes betrayed his uncertainty when he licked his bottom lip.

"Will ye tell me why ye carry those sticks, Rosa? Why ye dress as a nun and ride like a demon and kiss like a—"

When he bit off his words, Rosa smiled impishly. "Like a whore? Ye were the one to make that assumption."

He didn't so much pull her closer as just flex slightly, and she could feel his long, hard body pressed against hers. She flushed, remembering the pleasure he'd just brought her.

"And I cannae regret that, nor the kiss, lass," he growled.

Her smile grew. "I didnae start out that morning to kiss ye like a whore, but to follow ye as Charlotte commanded me. I've been taught to use all weapons at my disposal, and Mellie has always shown me how efficiently my *body* can be used as a weapon."

She could tell from his little frown he didn't understand.

Lifting her chin, she met his eyes. "I am no' a nun, nor a whore, nor a warrior. I'm an *Angel.*"

CHAPTER 14

*M*ayhap 'twas her smile. Mayhap 'twas how blasted *proud* she looked of herself. Mayhap 'twas the relief he felt, having finally unburdened his soul of all its secrets. Mayhap 'twas because he was lying, sated and naked, in a bed with Rosa.

Whatever the reason, Cam felt his lips twitch upwards.

"Aye, my angel. Ye are indeed."

Mysteriously, her smile grew, as she pushed herself upright to sit cross-legged beside him. She pulled his colors —the Fraser plaid—around her shoulders, which meant his legs were no longer covered, but he would *never* be cold around her.

He loved the way she was so free around him. The only things covering all that glorious skin of hers were her stockings and his plaid, and his palms itched to touch her again.

"Angels, my love, mean something different to everyone," she began, her tone settling into a lecturing cadence. "To Queen Elizabeth, they were women no one would suspect, but who could work for the good of the Crown behind the scenes. Her ladies-in-waiting have been trained the same way one of the King's agents might be."

"Wait..." His brows drew in as he considered this news. "Ye mean like...*spies?*"

When she shrugged, the tartan fell off one shoulder, but she made no move to pull it back. "A bit. We work for the Queen. She gives us missions or objectives to fulfill."

Incredulous, he propped himself up on one elbow. "Like stealing back letters," he whispered.

"Aye."

This was remarkable. "How many of ye Angels are there?"

She shrugged again. "I donae ken, which is irritating sometimes. Lady Charlotte Bruce, whose husband is cousin to the King and the head of the Queen's bodyguards, is our leader. She and the Queen are close friends."

Distracted by the dusky expanse of skin in front of him, Cam trailed his fingertip down her shin.

"I've heard of her," he murmured.

She hummed. "There are three of us on our team. I've never heard of other teams, but 'tis logical to assume Charlotte has others. We three Angels cannae be expected to meet *every* threat against the Crown."

God's Teeth, but he loved to hear the way her mind worked. He loved to touch her as well.

"Are ye listening, Cam?"

He glanced upward. "I can listen and admire the beauty before me at the same time, can I no'?"

She squirmed backward, reaching for the coverlet. "If ye continue to *admire* me that way, I'll no' get my secrets told."

His brow shot up. "Ye're finally telling me all yer secrets, lass?"

As she settled herself beneath the coverlet, she lifted her chin stubbornly. "I *might*, if ye cease touching me."

With a chuckle, he threw off his plaid and reached for the coverlet as well. "Then ye ask the impossible."

"*Cam.*"

"Aye, angel?" He was still chuckling as he settled himself beneath the blanket beside her in the too-small bed. "Three of ye. I was listening."

The noise she made sounded doubtful, but she was smiling. "Mellie, yer brother's betrothed, is one of our trio. She's no' only the most caring, but the one who understands people. She's the Angel who kens what our targets—or our enemies—desire, and figures out how to manipulate that."

He settled his head on his forearm. "Sounds like she's almost a match for ye, lass."

"Aye, well, as ye can imagine, Charlotte recruited me for the team for my memory."

He snorted. "She recruited ye for yer brilliant mind, love. I ken ye said ye could recall what ye read, and now ye can nae longer read…"

" 'Tis just it!" She shifted excitedly, rolling to face him. "Charlotte was so—so *accepting* of my secret!" Blowing out a breath, she shook her head slightly. "I've been so worried what would happen to my place on the team when they found out I could nae longer see the words on parchment, but Charlotte and Mellie just picked up the letters and read to me."

He remembered the look of joy in Rosa's eyes when he'd read her *Lanval* on that magical afternoon. It had been one of the best days of his life.

Now, her expression of wonder made his chest tighten.

"I'm glad," he whispered, reaching for her. His fingertips brushed against her lips, then caressed her cheeks. "They would be fools to lose ye."

Rosa Forbes had a place here in Scone. A purpose.

A future.

A future which didn't include a thief accused of treason.

No matter how much they loved one another.

But he couldn't make his fingers stop touching her, so he cleared his throat. "And yer third member?"

Her eyes sparkled. "Can ye guess?"

"I would *hope* 'tis Court, but..." But an orphan, sold to a band of footpads and cutpurses, branded as a thief and rescued from the gaol, would *not* be a proper lady-in-waiting.

Rosa tilted her head enough to press a kiss against his palm. " 'Tis Court."

He exhaled. His mission was complete. If Court was one of these Angels, she had a place here in the palace at the Queen's side. And Lachlan said she was happy, which is all Cam had ever wanted for her.

"I cannae tell her story for her, Cam, but she is an Angel, the same as I am. She is our leader, our strength. She's our brawn, who stands between us and danger. She taught me how to use a blade."

His throat was thick with emotion he tried to hide by asking, "And those sticks?"

She smiled as she shook her head. "Nay. My grandmother had those made for me when I left for Scone, and my grandfather taught me how to use them. He'd been the one, many years before, to show me Arabic treatises on the wonders of the human body, and how it could be controlled. But Court was the one to help me strengthen my muscles, to push my body."

Bless Courtney.

His lips pulled upward as he dragged his fingers down the side of her neck, past her hair and her shoulders, to the lines of her ribcage. Brushing against her skin, his smile grew as she sucked in a breath.

When he allowed his hand to drift lower to cup the

curve of her hips, then her arse, she growled playfully. "I'll never get my story told if ye continue to touch me like that."

At that moment, he couldn't decide if he wanted to learn her secrets, or her *body*, more.

"Then let's move things along," he murmured, his attention on the feel of her skin under his palm, and his cock twitching in anticipation already. "Ye've told me about the plot against the Queen, and I assume this is one of yer Angels' missions, aye?"

"Aye, and *ye* are our prime suspect."

He hummed, his hand drifting lower, down the back of her thigh, which he tugged toward him, until her leg was draped across his. "But *I* ken I'm no' guilty, and ye claim to believe the same."

She placed her hand on his cheek. "I *ken* it, Cam."

Her faith—when all the evidence seemed to point to him—humbled him. Still, his fingertips caressed the skin of her outer thigh, drawing small circles.

"So we have to discover who *is* guilty, do we no'? I'll help ye, Rosa. Tell me what ye need me to do."

Her fingertips played with the hair above his ears. "I'm rather torn right now," she murmured. "I *need* to tell ye what I've learned, but I also *need* ye to keep touching me."

"Oh, aye?" His fingers drifted back, around the curve of her arse, pulling her flush against his stiffening cock. This position—with her leg thrown across his—allowed his fingertips to brush against the sensitive spots he knew would drive her wild. "Like this?"

"*Cam!*" she gasped, arching against him, allowing him easier access.

"Ye were going to tell me what ye've learned, Rosa," he reminded her with a grin.

Then her arms were around him, her leg hooked behind

his, and she was tugging him atop her. "No' now, my love." She pressed her breasts against him. *"Please."*

And never let it be said he shirked his duty.

Smiling, he lowered his mouth to one exposed nipple, then reached between their bodies to stroke her into readiness.

~

*H*eaven help her, but she was *never* going to get anything told if they continued this way.

Rosa lay, boneless and sated, with Cam still nestled inside her. He was heavy, aye, but she would never complain about something which felt so glorious.

Instead, she brushed a kiss against his neck. "I love ye, Cam."

He grunted, then pulled her in his arms as he rolled. She ended up plastered against his chest, as he pushed a pillow beneath his head, which allowed him to meet her eyes.

"Good, because I love ye, Rosa. I'm humbled by yer gift."

Propping her chin upon his chest, she smiled. "My maidenhead is no' *that* much of a gift."

" 'Tis to me," he said solemnly. "And *almost* as precious as yer love, yer trust, and yer belief in me."

He was right, and she loved he recognized what truly mattered.

"I *do* believe in ye, Cam. But 'tis no' blind faith. Ye see, I ken ye're no' guilty of masterminding the plot against the Crown, because I ken who *is*."

One of his arms was still wrapped around her back, but the other shifted behind his head to prop him up further. "Ye could no' have led with that?"

She gave a little wiggle against his softening member. "And miss out on this glorious exercise?"

Chuckling, he shook his head. "Aright, my brilliant Angel. Tell me who wants to kill the Queen, and why."

Yer mother.

But instead of blurting it out like that, she closed her eyes and marshalled her thoughts.

"After the attack on Her Majesty, I determined—and the others agreed—that barring a personal hatred of Elizabeth, the likeliest suspect was someone who wanted to eliminate the Queen before she could bear a son."

His fingertips began to draw lazy circles on her back. "Aye. The whole kingdom is awaiting that blessed event."

"The two most logical reasons were because, either someone wanted to put forth a candidate for queen in her place, *or* there was a larger conspiracy against the Bruce, and the conspirators wanted to remove the chance of another post-humous heir, like the turmoil Scotland saw when Alexander the Third died and left Queen Yolande pregnant."

She heard the smile in his voice when he murmured, "Verra logical."

With a little smirk, she opened her eyes and raised a brow at him. "Logic is oft all we have when it comes to solving a puzzle."

He hummed, his fingers still teasing her bare skin. "But my uncle ruled out the first possibility, right?"

Her lips curled farther upward, as she realized he was making logical leaps right along with her. In excitement, she pulled her knees up on either side of him, nestling against the heat at the junction of his thighs.

"Aye. Andrew told Court—she was the Queen's agent who went to Kintyre, by the way—that the Frasers were behind the attack on the Queen, because they wanted to put the Comyn line back on the throne."

His hand was cupping her arse now, but he frowned

thoughtfully. "If that's the truth, why would they—whoever *they* are—start with the Queen?"

" 'Tis the interesting part!" Breathless with enthusiasm now, she planted her hands on his chest and pushed herself upright. "See, they *had* attacked the King, but we hadn't recognized them as being related. He's the *King*, after all, and is used to a certain amount of danger. But the accidents and deliberate attacks made nae sense, other than to eliminate him."

She noticed he seemed to be having trouble keeping his eyes on hers. He hummed as his gaze dropped to her bare breasts, then dragged upward once more. Pressing her lips together to stifle a smile, she reached for his plaid to wrap around herself.

"Ye see," she went on matter-of-factly, as if she didn't notice the disappointment in his eyes as she covered herself, "they were also intent on removing the King, sending individual attackers against him. But we wouldn't have recognized it as a wide-spread conspiracy, until the *Queen* was put in danger."

" 'Tis far less of a common occurrence, I imagine," he murmured, dropping his hand to her thigh, still uncovered, and sliding his palm down to her knee. "And the conspirators likely hadn't counted on a mind as brilliant as yers confronting them."

Rosa scoffed, but inside she was gleaming. "I am only one member of the team, Cam."

His hum sounded noncommittal, but he nodded to let her know he understood. "So with my uncle's confession, ye likely blamed the Frasers, aye?"

She nodded, pushing herself to straddle him upright, his member tucked snuggling against her arse.

"The Queen dispatched Mellie to An Torr. I said she's the one who understands *people*, did I no'? She once believed that meant seduction when it came to men—giving them what she kenned they wanted, in exchange for information. Well, Queen Elizabeth kenned that as well, and arranged a betrothal between her and yer brother, Lachlan."

With a frown, his hand stilled. "Lachlan believes they are betrothed because Mellie loves him."

"Aye," she hastened to reassure him, her own hands dropping to his chest. "They were lucky enough to find real love *and* prove his innocence."

"And thus, the suspicions turned to me."

It wasn't a question, and she winced.

With a sigh, she dropped her gaze to the smooth golden skin under her palms. "Aye," she whispered. "Ye were the logical suspect. Ye had the ties to the Red Hand, which had no' only sent the assassin, but also the attackers against Lachlan and Mellie."

"And what about that attack?" His hand left her leg to capture one of her hands, pressing it against his chest. "My men said the Fraser advisor had paid for their blades, but he wanted *Mellie* killed."

Rosa bit her lip and tilted her head back to stare at the ceiling. After all this time, she *still* couldn't make sense of that attack. "I donae ken," she finally admitted, with a sigh. "Gillepatric was found murdered in his bed the verra day of the attack. Court found him after Mellie reported Lachlan was with the healer."

"So 'tis obvious he was working on someone else's orders."

"Someone who murdered him," she agreed.

"And ye thought it was me?"

With a frustrated huff, she tried to tug her hand out from under his. "*Deus meus*, Cam, leave be! I didnae *ken* ye then!"

He refused to let her go, but his lips curled into a slow,

lazy smile. "I ken," he said softly. "But ye set out to find me soon enough."

"We *all* did." Her irritation faded as quickly as it took to remember the kiss they'd shared in the alleyway, when he'd tried to help her by giving her lessons on how to entice a man. "But I was lucky enough to find ye first."

He hummed again, turning her hand over in his so he could rub her palm with his thumb. "And what did the Angels have to say about *that*?"

She flushed and stared down at their joined hands.

"I didnae tell them," she confessed in a whisper. "I wanted to be the one to find ye, to discover yer secrets. I couldnae afford the guards capturing ye before I could question ye."

"And then my brother sent ye to Scone to fetch Simone instead."

She peeked at him and saw the twinkle in his eyes. "No' quite that simple, but aye."

"Which leads us to ye sneaking me into the palace to see my mother this morning. Was it only this morning?" He blew out a breath and shook his head, then pulled his arm out from under his head and placed his hand possessively on her knee. "So much has changed."

"Aye. And more than ye ken."

"Really?" He raised a brow. "Finding out I'm a bastard, my true father was a contender for the throne, rediscovering my brother and being accepted back into my clan, being accused of treason—"

"*I* did no' accuse ye!"

When she saw his lips twitch, she realized he'd been teasing her.

"Bah!" she said, smacking him lightly with her free hand. "Do ye want to hear what I've discovered, or no'?"

"Lass," he drawled with a put-upon sigh, "I've been

listening to yer logic and conclusions, and doing my best to tamp down what I'd *rather* be doing, to hear just that."

Come to think of it, there *was* something pressing against her backside, which hinted what he'd rather be doing.

And for that matter, what *she'd* rather be doing.

" 'Tis yer mother," she blurted.

He stiffened, his gray eyes widening. "*Mother?*"

Wincing, she hoped she hadn't made a mess of the confession. "Tonight at dinner, after I left ye in the garden, I confronted her. I'd finally pulled the right string, ye see."

"What? What in damnation does string—"

"Sorry," she was quick to interrupt. " 'Tis just a visual metaphor I use when puzzling through problems. Each clue is a string, ye see, and they're all twisted and tied up, and if I can just find the right one to pull, or the right place to pull it in…"

He hummed. "The knot comes undone."

"Exactly. I figured it out in the garden, ye ken. I'll admit ye surprised me with yer confession of love for me, but I couldnae linger, no' before I solved it."

Taking her free hand in his, he placed them together and pressed them against his heart. "And what did ye find, love?"

"Yer mother has a letter, signed with Red Comyn's seal, declaring ye to be his son. She's anxiously awaiting the arrival of a few nobles in particular, and we're certain the Bruce's return to Scone will no' only bring his sycophants in droves, but the conspirators as well. I couldnae tell Charlotte, but Court and Mellie will take turns watching her and looking for the nobles yer mother named. We'll stop them before this goes any further."

"Ye think my mother is the—the what? The *leader* of these conspirators?"

That was one thing she couldn't guess. Shrugging, she said, "I donae ken. 'Tis hard to believe she's the mastermind, but she definitely believes Comyn's heir—*ye*—belongs on the throne instead of Robert. She all-but-admitted to the *accidents* which have been plaguing him."

"*God's Teeth*, Rosa," he breathed, his eyes intent on hers. " 'Tis *treason*. If she has that letter, any noble who wants Robert off the throne will hold *me* up as an alternative. It could mean another war!"

Solemnly, she nodded.

His hands tightened around hers, as if he could make her a part of his heart. "Ye must believe I want nae part in that! I would *never* stand against the King—"

It was the desperation in his eyes which caused her to ache for him. "Shh, my love, I ken it."

Shifting, she leaned forward, and as she pulled her hands out from under his, she pressed her cheek to his shoulder and slid her body along his. His hands fell to her thighs, then stroked up to her backside.

"I ken ye, Cameron Fraser," she whispered against his skin. "I ken ye want nae part in yer mother's scheme. But I also ken that, as long as she has ye and that letter to prove yer birthright, she'll be able to rally all those dissatisfied with Robert's rule."

He was silent for a long moment, his fingers brushing against her skin and causing the most delicious, confusing sensations.

Finally, he exhaled. "Ye are right. And the only solution is to ensure she does *no'* have that letter."

Lifting her head just enough to meet his eyes, Rosa frowned, confused.

In response, he smiled.

"I'm a thief, love, remember? I ken where her room is. 'Twill be a simple matter of searching it and removing the letter. Without it, she cannae hold me up as a possible contender for the throne. Nae one would back such an enterprise, no' without proof."

Her frown deepened; the way his hands were playing with her body made it *exceedingly difficult* to concentrate. "Ye're...ye're right."

"Aye," he said confidently, his fingers finding the backs of her thighs and pulling her legs farther apart, as he scooted her down his torso just a bit. She sucked in a breath and pushed herself off his chest as the hard length of him nestled against the seam of her arse.

"Cam, I cannae concentrate when ye..." She ended in a sigh, as one large hand cupped her breast.

"I ken, love," he chuckled wickedly. "But ye have nae need to *concentrate*, no' for a while. I'll steal the letter, we—and yer Angels—will stop whatever conspiracy my mother's a part of. But for now..."

Rosa moaned as he lifted his head and kissed a trail from her neck to her nipple. She could feel the liquid heat pooling in her core, but she was still new at being loved. "Cam..."

With a growl, he wrapped his arms around her and rolled. Before she could suck in a gasp, she was flat on her back, with him kneeling over her.

His hand went to the junction of her thighs, and as his gaze eagerly feasted on her, he murmured, "So wet for me."

The familiar pressure was building in her, and she squirmed under his touch. No matter that her body was unused to his; she'd happily endure whatever he had planned if it meant—

"*Deus in caelo!*" she gasped, as his finger slipped inside her.

"Aye, lass." When he looked up at her, there was a wicked look in his eyes. "Ye're too sore for another round, but there are other ways to find pleasure."

As he moved between her legs and his grin grew, Rosa

realized what he intended to do. Sometimes, having a friend like Mellie really had its advantages.

"Cam, I donae think—"

"Then donae think, my Angel." His tone turned commanding. "Just *feel*."

And as he lowered his lips to her aching core, Rosa decided to obey his order.

She allowed herself to just *feel*.

CHAPTER 15

*H*e'd...failed?

He'd failed as a son, failed as a brother, failed at being respectable. He had no idea how in damnation he was going to keep from failing when it came to loving Rosa, building a *future* for her.

But one thing he'd never before failed at was *thieving*, and the realization left a bitter taste in his mouth as he slipped out of his mother's room in the pre-dawn hour.

He'd spent the last fifteen years of his life as a thief, and now he couldn't even find one blasted letter in one guest room?

Scowling down at his hands, Cam had to acknowledge he wasn't a complete failure. If the letter had been in that room, he would've found it. It wasn't the first room he'd searched with the occupant snoring happily in the bed, and he knew how to be silent.

The letter hadn't been on the desk or in any of the cubbies. He'd moved to the trunk next, then the bags. He'd even searched the gowns hanging along the wall, and the bedside table with the candle atop it.

No letter.

Either his mother slept with it, or it wasn't in the room.

Or it didn't exist.

Nay, then why would Mother have told Rosa it did?

It had been...*odd* to see his mother lying there in that bed. In the moonlight from the shutter he'd opened, he'd studied her. Studied her face, her form. She was older, aye, but still had the same haughty beauty he'd remembered as a child. The same beauty which might've attracted a man such as the Red Comyn.

And Cam had been surprised he'd felt nothing more than disappointment. There'd been no longing, no urge to gather her in his arms. As a child, she'd never offered him comfort or love, but had treated all her sons with a *distance* her husband had modeled. Cam might've forgiven her that—God knew their family wasn't the only one like that—had she protected him from Hamish.

But she hadn't, and he'd left. And now, fifteen years later, she was *using* Cam. Using him, but didn't know him. She hadn't even been willing to spend more than a few moments' time with him yesterday morning.

All these years later, and she only wanted him here so she could use him.

Footsteps down the corridor jerked Cam's attention away from his introspection, and he forced himself to breath carefully as he strolled in the opposite direction.

Toward Rosa.

He'd left her in her small room, smiling in her sleep. As a man, it had been hard to leave her, especially remembering the pleasure they'd given one another. But as a thief, he knew the best time to burgle was in the hours before dawn, when the target was sleeping deepest.

Aye, it had been hard to leave Rosa, but he'd been doing it

for the best reasons. To finish this, so the two of them could start planning a future.

She loved him, and he planned to spend the rest of his life trying to be worth her love.

Ahead, a man wearing a Bruce tartan stood with his back to a door, arms folded across his chest.

A guard?

He hadn't been there when Cam had passed that way two hours before.

'Twas too late to turn back now; that would be even more suspicious. So Cam lightened his steps, tucked his thumbs in his belt, and smiled like a man who'd spent the night in his cups or in a wench's arms.

" 'Tis a beautiful morning, is it no'?" Cam called cheerfully with a smile.

The guard scowled, his eyes darting to the plaid wrapped low on Cam's hips, then to the window. " 'Tis no' yet morn," the man grunted.

Cam kept walking, his silly grin in place. "Then I had better get what sleep I can!"

He held his breath until he turned the corner in the corridor, but there were no suspicious sounds behind him. The guard had believed him to be what he appeared, and Cam was pleased he'd left his sword in Rosa's room.

Truthfully, that had been a last-minute decision, the same as the decision to wear the plaid. It would've been easy to dress in his trewes and tunic, same as every day for the last fifteen years.

But...

Yesterday, his brother—the new Fraser laird—had offered him a tartan and a place in the clan.

Yesterday, Rosa had told him she loved him.

Yesterday, he'd discovered a chance to clear his name and build a future with the woman he loved.

And so, early this morning, just before he'd slipped out to perform a bit of thieving, he hadn't *wanted* to go back to the way things had been for the last fifteen years. He'd left his sword, aye, and had chosen to don his new plaid instead.

As a reminder of what could be.

He reached Rosa's room without incident, but before he could lift the latch, the door swung open.

"There ye are!" Rosa was fully dressed, her hair pinned up underneath a netting which managed to look proper and respectable for a royal palace...and also sexy as hell.

Or mayhap he was just remembering the way she felt in his arms last night.

She tsked. "Don' look at me like that *now*. We have work to do," she scolded in a low voice. "Here, take this."

When she offered him his sword and scabbard, he tied it to his belt with only a raised brow.

Then she peeked her head into the corridor, looked both ways, and stepped out. Taking his arm, she began a sedate stroll toward the heart of the palace. Any on-looker might think he was just escorting a lady to break her fast early, but she was most definitely leading him.

"Are ye willing to offer me any clues, milady?"

"What?"

A smile tugged at his lips. "About where ye're taking me this early? I was hoping to find ye still abed."

Naked. And willing.

The way she flushed—subtle against her darker skin, but obvious to him—told him she'd heard the unspoken words.

But she lifted her chin. "Too much to do to spend the day in bed, my love."

"Oh well." He pretended to sigh, when in fact he adored this chance to banter with her. "Mayhap tomorrow, then?"

But her nod was too serious. "Mayhap. If we are lucky."

Before he could ask what worried her, they reached a door and she paused.

"This is Charlotte's solar. The Angels often meet here, but she's no' here."

He didn't like how nervous she was acting. "Are ye still afraid she'll call the guards the moment she sees me?"

"Nay. Well, aye," Rosa confessed. "But for now, we just needed someplace to meet. She came to me this morning, 'twas how I kenned ye'd left—no' Charlotte, but—oh, ye'll see. I'll give ye as long as I can, alone, before returning with the others. And mayhap some food."

She wasn't making any sense, and the way she was chewing on her lip wasn't normal either. Her worry was beginning to affect him.

"Rosa, love?" His hand dropped to hers. "What is it?"

She didn't answer, but took a breath and pushed the door open. Instinctively, Cam's gaze swept the room, but made it no further than the tall woman in trewes near the window, who spun around at the sound of their entrance. She'd instinctively reached for the bow propped beside her, but as she recognized him, she slowly straightened, her hand falling back to her side.

Courtney.

He felt Rosa's hand tighten around his. "I'll be back soon," she murmured, then pulled away.

He wanted to thank her, to at least acknowledge her words, but no sound emerged. He could only listen to the sound of the door shutting behind Rosa, as he stared at the woman he'd raised as a sister.

Court.

He owed her so many apologies, but didn't know where to start. Didn't know what to say to make her accept him. Didn't know how to make up for—

"Cam," she breathed, and then she was in front of him, her hands reaching, pulling him into a hug.

He wrapped his own arms around her and hugged her back, praying for her pardon.

It felt like ages before they pulled apart, standing close enough together to examine one another. Her hair was longer than she'd kept it among the Red Hand, but still shorter than was likely proper. It had darkened some in the years since he'd last seen her, now a color somewhere between her childhood blonde and a light brown.

And she was taller, if such a thing was even possible. She'd never been a small lassie, and now stood almost eye-to-eye with him. There was a reason she'd never succeeded as a housebreaker.

That reminder—the reminder of what she'd endured after he'd sent her away—caused him to suck in a sharp breath.

"Court, I—" he began, but his voice caught, and he pressed his lips together.

She was the one to take his hands, to squeeze them.

"I ken, Cam," she said in a low voice. "I ken. Andrew told me why ye sent me away."

Shaking his head, he refused to accept her forgiveness so easily. "I should no' have done it. I—" Glancing down at their joined hands, he saw the brand on the back of hers, and twisted it up to bring it into the light. "Oh, God in Heaven, Court. I am sorry." He dragged his anguished stare back to her eyes. "Ye'll never ken how sorry I am, how much I've regretted sending ye here, to face the—the *King's justice*"—he spat out the word, lifting her branded hand higher—"on yer own. I should've been here. Nay, I should no' have let ye go in the first place."

She swallowed, then shook her head. "Ye could no' protect me from Andrew. I've had time to think it over, Cam, and 'tis why ye sent me. Before we killed him—and I ken I *should* apologize to ye for killing the bastard, but—"

"Nay," he interrupted, certainty in his voice. "I kenned him, remember. He was well-suited to lead the Red Hand—vicious, power-hungry, and angry. 'Twas one of the reasons I held onto power so long, merely so *he* wouldnae take it. I left my family because of their sins, and my uncle was nae different." Bitterness crept into his tone. "The only difference was I had to live with *him* for another ten years, after I thought I was done with them. So nae, lass, I understand why ye might want to kill him, and now I understand his role in the current mess."

Court peered at him for a moment, as if uncertain, then shrugged. "Well, before we killed him, Ross and I, Andrew said he'd wanted me, and that was why ye had sent me away. I didnae ken he was yer uncle, no' til Ross told me. But ye couldnae maintain yer power as leader if ye were protecting me from him or anyone else. 'Twas why ye sent me away, was it no'?"

Slowly, he nodded, more than a little amazed how easily she understood and accepted his motives.

"Aye, lass," he croaked, then shook his head again as he exhaled. "Aye, 'twas it exactly. But I couldnae live with my decision, no' for long. 'Twas only a few years later I gave up my spot to Andrew and came to Scone to find ye."

"That's what Rosa deduced."

Rosa.

The reminder of his love's brilliance reminded him of another miracle.

Stepping back slightly, he held onto his sister's hands as he looked her up and down. "And look at ye now! One of the Queen's Angels." A flicker of surprise flashed across her normally impassive expression. "Rosa told me everything—

about yer real role and the current investigation. But she didnae tell me how *ye* came to be an Angel."

Court's dry chuckle was a surprise; the woman he remembered didn't laugh, or even smile, easily.

" 'Tis a hell of a story," she muttered, as she tugged him toward the chairs near the cold hearth.

The two of them sat, and she told him of her failed career as a thief in Scone. He winced when she spoke of being caught and branded, and he cursed when she told him of all she'd endured while in prison.

"Court, I'm sorry I didnae—"

"Nay, 'twas for the best." A rare smile flicked across her face as she stared at the hearthstones. "I was due to be hanged in the morning, ye see. The gaoler announced I had a visitor, and I assumed 'twas a priest, come to shrive me. But then *she* walked in: Queen Elizabeth."

When she met Cam's eyes, he saw the love and devotion there.

"She told me she was putting together a team and needed someone of my talents. Well, I would've done just about anything to escape, but the chance of a future with a real purpose, no' to mention food and a warm bed?" She shook her head. "I couldnae pass that up."

"Thank the saints ye didnae, lass," he breathed. Then with a small shake of his head, he chuckled. "I was able to track ye to the gaol, but no' what happened to ye. It took almost a year before I heard of a lass matching yer description in the palace. I hoped that meant ye'd gotten a position as a servant or something. But look at ye—a proper lady!"

Her expression settled into a frown. "I'm wearing leather trewes and carrying a bow—"

"Nae, ye're no'," he teased her.

Her eyes flicked to the weapon, still propped beside the window. "—and when I'm no', I'm nervous."

One side of his lips pulled up, acknowledging the way she'd finished her claim.

"The point is, Cam, I'm nae lady. But Elizabeth—the Queen, I mean—doesnae seem to care. I'm *useful* here. I've done more good than I could ever imagine. I have sisters and a family, and—and Ross."

And damnation, if she didn't flush and stare down at her hands. "Ross loves me just the way I am, and he's determined to stand by my side between the Queen and danger. We're a good team."

Ah. Love.

"And who is Ross?" Cam prompted gently, not about to turn protective big brother on this woman he'd seen raised.

She peeked up at him. "A Fraser, same as ye. Lachlan's friend and advisor. He used to be a bodyguard for the Queen, but had returned to An Torr to help Lachlan after Hamish died. Now Ross is back in Scone again."

"And he loves ye?"

Her chin came up, that same mulish set of her jaw he remembered. "Aye. And I love him."

God's Teeth, she was—in the same moment—so much the lassie he'd raised *and* the strong independent woman who'd saved the Queen.

His heart swelled as he reached for her hand once more and held her gaze. "I am happy for ye. And, Court…I have absolutely nae right in the world to feel this way, but I'm proud of ye. Immensely proud of everything ye've accomplished. And ye have nae idea how much joy it brings me to see ye again."

She squeezed his hand. One side of her mouth twitched, and someone else might've dismissed it, but he knew it was a smile.

"And ye, Cam? Rosa—who is one of my dearest friends,

by the way—seems awfully taken with ye. She stood up to Charlotte for ye, claiming yer innocence. I believe her."

"Thank the saints." Cam dropped her hand and leaned back in the chair with a groan, scrubbing his hand across his face. "I'm no' even sure I understand the whole plot. And now my *mother's* involved."

"No' just involved," Court said seriously. "But mayhap the leader. I am sorry, Cam."

"Nay, she means little to me at this point. Lachlan's the one who must be mourning."

"Aye, Mellie says he's no' as accepting of Isla's guilt as we are. No' yet, anyhow."

Cam yawned, then waved in apology. He'd been up all night, first with Rosa—which he would *not* complain about—then with trying to find the letter. "So what's the next step?"

She leaned forward, propped her elbows on her knees, and took a deep breath. "That's what we need to discuss."

CHAPTER 16

It was after dawn when Rosa returned to Charlotte's solar, carrying a tray of food and leading the others. When Ross opened the door, she slipped inside and placed the food on the large desk which was still—in typical Charlotte fashion—covered in untidy stacks of letters.

Then she took a deep breath and turned to Cam.

He was smiling at her. Sitting beside Court by the hearth and *smiling*.

A weight she hadn't realized she'd been carrying seemed to lift from her shoulders, and she smiled in return.

"Are ye hungry?" she prompted quietly.

And Heaven help her, but he winked.

"Aye," he drawled, "I've had an active night."

Mellie was helping Lachlan sit at the window seat, but she couldn't pass up that opening. "Oh, really?" she quipped, her blue eyes sparkling in the morning light. "How long? And was it *hard*?"

Rosa flushed, Cam's eyes widened, and Court rolled hers.

It was Lachlan, however, who scoffed at his betrothed's lewd joke.

"If ye don' mind, I have nae need to hear details of my brother's conquests."

Mellie nudged his shoulder—the uninjured one—with a wink. "No' his *conquests*. I was referencing his—"

Lachlan caught her hand and brought it to his lips with an exasperated sigh. "I *ken* what ye meant, Mellie."

"Aye, hush, Mellie," Cam called out, nodding seriously, while one side of his lips curved upward. "Nae need to shame my brother when he finds out how much larger my cock is than his."

Rosa nearly choked, so quickly did she suck in a breath. Cam had naught to worry about in the *size* department, but to make so bold a claim...!

It was Mellie's turn to snort, her fingers lacing through her husband's. "Doubtful, Cam. Still..." She smiled conspiratorially at the blond man. " 'Tis glad I am to finally meet ye officially."

"Oh?" Cam stretched his legs out in front of him. "To thank me for saving yer life?"

Mellie's eyes rounded innocently. "Nay, to have someone to joke about cocks with, of course."

While Cam's smile grew, Ross crossed to Court. "God help us, lass. Yer friends are incorrigible."

"My friends are mad," their leader replied stoically.

"No' mad," Rosa joined in. "They just like cocks."

It was obvious no one expected her to participate in the teasing, judging from the incredulous looks Ross and Court sent her way, and how Lachlan and Cam both make choking sounds.

Her grin grew. "Roosters, aye? 'Tis what we're speaking of?"

Lachlan's choking turned to full-on laughter, and Mellie's

grin grew. "Lord help us, Rosa's discovered naughtiness!" She winked at Cam. "Good work!"

Cam managed a mocking bow from his chair, which set everyone else to chuckling—except Court, of course, who just snorted. Rolling her eyes, and blushing in happiness, Rosa snatched up a loaf of still-warm bread and crossed to her love.

"Here," she murmured, shoving it at him. "Since ye're so *hungry.*"

"No' for bread, lass," he murmured right back, wrapping one arm around her waist and tugging her closer to him.

With a squeal, she dropped into his lap. But her breath caught when he lifted her hand holding the bread and took a bite from it, directly from her hand!

They were here to make a battle plan. They were surrounded by her teammates. This was entirely the *wrong* time for flirtations.

But that didn't stop the rush of warmth spread through her chest. And when he looked at her like that, as if there was *more* he wanted to taste, the warmth turned to a pulsing deep in her core.

He'd brought her so much pleasure last night, she was a bit sore this morning. But that didn't stop her from wriggling against his lap, and his hardness. His hold tightened on her in warning, and humor flashed in his gray eyes.

Across the room, a throat cleared. "Ye look good in my plaid, Cameron."

Cam's hold on her loosened, and he shot a smile at Lachlan. "*Our* plaid, brother."

Twisting in his lap, Rosa was quick enough to catch the look of pleasure which flashed across the Fraser laird's face.

"Ye've made a decision then? About yer future?" she asked Cam.

"Aye." Cam nodded, and she watched him glance around

the room, his gaze sweeping over all these people who meant so much to her. Then he met her eyes.

"If ye'll have me, lass, after my name is cleared of treason, I'll do whatever ye ask to be worth yer hand."

Her hand.

A future.

With Cam.

There was so much uncertainty on the horizon, so much to fear. But in that moment, none of it mattered. Rosa lifted her palm to his cheek, cupping it gently, hoping he saw the love in her eyes.

And when words failed her, she stretched up and kissed him.

Kissed him with everything she was and ever would be.

Kissed him with her whole heart.

Behind her, someone chuckled. "I guess that answers *that* question," Ross said drily.

But it was longer still before Rosa could force herself to pull away, and the heat in Cam's eyes almost made her lose her resolve again. "Cam..." she whispered.

"*God's Blood*, little brother," Lachlan groaned from across the room, "we *don'* need to see this."

Mellie giggled. "Can I make another joke about cocks?"

"Aye," Court said sardonically, "Something-something-rooster-something."

Even Cam burst into chuckles at that, and Rosa quickly scrambled from his lap, thrusting the bread at him and hurrying to pick up another piece, sure her friends could see how warm her cheeks were.

Ross earned her appreciation for distracting everyone when he cleared his throat. He leaned against the hearth, his arms crossed in front of his chest, and his sword hanging alongside his Fraser plaid.

"No' to ruin everyone's fun, but what is our next move?"

"*My* next move is to ask where that beast of yers is?" Lachlan drawled. "Does he no' follow ye everywhere?"

Ross nodded. "Aye, but that was until yer daughter arrived. Now I cannae drag Honor away from wee Simone. I think she slips him treats. I checked in on him last night, and he was lying in bed with her."

Lachlan chuckled. "She fed him when he was a wee pup. He likely recalls it. Do ye want the hound to join us?"

"Nay." Ross shook his head. "Let him guard the lassie. We are here to discuss our next steps, aye, Court? Ye called us here."

All business now, the tall woman straightened in her chair. "Aye. Yesterday, Charlotte said some things about this investigation, but I'm choosing to ignore them for the good of Scotland and our Queen. Are ye all with me?"

Remembering the way Charlotte had forbid her to see Cam—whom she believed was their prime suspect—again, Rosa nodded resolutely, along with the rest of her friends.

"Rosalind assures us Cam isnae behind the plot against the Crown. We have him here with us, but I need to ken ye all agree with this assessment."

Mellie was the first to nod. "He saved Lachlan and me, and protected Simone. I believe he's a good man."

Her betrothed agreed. "He's my brother, and I'll support him because I never truly believed he was guilty in the first place."

Rosa met Court's eye, and the two women nodded slightly to one another. Both of them would support Cam.

Ross stepped away from the wall, closer to Cam. "Do ye remember me?"

Squinting, as if thinking, Cam stood slowly.

"Nay," he finally admitted, shaking his head. "Although ye're a Fraser, Court tells me."

"Aye. A bit aulder than Lachlan, so ye and I share nae

history as lads. But I remember ye. I remember yer brother Hamish, and I remember the rumors about why ye ran away."

Sucking in a breath, Rosa's eyes darted between the two men, wondering why Ross would bring this up. A muscle in Cam's jaw jumped, but that was his only reaction.

"The rumors are likely true," he finally said, too mildly.

Ross nodded. " 'Twas my blade which ended yer uncle's life. Besides Lachlan, I have nae love for yer family. I saw what kind of life ye've led, and I was quick to believe ye were guilty of this treason." Then he shrugged. "But I was a suspect once myself. Now Lachlan and I are cleared of this suspicion, and I'll do everything I can to help clear yer name as well."

Ross held out his hand.

Cam seemed to exhale as he stepped closer and clasped the bigger man's forearm.

They were all in accord.

Court nodded. "So what do we ken for certain, Rosalind?"

Relieved now, and knowing she was able to do what she did best, Rosa tilted her head back to look at the ceiling.

"The accidents and attacks against King Robert are tied to the attack against Elizabeth. Someone wants to put a Comyn on the throne. This points to a conspiracy. Now we ken there *is* a Comyn available for the position, and proof allegedly exists."

When she paused, no one interrupted, so she continued. "We also ken Robert arrives soon in Scone, which explains why there's been so many more nobles and visitors lately. They are likely gathering to petition him."

"Or kill him," muttered Mellie.

Rosa nodded. "This could be a clever cover for the conspirators, or 'tis possible—if unlikely—they're *all* conspirators. We have the names of two, and I've alerted the royal guards to search for more."

"And where does my mother come into this?" Lachlan asked. "I ken her madness is eating at her, but ye believe she's a part of this?"

It was enough to drag Rosa's concentration to him. Then she glanced at Mellie, surprised she hadn't told Lachlan the truth. Actually...she turned to peer questioningly at Cam. *He* should've told his brother the truth.

Cam dragged his hand through his hair, and she saw the hesitation in his eyes. "I..." He shook his head, dropped his hand, and set his jaw. "Red Comyn is my sire, Lachlan." He spat out the words, as if daring his brother to doubt them. "Mother confessed to me."

Silence stretched, and Lachlan's only reaction was a slight flaring of his nostrils.

Finally, he inclined his head. " 'Twould explain much about our childhood." His gray eyes flicked to Rosa. "And also prove Mother isnae just *a part* of this conspiracy."

"Nay," Rosa agreed quietly. "I believe yer mother is the heart of it. She possesses a letter from the Comyn himself, acknowledging Cam as his son. The nobles who would remove Robert from the throne wouldnae dare to do so without proof of the next king's rightful blood."

Court snorted quietly—probably at the idea of Comyn's illegitimate son being *rightful*—but it was Mellie who spoke.

"So without that letter, without proof, the conspiracy would no' stand?"

Nodding, Rosa turned to Cam. " 'Twas my conclusion as well."

But to her surprise, Cam winced and blew out a breath. "I couldnae find it. I'm sorry."

"Find what?" Lachlan asked.

Rosa answered without dropping Cam's gaze. "Sometimes there are benefits to having a thief on yer side. Yer mother didnae have it in her room?" she asked Cam directly.

He shrugged, looking pained at his inability to steal the letter. "It should have been, but I searched everywhere. I couldnae find it."

"That was quite the risk," Ross rumbled quietly.

Court was the one to defend her childhood friend. "If Cam was in Lady Isla's room, she would have *never* kenned it."

One side of Cam's lips curved upward at her impassioned defense, but he didn't respond.

"So now what?" Mellie asked.

"*Acta non verba*," Rosa murmured. *Actions instead of words.*

Cam snorted, his smile growing. " 'Tis hard to believe *ye'd* have us rush into action."

"I am no'" she was quick to point out. "But we need a plan, and soon."

He shrugged. "*Faber est suae quisque fortunae.*"

And it was *her* turn to smirk. How could she *not* love a man who argued with her in Latin and could bring her so much pleasure? "Whether ye create yer own fortune or no', ye need a *plan*."

Before he could reply, Mellie interrupted. "What we need is that letter."

Expression sobering once more, Cam nodded. "I'll try again tonight. Mayhap she has moved it."

Humming, Rosa tilted her head back once more. "Or mayhap she carries it with her at all times. We cannae deny she kens the letter's importance. If she *sleeps* with it, searching her room will no' work."

"Besides," rumbled Ross, from his spot by the hearth, "we don' have the time." When they all turned to him, he shrugged. "King Robert will likely be here by the evening meal, assuming he rides ahead with only his guards to see his lady wife, as is his wont."

Both Cam and Lachlan cursed quietly, and Rosa felt like repeating it.

Court's hands curled into fists on her knees. "Then we have to move today. *Now*."

"To steal the letter in broad daylight?" Cam frowned.

The tall woman pushed herself to her feet with a dangerous grace. "It might be too late to steal the letter. We need to eliminate the threat to the Crown before the King arrives. Once he *and* the conspirators *and* the Queen are in one place, we'll have lost the advantage our knowledge grants us now."

Mellie hummed, exchanging a glance with Rosa. "She has a point." She sounded almost apologetic.

But Rosa nodded. "Court's right. We have the element of surprise now. Once the King is in the palace, the conspirators will have the advantage of being able to either implement their final plan, or choose the time and place they need to give them the best chance of success. We cannae allow them that advantage."

"So the question then becomes..." Ross straightened away from the wall. "When do we move against Isla Fraser? And how?"

"And do we have yer approval?" Court asked both Lachlan and Cam.

Cam jerked back, surprise in his expression, as he glanced at his brother.

Lachlan was frowning, his gaze locked on the floor. "I cannae deny her madness has gotten worse over the years. 'Tis hard to believe she'd be involved in something this *stupid*, but she and our—*my* father were always staunch Comyn supporters." With a sigh, he looked up and met Cam's gaze. "If she's guilty, she needs to be punished."

Rosa wondered if anyone else could see the emotions

warring behind Cam's eyes, or if she just understood him well enough.

Finally, he dropped his chin in acceptance. "Aye," he quietly agreed.

"Today then?" Ross rumbled.

Court shook her head. "*Now.*"

Cam took a deep breath, the plaid across his shoulders making him look somehow larger and more noble. "She was sleeping when I left her chambers. 'Tis possible she's awake now."

Lachlan grunted as he reached for his betrothed's hand and lifted himself to his feet with a wince. "Then we go there now." He met his brother's eyes. "We confront her."

Cam's nod was quick, final. *Certain.* "We end this."

CHAPTER 17

Mother wasn't in her chambers.

Cam insisted on going in first, while Ross stood watch. When he determined they were alone, he alerted the others to join him.

The six of them filled the room, which hadn't seemed this small when Cam had been there before dawn.

Had that only been a short time ago?

And a few hours before then that he'd wrapped himself in the Fraser plaid for the first time?

That he'd made love to Rosa for the first time?

That he'd lost his heart?

She moved to stand beside him near the bed. Her dark eyes were serious, her expression grim. But when she slipped her small hand in his, he felt strength radiating through her.

She was an *Angel*, and he had to keep reminding himself she was no weaker than Court. The lass—the *woman*—he'd thought of as his little sister now stood tall and strong beside Ross, her stance the easy battle-ready one he'd taught her so long ago. Her strung bow was clutched in one hand, three arrows in the other. He knew she could nock and fire those three in a blink and found himself praying they wouldn't be necessary this morning.

Mellie was seated at the window, but not out of choice, it seemed. Lachlan had pushed her behind him, and now stood, feet braced, hand on the hilt of his sword.

Cam had only just found him again, but even *he* could see his older brother's lips were pressed into a hard line; his face paler than normal. He'd been wounded only a short time ago, and it was possible he was pushing himself too hard.

But far be it for *Cam* to tell him he should sit down and rest. The way Mellie's blue eyes were shooting daggers at Lachlan, she'd already tried and failed.

Nay, the Fraser laird would stand between danger and the woman he loved.

And so would Cam.

Rosa's shoulder pressed against his arm, and he squeezed her fingers.

"Will ye stand behind me, love?" he murmured.

She peeked up at him. "Do ye fear yer mother will hurt me?"

"Nay, I—" He shook his head. "I donae ken what is coming, and I cannae stand the thought of ye in danger."

"Donae worry. I am armed." She offered him a slight grin and touched her forearms, where he imagined her steal shafts were hidden. "I am smart, aye, but fast. Also, smart enough to ken when to stand back and let someone with a sword enter the melee on my behalf."

With a grin, he lifted her hand to his lips and brushed a kiss across her fingers. "I love ye, Angel."

"Enough to marry me?"

So she'd understood what he'd been asking when she'd sat on his lap in the solar?

He knew she was brilliant.

"*Please.*" He swallowed, knowing that wasn't much of a proposal. "I ken I'm no' worth—"

"Shh." She stretched up on her toes and planted a kiss on his cheek. "Ye are worth *everything* to me."

Had he thought himself lucky before?

When he'd held her, been *inside* her?

Nay, 'twas nothing compared to the joy he felt knowing she loved him.

No matter what the next few hours brought, no matter how much danger returned along with his mother, he would hold on to that knowledge.

And he'd hold on to the certainty that, when his name was cleared, he had a chance at a new life with Rosalind Forbes.

But as it turned out, no danger arrived with Mother.

In fact, as she stepped into the chamber, it was hard to imagine this elderly woman was the *enemy*.

But on the other hand, it was hard to consider her his mother, as well.

Mothers protected their children from harm; they didn't encourage it. Mothers didn't *use* their sons to advance their own careers.

This woman—*Isla Fraser*—was frowning when she looked at all the people in her chamber. But her expression cleared as her eyes fell on Lachlan.

"Cameron! I kenned ye would return!"

Lachlan's expression didn't change, but his gaze flicked to Cam, questioningly.

Aye, they'd said Isla's mind had begun to break the day Lachlan had been wounded, and she had begun calling him by different names.

Mellie slowly stood behind Lachlan, and when she saw her, Isla's expression clouded once more.

"Why'd ye bring *her*, my lad? I'll no' make *her* queen."

Beside him, Rosa sucked in a breath, and Court spat out a curse, which drew Isla's attention.

"What are *ye* doing in my chambers?"

"Lady Isla Fraser," Court spoke in a commanding voice, "ye seek to make yer son king of Scotland, do ye no'?"

When Isla glanced at Lachlan, Court's voice stopped her, snapping out, "No' Lachlan. *Cam.*"

It was obvious how confused the old woman had become. She shook her head, her gaze flitting around the room and not landing on anything in particular. "I—Cameron is my son. The *Comyn's* son. He will be King!"

Rosa's fingers tightened around Cam's, and he was torn between pity and anger at his mother's treason.

Court had no such compulsions. She lifted her bow as Ross's hand went to the hilt of his sword. "I accuse ye of treason, Isla Fraser. Ye *will* name yer conspirators, those who helped ye in this plot. Was it de Soules and the Countess of Strathearn? Who else?"

The old woman was shaking her head harder, her hand pressed to her hip in what seemed to be a comforting gesture. Her frantic gaze landed on Cam, finally.

"Cameron! Ye will no' let them harm yer mother, would ye?" she called, reaching for him.

Instinctively, he leaned away, pulling Rosa away from this woman's madness.

And the look in Isla's eyes turned from desperation to anger, in one heartbeat.

"So be it!" She whirled around and lunged for the door. "I'll see ye all in hell before I betray our plans!"

"Nay!" cried Lachlan, at the same time Court loosed one of her arrows.

It flew over the old woman's head when she ducked around the corner.

Then Cam was moving, tugging Rosa out the door, following Isla.

Following his mother.

"Mother!" he bellowed, knowing of all of them, he might be the only one who could stop her. "Mother, *please*."

It worked.

At the top of the grand staircase leading to the lower level—were her conspirators there, even now?—Isla stopped and turned around.

Cam skidded to a stop, dropping Rosa's hand, and praying she had the sense to stay behind him.

He wanted to rail at his mother.

He wanted to shout, to ask her how she could be so *stupid* as to believe she could kill the King of Scotland.

And part of him wanted to cry, to ask her how she could abandon him and use him this way.

Instead, he lifted his hands, palms down.

"*Mother*," he said softly, his stomach twisting at the thought of acknowledging this woman as his relation, "please stop. *Talk* to us."

"Talk?" she spat, as her hand curled around the silk of the gown at her hip. "*Talk*? I should've kenned ye wouldnae understand."

"Ye want to put me on the throne, do ye no'? Is that no' worth some discussion?"

There were people about—servants and courtiers and holy men—who'd stopped to watch the drama unfolding. Court stood off to one side, staring down the length of her arrow at Isla's heart. Mellie and Rosa stood together, but Lachlan and Ross had their swords half-drawn already.

They'd all frozen when Cam had begun to speak to Isla, but now Lachlan took a cautious step forward.

"Mother, tell us of yer plans," he cajoled softly.

The old woman sneered at him. "And have ye run to the

royal guards, Lachlan?" At least she recognized her sons now. "Do ye think me *simple*? Nay!"

" 'Tis only us," Cam said soothingly, remembering how he'd spoken to the frightened lassie—Tess had been her name—who'd tried to make off with his purse all those days ago. "We only want to speak to ye."

With a deep breath, Isla straightened, brushing down her gown there at the top of the stairs. Then she pierced Cam with a haughty look.

"Ye are the son of *greatness*, Cameron, and I will ask ye to act thusly. Yer father should've been king, but *ye* will be."

"Ye speak treason, Mother," Lachlan growled.

Silently, Cam urged his brother to shut up. They weren't going to get anywhere by upsetting this mad woman.

"Nae one wants me on the throne," he hurried to speak before she could respond to Lachlan. "Robert is a good king."

She tsked, the look in her eyes turning almost pitying. "Ye really have nae idea, Cameron. There are men who hate him, who want another. Yer Uncle Andrew kenned this as well as I. 'Twas his plan to mold ye into a leader of men, to assure ye were ready for yer role when the time came."

It made his stomach hurt, this reminder that she'd known where he was for all these years. Known where he was and what he was doing, and still hadn't tried to contact him.

She sniffed, raising her chin proudly. "My husband might've been a blind fool, but Andrew and I both kenned what power we would one day have. Until he was *murdered*," she spat angrily.

Did she know Court and Ross had been the ones to kill Andrew?

Cam risked a glance, but both the Angel and the Fraser warrior stood still and silent, their weapons at the ready.

"I heard," Cam offered drily, trying to keep Isla's attention on him. "But 'tis no' enough to think I might be…" His voice caught, still hating to voice the idea. "I might be *king*."

"Might be?" she scoffed, lifting her head and chin high, as regal as the queen she'd tried to assassinate. "With the nobles behind ye, there is nae *might be*."

God's Teeth!

She was standing here, clutching her fine gown before all these witnesses, and was casually declaring treason.

Cam's gaze darted to Rosa, and saw his love staring intently at his mother.

Nay, not just staring at the old woman…but at her hip.

Understanding slammed into Cam.

His mother had a pocket under her gown.

'Twas an uncommon modification, but effective in hiding one's purse instead of hanging it from a belt.

Hiding a purse…or something else?

Isla Fraser clutched at that hip, that pocket, as if desperate.

Was that where she'd hidden the letter?

The letter which would provide the proof the conspiracy needed to challenge King Robert?

It *had* to be.

"Mother…" His voice caught on the word, but he pushed himself past his disgust. "I've returned from the dead. Now ye think to use me for power?"

By all the saints, he *hated* how hurt, how *broken*, his tone sounded.

Mayhap Isla heard it, because her lip curled with disgust. "Ye have no' been dead, lad. But aye, ye're back where ye belong now. What would ye have me offer, if no' a throne?"

A throne?

'Twas the last thing Cam wanted.

"A hug."

Her head jerked back. "What?"

Cam lifted his chin. "A hug, *Mother*. A hug to welcome me home."

Indecision warred in her eyes, as she seemed to shrink back.

Was she considering his request?

Wondering at his motives?

Or did she just not want to hug him?

Finally, with a sigh, she rolled her eyes.

"Fine," she snapped, throwing her arms open. *"Here."*

And behind him, he heard Rosa exhale. She understood his plan.

Slowly, careful not to impeded Court's line of sight, Cam stepped up to his mother. He was surprised to find her barely to his chin. The last time he'd been hugged by her, he'd barely reached her shoulder. Now he'd far surpassed her.

Carelessly, she closed her arms around his shoulders, pulling him down toward her. He placed his hands on her hips, and held his breath.

As she tugged him into a hug—of course the hug would be on *her* terms—Cam's feather-light touch probed at her hidden pocket.

There are benefits to being a thief, sometimes.

As soon as he touched the parchment—small and folded —he murmured, "Thank ye, Mother," against her hair to distract her as he pulled it free.

And she turned her head and placed a kiss on his cheek.

As if he were a boy.

As if he were a boy she *loved.*

Swallowing, Cam stepped back, out of her embrace. He'd gotten the proof they needed, but had also received a *hug* from his mother.

Finally.

Taking another step back, he tucked the parchment into his belt in the small of his back, so his companions would all see it. Now that they had the letter—the proof—in their possession, the conspiracy would be foiled.

Now they just had to deal with his mother.

Who'd hugged him as if she cared about him, in some small way.

God's Teeth, why did his stomach clench at the thought?

Was it from anger?

Or longing?

Mayhap Lachlan saw the indecision, the confusion in his eyes. Or mayhap he was just restless. Whatever the reason, Cam's brother stepped forward again, his hand still on his sword.

"Mother, come with us. We'll alert the guards, aye, but I will do my best to ensure ye are treated well."

Isla's head snapped up, her shoulders back, as she gaped at her son.

"*Surrender?*" Her chuckle sounded half-desperate. "When *I* hold the power?"

"Look around," Lachlan ordered, gesturing with his free hand to Court's weapon, pointed at Isla, and all the witnesses. "Ye have nae power."

"I have *all* the power, ye clot-heid!" She shook her head, a look of disgust crossing her features. "*Ye* have always been the simple one."

"As opposed to Cameron?" Lachlan drawled in a deceptively lazy voice. "The *thief?*"

Cam winced. He *knew* his brother called him that only to rile Isla, not to insult Cam, but still…

He'd made his choices in the past, but now he wanted a real future.

With Rosa.

As if he'd conjured her, his Angel stepped up beside him. They didn't touch, but they didn't *have* to for him to draw strength from her nearness.

Meanwhile, Isla was continuing to spit insults at Lachlan. "And my Cameron is twice the man of any here!" she called triumphantly, reaching for her hip. "His father was the great Red Comyn, and I have proof!"

"Nay," Lachlan drawled, "ye do no'."

She sucked in a breath as she fumbled for her pocket, discovering it was empty and frantically patting about, as if the parchment had just shifted.

"Where is it?" she shrieked.

No one answered her, but Rosa's shoulder pressed into Cam's arm, a silent reminder she stood with him.

Isla's head snapped up; her eyes boring into Lachlan's.

"*Ye* did this, did ye no'? *Ye*, who has nae true understanding of power or leadership," she bit out. "Ye, who prefers to lower yerself among the servants, rather than stand above as a true laird does."

Lachlan frowned. "Ye mean the way I work beside my clan to strengthen our wall? The way I work in the fields and labor for our future?"

"Bah!" Isla spat. "Hamish kenned how to be a laird, and so did my poor James. *Ye* are naught but the youngest—and least worthy of yer father's get. I *kenned* I couldnae allow ye to sire a son. Yer whore should have had the good grace to die in that attack."

A dangerous glint came to Lachlan's eyes as he took a step forward. "What are ye saying, Mother? That ye had a hand in the attack which nearly killed me?"

" 'Twas no' supposed to kill *ye*, my lad!" A crazed look had come to her eyes as she gathered her skirts in her hands, clearly ready to run. "Ye—however unworthy—are still the Fraser! But I cannae allow ye to marry, to sire the next laird. Yer brother Cameron's son will bear that title."

Cam growled, "*Nay*," at the same time Lachlan barked, "Mother! Did ye set the footpads who attacked us?"

She took a step back, poised to flee down the staircase.

Why?

Because she was genuinely afraid of Lachlan, or because she knew she was lost without the letter?

Lachlan wouldn't accept her silence. *"Answer me, woman! Did ye send the footpads who threatened Mellie? All because ye didnae want me to sire a legitimate son?"* He was yelling now, his rage palpable. *"Ye tried to kill the woman I love?"*

Isla sneered. "Nay. I instructed Gillepatric to do so. The poor idiot thought I was in love with him, just because I occasionally shared his bed. 'Twas a surprise, I suppose, when he found me waiting with that dagger! *He* was the one who made contact with the Red Hand—"

With a roar, Lachlan ripped his sword from his scabbard and took a step forward.

Cam lunged forward, even as he tried to stop himself. His mother did not deserve their leniency. Did not deserve their pity. But still, he stepped in front of Lachlan, using his hip to push the blade to one side.

Behind him, he heard his mother shriek.

Keeping his grip on his brother's arms, Cam turned them both to watch the moment when Isla tripped on her gown, her gray eyes widening with terror and anger both. She fell backward, her mouth opening on another scream.

Then she disappeared from their view with a series of sickening crunches.

It was Rosa who darted forward to peer over the lip of the staircase. "She is dead."

There was no question in her tone.

Dead.

His mother. The woman who'd hugged him. The woman who'd betrayed him. The woman who'd committed treason against the throne.

And in his arms, Lachlan sagged.

It had been easy to forget his brother was wounded, but now…

Cam met his brother's identical gray eyes. There was anger there, but also sorrow.

"I couldnae," Cam whispered, willing his brother to understand. "I couldnae let ye bear the guilt of her death."

When Lachlan dragged in a breath, it sounded suspiciously like a sob.

And then his sword clattered against the floor, and he was pulling Cam into a hug fiercer and more *real* than the one their mother had offered. Lachlan burrowed his face in Cam's shoulder, his arms shaking.

Cam wrapped his own arms around his brother and closed his eyes.

Their mother was dead, the threat against the throne eliminated for now.

And he had a place, a future.

A home.

"Thank ye, brother," Lachlan whispered roughly.

Cam nodded, understanding without more words being needed.

When he opened his eyes, Rosa was there. Her smile was sweet, and he knew—with his brother and his love—he had all the home he'd ever need.

"It's over," he whispered to both of them. "*Over.*"

CHAPTER 18

It's over.
It was, wasn't it?

Rosa stood beside Cam in the Queen's private solar, their clasped hands hidden in the folds of her skirts.

Despite his own words, despite his assurance to his brother that their worries were over, she could feel her love's coiled tension. His sharp gray eyes were locked on the Queen, who was listening to Charlotte's murmurs. Cam's other hand was resting on the hilt of his sword, but she could tell from the way he rocked slightly on his booted heels that he was far from at ease.

And she shared his nerves.

Aye, they'd defeated Isla and stopped the conspiracy to overthrow the King. And aye, Cam had been the one to steal the Comyn's letter, therefore assuring there'd be no further plots with him at the center.

But he was a criminal, a thief. The royal guards were looking for him…

And here he stood in the Queen's private solar, being glared at by her bodyguard.

Rosa's heart lightened a little at the sight of Liam Bruce, the King's cousin, holding his wee son against his shoulder. Liam took his job as head of the Queen's guards very seriously, but apparently, that job came second to the chance to care for his firstborn.

Mayhap his glare had less to do with Cam's presence, and more to do with the dark circles under his eyes.

Was Roger still not sleeping well?

Rosa tilted her head back slightly, trying to recall if she'd ever read or heard anything about infant sleep cycles…

It wasn't until Cam squeezed her hand, that she realized she'd drifted off into her mental library of knowledge.

When she glanced at him, he was looking at her in concern.

So she offered him a small smile, trying to reassure him she was alright.

Or would be, once Charlotte finished her retelling to the Queen.

Surely.

Court and Ross stood silent beside the hearth, her bow unstrung in the Queen's presence, but propped in front of her. Mellie was seated beside her betrothed on a bench across the room, the corners of her lips curled upward just slightly as she lounged.

Lachlan, on the other hand, was frowning, and not with pain. Nay, his gaze flicked between the Queen and his brother, occasionally glancing down at his empty hands.

Was he remembering what he'd almost done?

Or how Cam had saved his soul from the blemish of having to kill his own mother?

Rosa lifted herself on her toes to bump Cam's shoulder with hers, and when he jerked his gaze back down to hers, she smiled.

A *real* smile, letting him know—whatever happened—she would stand by him.

And judging from the way his shoulders relaxed just slightly, he understood.

"How...*intriguing*." The Queen nodded to Charlotte as she sat in the chair behind her desk and folded her hands atop the pristine surface. "Thank you all for gathering this afternoon."

It had taken a few hours to explain everything to a glaring Charlotte and all the guards, then to assure them all Cam wasn't the threat they'd believed, and that Isla's head didn't *need* to be displayed atop a pike.

And now they had one more explanation to make.

To the Queen of Scotland.

Charlotte crossed her arms in front of her chest, propped one hip against the Queen's desk, and glared at Cam.

"So, my Angels have done a good job of catching me up on the investigation, which has taken a hell of a turn since I saw ye all last. But would someone explain to me exactly what *he's* doing here?"

Rosa's lips thinned into a line. Charlotte knew perfectly well why Cam was here, and his role in the recent success. Their leader was just being stubborn.

It was Court who defended her childhood friend, yet again. "Cam was essential to our victory, Charlotte. He is *no'* the guilty man ye believe him to be. Aye, he was being held up as the King's heir—"

"As I understand it," Queen Elizabeth said drily, " 'Twas more than that. His mother was behind the conspiracy which was actively attempting to remove my husband from the throne...by death."

Reluctantly, Court nodded. "Aye, Yer Majesty. But Cam wasnae aware of her plans."

When the Queen quirked a brow, Rosa jumped into the

conversation. "Truly, Yer Majesty. He wasnae even aware of his true parentage until yesterday."

The Queen hummed. "So I have heard. And although I can see my dear friend is unhappy about it"—she sent Charlotte a little smirk—"I know when to believe my Angels. Rosa is intelligent, and I trust her judgement."

Charlotte rolled her eyes and sighed. "*Fine.* Cameron Fraser is innocent of our suspicions."

Across the room, her husband Liam pressed his lips together, as if he was trying not to laugh at his wife's irritation, and Mellie smiled happily.

Beside her, Cam shifted. "Cam, milady."

When the Queen's regard turned to him, and she asked, "What?" regally, he cleared his throat.

"My name is Cam, Yer Majesty. I've been *Cam* far longer than I was ever Cameron Fraser. Only—only my mother called me that."

"Yes. And she is dead," Elizabeth stated baldly.

Cam's chin rose. "Until yesterday, I had no' seen her for fifteen years. And instead of an embrace, her welcome to me was to announce I was her path to power. Do no' ask me to mourn her."

At his words, the Queen's countenance softened. She was a mother twice over, with two beautiful daughters, and the hope for a son in the future.

Was she imagining how twisted Isla Fraser's mind must have been, to know where her youngest son was all these years, and never reach out?

And Rosa wondered if anyone else had heard the pain beneath the bitterness in Cam's voice.

Had she been the only one to see the longing in that hug he'd given his mother, moments before he'd sealed her fate by stealing the letter?

Her heart ached for him, and her fingers tightened around his.

"Nevertheless, I am sorry for your loss, Cam," Queen Elizabeth finally said, inclining her head slightly. "Sorry for *all* your losses."

Cam's gaze flicked to Lachlan, then back to the Queen. "Thank ye, Yer Majesty."

Charlotte sighed. "Isla Fraser was either the mastermind behind the plot, or at the center at least. We can agree on that?"

"Aye." Ross nodded. "She confessed to trying to have Mellie killed, so that Lachlan wouldn't marry her and father a son."

As Lachlan's arm went around his betrothed shoulders, Mellie nodded, obviously not needing comfort. "As if, with me dead, Lachlan couldnae find another willing lass to marry and sire an heir."

"If ye left me, my love," the Fraser laird said seriously, "I would never look at another woman again for as long as I lived."

Mellie's smile turned mischievous. "Ye'd better no' do that anyhow," she quipped, right before she leaned over and brushed a kiss against his lips.

Court made a noise somewhere between a snort and a laugh. When all eyes turned to her, she frowned, as if startled. "Isla admitted to sending Gillepatric, her advisor, to offer the remnants of the Red Hand gold in exchange for Mellie's death."

"And Gillepatric's death?" the Queen prompted.

Court answered promptly. "At Isla's hand. She intimated they were lovers—"

"They were," Lachlan cut in.

"And that concurs with the evidence discovered when we found his body."

"That's right," Charlotte murmured. "Ye said 'twas as if he'd been awaiting an assignation."

Rosa nodded. " 'Twas likely he *was*. But Isla, kenning all would be lost if he ever told the truth about who ordered Mellie's death, stabbed him instead."

Queen Elizabeth hummed, still eyeing Cam speculatively as her sharp mind whirled.

Finally, she said, "And the letter? The one which Lady Fraser believed would support this young man's claim to the throne?"

Cam stiffened, but Rosa doubted anyone noticed. "Cam stole it from his—from *Lady Fraser* without her kenning. The letter was fairly damning, Yer Majesty. Cam gave it to Charlotte, who burned it while waiting for ye to join us."

With the Queen glanced at Charlotte, her friend nodded, confirming the story.

" 'Tis destroyed, Elizabeth."

"How *fairly damning*, would you say?" the Queen asked.

Rosa tilted her head back, closed her eyes, and began to recite the relevant parts of the missive.

"I can tell by the lad's build that he is mine. He bears a remarkable resemblance to my heir, John. Raise him well, my lady, for one day he may be powerful indeed. Now that the pretender king has surrendered to the English and fled, 'tis only a matter of time before Scotland produces a strong leader. I have every intention of being that man, and I will not rest until a Comyn sits upon the throne. Never let young Cameron forget he is a Comyn."

Silence stretched.

Liam broke it with a long whistle, which caused his son to jerk in surprise. The man was grinning wryly as he soothed the lad and shook his head. "*Toom Tabard* was stripped of his crown almost twenty-five years ago, when Edward of England stole the stone, aye? So Lady Fraser has been hanging on to that letter for decades."

"She was waiting for it to be useful," Charlotte replied to her husband. "Even six years after defeating the English, there are still many in Scotland who bear grudges against the Bruce."

But the Queen was staring at Rosa critically. "How did you manage to remember those words, Rosalind?"

Rosa flushed, understanding what her monarch was asking. She wasn't questioning her memory, but Charlotte must've told the Queen about Rosa's eyesight.

For the first time, Rosa shifted away from Cam. But only enough to pull their joined hands from her skirts to show the Queen that they were a team, a pair.

"Cam read it to me, Yer Majesty."

Cam understood my problem right away, she wanted to say. *He didnae shame me. He didnae question why I needed to ken such things, or why I wanted to learn. He just read to me.*

Mayhap Queen Elizabeth heard the unspoken words.

Humming, she sat back in her chair, her gaze sweeping over those gathered.

"So the only question remaining is, who else is involved in this plot against my husband?" she stated.

Liam spoke, patting his son's wee bottom comfortingly. "Dinnae fash, Yer Majesty. Yer guards are alerted to the danger, and as soon as Robert returns, his men will be made aware. Between us, we'll ken all the traitors ere long."

"And ye'll have my Angels, don' forget," Charlotte reminded him.

When the bodyguard inclined his head in acknowledgement, his wife smiled at him.

"I willnae be here long, remember?" Mellie reminded them, a flash of something akin to sorrow in her eyes. "My place is at An Torr, with my husband."

Court nodded. "Aye, but ye'll always be an Angel, even if we're no' always working together."

"Mayhap ye should find another to take my place?" Mellie offered.

"And have to get used to someone else's naughty stories?" Court quipped in return.

Mellie gasped theatrically. "Rosa! Did ye hear that? She made a *jest*."

"Aye," Rosa drawled. "I kenned falling in love would change her."

When the Queen rose to her feet, all eyes immediately went to her, and all jests ceased.

"Mellie and Lachlan have agreed to be wed here in Scone, now that the danger is passed, and their daughter is present."

When the couple nodded their agreement, she turned to Court and Ross, who still stood at attention. "And the two of you have stated your intentions to remain here at my side in whatever capacity I will accept?"

"Aye, Yer Majesty," the two warriors murmured in tandem.

Queen Elizabeth's gaze fell on Rosa and Cam. "So now we are left with the question of you two."

Cam released her hand, but not for long. A heartbeat later, his arm was around Rosa's waist, pulling her against him. When she glanced up at him, she saw the resolved set of his jaw, but also the worry in his beautiful gray eyes.

The Queen eyed the place where they were joined, one brow rising delicately. "Are you letting me know you do not wish to be parted?"

"Aye, Yer Majesty," Cam ground out. Then he cleared his throat and tried again. "I ken who I am, what I've done. But loving Rosa…"

When he trailed off, obviously unsure how to finish, Rosa rested her head against his shoulder, willing him to feel her love.

"And you, Rosalind?" Queen Elizabeth asked mildly. "Do you love this man?"

"With all my heart, Yer Majesty," came her quick reply. "I would give all my days, all my futures, to be with him."

The Queen hummed, one corner of her lips curving upward. "Then I would hear the question from the thief's own lips."

Immediately, Cam turned to Rosa, both arms wrapping her snuggly in his embrace. "Marry me, Rosalind Forbes. I ken I'm no' worthy to even hold ye, but I love ye more than life. Marry me and let me spend the rest of my days trying to be worthy of yer love."

Deus in caelo.

It was the most perfect proposal of marriage Rosa had ever heard.

With a soft sigh, she pushed herself up on her toes to brush her lips against his. "Aye," she whispered. "Aye, Cam. I love ye, and will adore being yers, and only yers."

With a relieved sound, Cam pulled her against him, his lips claiming hers in a joyful dance.

Mayhap it wasn't proper to kiss so soundly before the Queen, but neither could seem to make themselves care. It wasn't until the laughter penetrated the fierce tempo of her pulse pounding in her ears that Rosa pulled away.

Mellie was still chuckling, and Charlotte was staring at the ceiling in exasperation.

"God's Blood, brother" Lachlan sighed. "*Again?*"

"Like *ye two* are any better?" Court drawled.

"Aye," Ross quipped, the twinkle in his eyes belying his serious expression, "ye should all be like us: Totally impervious to any desire whatsoever."

More chuckles sounded at that, and the Queen rolled her eyes. "You Angels make me long for my own husband."

Which, of course, led to more jests about the *royal succes-*

sion and kisses. Finally, Queen Elizabeth raised her hands to cease the chatter.

"It seems to me our futures are set, except Rosalind's. My dear, I should give you the choice of a future away from Scone, but I confess I am greedy. I'm allowed to be, you know, being Queen and all."

Rosa's heart began to slam against her ribs, and she exchanged a worried glance with Cam. "Aye, Yer Majesty?"

"As such, I am unwilling to allow you to retire from your duties here with me. You are still a Queen's Angel, until such a time we both decide otherwise."

Rosa's tongue flicked out over her lower lip. "And...and Cam, Yer Majesty?"

Queen Elizabeth lifted her chin imperiously. "I *could* order him punished for crimes against the Crown—surely we could come up with something—but instead, I will put him to work. It has been clearly demonstrated to me today that there are benefits to having a trained thief on hand. Mayhap Cameron is not a woman, but as far as I am concerned, he is now an Angel." Her gaze swept those gathered. "Does anyone object?"

As the others—even Charlotte—agreed, Rosa felt the tension in her love's body slowly flow from him. When he took a deep breath, she felt his *hope* flowing through her now.

"And you, Cameron Fraser?" the Queen asked, piercing him with her sharp gaze?

He smiled.

"I would be honored, Yer Majesty, and will give all I can to yer cause."

Then he released Rosa, and placing his fist over his heart, bowed.

Rosa lifted her skirts and curtsied

Court and Ross both placed their fists over their hearts and bowed, and Mellie came to her feet to curtsy.

The Queen nodded regally.

"I am eternally grateful to *all* my Angels," she said softly.

Just then, a soft knock came from the direction of the door. Before she—or anyone—could bid the knocker to enter, the door opened.

Ross's sword was halfway removed from his scabbard before the figures in the door were recognized, and he relaxed.

Rosa frowned.

What were *they* doing here?

And entering such an intimate gathering with such ease?

The three women slipped into the room, looking as if they belonged there.

Rosa recognized Lady Avaline as the dark-haired woman who inclined her head to the Queen. And the one with the wild curls who curtsied cheekily was Brigit, the lady's maid who'd accompanied Mellie to An Torr.

Wasn't she also one of the Queen's maids?

Or maid to Lady Isabel?

Because Isabel de Strathbogie was the third woman. The beautiful, regal woman smiled and bobbed a greeting to her friend the Queen. The twinkle in her eyes told Rosa she had good news.

"Aye, Isabel?" Queen Elizabeth prompted.

The beautiful noble woman's smile grew. "Yer husband has returned. Robert's ordered a bath and awaits ye in yer chambers."

It was almost funny the way the Queen's eyes lit with excitement, and how hard she tried to hide it. But those who knew her best could see how badly her regal expression wanted to pull into a smile when she swept her gaze around the room.

"We are finished here then, Angels?"

There was a chorus of *ayes*.

Including, Rosa noted, from the three newcomers.

Hmm.

Without another word, the Queen swept from the room. Ross and Liam exchanged a glance, and when Liam gestured to the infant in his arms, Ross nodded quickly and followed Elizabeth from the chambers. She would be guarded, even for the walk to her own bedchamber.

A moment of awkward silence reigned after her departure.

Court was glaring at Isabel, Avaline and Brigit, as if wondering why they were there. Mellie was watching Rosa and Lachlan, and Charlotte's lips were pursed.

Finally, she pushed herself away from her desk. "Aright, ye three!" When Court, Mellie and Rosa turned to her, she sighed. "Go away. Ye have until the wedding to get yer affairs in order, but then I'm sending ye all to An Torr."

"Why?" Court growled, confused.

"Because ye need a break. Oh, don' look so worried, Courtney. I'm sending Ross too. The six of ye'd better enjoy some rest and relaxation—and I *donae* need to hear about what kind of *relaxation*, Mellie," she cautioned, when the Angel began to giggle.

Exhaling, Cam was already in motion, tugging Rosa toward the door, mayhap hoping for an escape. But Court wasn't done arguing.

"Ye want us to just *leave*?"

"Aye. Start practicing now," Charlotte snapped, making little shooing motions with her hands. "And I want ye—*all of ye*—married afore ye even think about coming back." She sent her husband a wink. "Two fortnights, at least. Go. Enjoy yerselves."

"Ye heard the lady," Cam whispered in Rosa's ear. "We've been commanded to marry. And *enjoy* ourselves."

Smiling, Rosa exchanged glances with Mellie, who had helped Lachlan stand and was already halfway across the solar.

Only Court seemed to object. Her expression was incredulous, her bow gripped tightly in her hand. "*Charlotte*. Ye cannae expect us—*me*—to leave the Queen unguarded. We are her *Angels*."

The others were near the door when Charlotte sighed. "She will be guarded. Surely ye donae think ye three are my *only* Angels?"

At that moment, Rosa's gaze met and held Lady Isabel's. The regal blonde woman's lips were curled into a slight smile, and suddenly, Rosa understood the truth.

Her team had been put together five years ago, right after the Queen's return to Scotland.

But 'twas hubris to think she wouldn't have replicated their success.

There were other teams of Angels here in the palace...and she was looking at one right now.

She inclined her head briefly to Lady Isabel, whose smile grew. And then Cam was tugging her out the door.

In the corridor, he swung her into his arms and pulled her into a niche, away from any watching eyes. Rosa was happy to let him, even curling her arms around his neck to allow her to stretch closer to him.

"Well, my Angel?" he murmured, his lips inches from hers and his gaze intense. "How does it feel?"

"To be so thoroughly dismissed? Told to marry and *relax*?"

His lips twitched. "Aye. But I meant, how does it feel to be betrothed? To someone like me?"

Stretching on her toes, she brushed a kiss against his

mouth. "I will spend the rest of my life proving to ye what a wonderful man ye are, Cam Fraser. Have I told ye how handsome ye look in that plaid?"

"No' nearly often enough."

"Well, remind me to do it at least once a day." Another light kiss. "Around the same time I tell ye how worthy ye are."

He hummed. "Worthy? Of ye? Never, my love."

Her heart swelled. "Ye read to me, Cam. Ye are my other half. I cannae be without ye, and I'll tell ye such every day until we're auld and gray."

His hold on her tightened. "And I'll tell ye each and every day how much I love ye, my wee flower."

"*Decet*. Because every day I plan on telling ye how much I love *ye*."

They were both smiling when their lips met.

EPILOGUE

𝒥t was fitting she spend her wedding night at An Torr.

If only it hadn't taken so long to reach this night!

Mellie and Lachlan had been married a sennight before at Scone, where the King and Queen themselves had blessed the union happily.

Simone had been an ecstatic part of the ceremony, and Rosa suspected it was likely the lassie had had plans to be a part of her parents' evening as well, had Cam not interfered.

While Mellie and Lachlan had been able to retreat to their chambers at the palace in private—and undue haste, likely having to do with the heated glances they kept sending one another—Cam and Rosa had played with Simone.

And then, on the trip north to Loch Ness, the lassie had been attached to her Uncle Cam like some sort of ocean bivalve.

Cam didn't seem to mind, but he *had* sent a few heated glances of his own Rosa's way, in between his niece's attempts to get him to run footraces, go fishing, tell her about horse genitalia, explain the current political situation with England, and compare their accuracy throwing rocks.

Rosa found herself giggling more on that journey north than she ever had in the past. Simone was such a delightful, exasperating, curious, *exhausting* child, and Cam seemed to have infinite patience. She remembered what he'd said about wanting to help others, and knew he was right where he needed to be.

He'd also said he wanted bairns of his own.

Sitting atop her horse, Rosa's hand strayed to her abdomen.

Was it possible she was even now carrying Cam's longed-for bairn?

For years she'd counseled Mellie on carefully counting days to ensure she didn't conceive, but now she herself was in love, she realized *counting* didn't matter so much. When the opportunities arrived to find joy in Cam's arms, she never stopped to count.

And *gratias Deo* for that!

Over the last fortnight, the two of them had been blessed with much time alone, away from her duties. At the palace, they'd made love in her room, in secluded nooks in the garden, and once, in a niche along the corridor when they couldn't make it someplace private in time.

It was *glorious*.

Of course, there was less privacy here on the road, but Mellie and Lachlan seemed to find opportunities to sneak off often enough, now Lachlan's shoulder had healed.

Their arrival at An Torr was met with much celebrating and joy, especially once Lachlan announced Mellie was now his wife—and not just by the Queen's decree.

That eve at supper, he stood in front of his gathered clan and told of their wedding ceremony, which prompted many toasts. But when he had Cam stand, and he told the Frasers of his brother's return from the dead, his words were met with silence.

Rosa had stood beside him, with Simone holding his other hand, and had beamed with pride at the way he met those stares with acceptance. He knew who he was, and what he'd done...and now he was ready to build a better future.

It was Martin, the old seneschal, who stepped out of the crowd first. On creaking knees, he stopped near the dais and met Cam's gaze. "I remember ye, lad, and I am overjoyed to ken ye are safe and happy. Welcome home."

When he bowed, it seemed to trigger an eruption of cheers from the clan, each member anxious to greet Cam, to assure him of his welcome to An Torr.

Rosa *might've* gotten a little weepy, seeing Cam's incredulity and joy.

Today, their wedding had been no different. Lachlan and Mellie, as Laird and Lady Fraser, had hosted a grand event, and the entire clan had turned out in their finery to celebrate the two marriages.

Rosalind wished her own family could have been there to celebrate with her, but she and Cam still had a fortnight before they needed to return to Scone, and she had every intention of dragging him to Aberdeen. She'd already sent a missive ahead to warn her parents of her nuptials and knew Mother would be thrilled to welcome Cam—a man who could banter in Latin and who had read Marie de France's Lais—into the family.

Court and Ross—followed by his giant, shaggy hound, Honor—had been spending time with Ross's family, but had showed up at the wee chapel right on time. Rosa's friend was stoic as always throughout the ceremony, but gripped her betrothed's hand as if it were a lifeline, and she were dangling from a cliff.

Ross, of course, beamed throughout. That giant beast of

his even let loose a series of frantic barks—which sounded joyful—when the priest blessed their union.

The wedding feast was overwhelming, but Rosa found she didn't mind. There was one moment where she, Mellie and Court gathered near the castle's wall to observe Simone and the stable lads playing with Honor, each content to watch and enjoy this new life they were now a part of.

"Ye ken," Court said quietly, "everything's going to change now."

Rosa shook her head. "Nay. Mellie might be here most of the time, while ye and I and Ross and Cam are back in Scone, but that matters naught. We'll always be partners. A team."

"Aye," Mellie said with a smile. "We'll always be Angels."

As they grasped one another's forearms, the familiar and unbroken triangle—*Tri-Angel*, her mind whispered—of support and love, Rosa smiled into her teammates' eyes. She'd trusted these women with her life on more occasions than she could count. And now she was trusting her future to them as well.

"I love ye both," she whispered.

Mellie threw her arms around Rosa, making a noise somewhere between a laugh and a sob. "I love ye too, Rosa! And ye, Court," she cried, reaching out and pulling their recalcitrant friend into their hug.

Court's strong arms wrapped around both of them, cradling them and protecting them the way she always had, and she grunted slightly. "Aye, and I love ye both as well, but don' expect me to be telling ye more than once."

With that, Rosa and Mellie burst into laughter, and Rosa knew, no matter where they went or what the future held, they would always be a team.

Not long after, Ross arrived with a folded plaid and took Court's hand. She nodded her goodbyes, and the two of them went off into the failing evening light.

"I ken his family lives in Durris," Mellie murmured, "but kenning those two, they'd be just as happy to bed down beside the loch."

"I'll avoid the beach tonight then," Rosa quipped in return.

She needn't have worried. Once Cam managed to break away from his clan's well-wishes, he wasn't letting her go anywhere. Swinging her up into his arms, he grinned down at her.

"I'm taking ye to bed, *wife*. Any objections?"

Her fingers played with the hair at the base of his neck. "None whatsoever, husband."

They'd been given a guest chamber, which meant Cam didn't have to return to his childhood chamber.

When they'd first arrived at An Torr, she'd seen the tension and bitterness in his gaze as he'd parsed through the painful memories his former home held for him, before acceptance and hope took their place.

Now, however, he had only love in his eyes as he slowly undressed her.

Soon, she was standing nude in the center of their chamber, her hair loose down her back, and trying not to feel self-conscious.

The heat in his gaze soon warmed her enough to feel bold.

Placing her hands on her hips, she lifted her chin. "Like what ye see?"

Blowing out a breath, he raked his hand though his hair, then shook his head. "Rosa, I—I cannae…"

When he trailed off, she realized she was chewing on her lip. "Aye?" she prompted cautiously.

"When I look at ye, lass, I cannae believe my good fortune. I cannae believe someone like *ye* could love someone like *me*."

She decided she didn't need to be bold; she needed to be in his arms.

In a heartbeat, she was there, her cheek resting against his chest. "Believe it, Cam. I love ye, and I'll love ye forever."

His palms skimmed across her bare back, dropping to cup her arse and pull her against his hardness.

"Are ye sure, my wee flower?" he asked in a choked voice.

As promised, she'd told him every day of her love, but she didn't mind telling him again.

"Aye, my thief."

Stretching up on her toes, she kissed him, and continued kissing him until he was breathing as heavy as she was, until her leg was hooked around his thigh, until his thumb was teasing her nipple.

She kissed him until he *understood.*

"Ye stole my heart, Cam," she said, panting, when she pulled away. "How could I no' love ye?"

With a groan, he picked her up, whirled around, and reached the bed in two strides, where he unceremoniously dropped her. While he made short work of his clothing, she scooted under the coverlet.

She shouldn't have bothered though, because when he joined her, he just ripped the covering away, baring both of their bodies to the moonlight streaming in through the window.

"*God's Teeth*, lass. I have to have ye...*now*."

Eyeing the thick length of his manhood, jutting toward her as he knelt on the mattress, she hummed in agreement. Her core was already wet and pulsing for him.

"We can go slower next time, husband," she managed to say.

With a relieved sound, he dropped beside her, pulling her to him, until their limbs were wrapped as tightly as any knot.

Facing her, he held her gaze as he entered her, and at her whimper of pleasure, he growled.

She hooked her leg around his hip, giving him a better angle, as he reached between their joined bodies and began caressing the nub of her pleasure. His strokes became faster, each one accompanied with a panting sob from her, the spiraling joy building between them.

When it burst, she had to clamp her eyes shut tightly, lest the white lightening flashing behind her lids blind them both.

With a shuddering roar, he found his own release, spilling his seed against her womb.

Spent, facing one another, they held tightly as their breathing returned to normal. As he softened and slid from her wetness. As they slowly relaxed.

"Ye're mine now, Rosa," he finally whispered, his gray eyes so serious, so near hers. "My wife."

She shifted slightly, giving them each room, although still facing him. "Nay, husband. Ye are *mine*."

His fingers toyed with her hair. With a wry smile, he lifted a lock of it, brushing it against her bare shoulder.

"The first time I saw ye, my Angel, I loved yer hair. Remember that?"

She remembered him telling her to let her hair down because it would entice a man.

"It smelled of flowers," he whispered. "I remembered that smell, long after ye ran off. I took myself in hand, thinking of ye. Imagining ye wrapped around me exactly like this."

The confession made her feel...*powerful*. To know she'd influenced him so strongly, from their very first meeting.

He dragged the lock of hair against her skin. "I couldnae believe my good fortune when I found ye again."

"Ye thought me a whore," she pointed out.

"I thought ye a *nun* at that point."

Her smile bloomed. "And now?"

"Now…" His fingers replaced the hair, and he began caressing her skin. Down her arm, up her side. Across her breast, light touches on her neck and under her ear, which had her sighing in pleasure.

"Now, I ken ye are a scholar," he murmured. "A warrior. Ye are the most brilliant person I ken, and brave besides. Ye are—"

"Now I am a wife, Cam." She untangled her own hand enough to clasp his. Partly to stop his wonderfully distracting touches, partly to bring it to her lips to kiss his palm. "I am *yer* wife, and ye are my partner. Are ye ready to return to Scone and help me preserve the Crown? Ready to become an honorary Angel?"

The gleam in his eye turned wicked as her lips caressed his palm, then traveled to the inside of his wrist.

"Aye, *wife*," he growled.

When he flipped her onto her back, she squealed happily and wrapped her arms around his neck.

"Aye," he repeated, his breath feather-light against her breasts as he kissed his way between them. When he reached her belly and kept going, she understood his intention, and willingly spread her legs and arched her back.

When he reached the junction of her thighs, he planted a kiss atop the cluster of dark hairs there and looked up to meet her gaze. He was grinning, happiness in his eyes.

"I'll return to Scone with ye, my Angel, but…"

"But?" she prompted breathlessly, her core already *aching* for him.

And just before he lowered his lips to her, he winked. "But no' yet."

AUTHOR'S NOTE ON HISTORICAL ACCURACY

You made it! All the way to the end of *The Highland Angels* series! Huzzah!

Wait, Caroline. *Is* it the end? Or is there more coming? Better keep reading...

But first, let's talk some history. Actually, most of what I want to say has been covered already in earlier *Author's Notes:* kilts good, but historically inaccurate; Queen Elizabeth largely unrepresented in history books, but still cool to extrapolate about; Highland history complex.

Bam. Author's Note done.

Hahahaha, just kidding.

I *did* tell you all about Red Comyn's claim to the throne in a previous Author's Note—I hope you were paying attention! —and how his son died at Bannockburn. There were plenty of Scottish nobles who believed he had the stronger claim, but Robert was the one who ultimately took the throne (causing Red's death along the way, if not actually killing the man himself).

Even in 1320, a decade and a half after Robert became

King, he had to put up with conspiracies against him. The most famous one was the de Soules conspiracy (yep, which included Agnes, Countess of Strathearn, who was ultimately the one who ratted them all out in exchange for lenient sentencing). There's no reason to think William de Soules planned treason against King Robert in support of the Comyns, but because of his own power among the nobles, historians believe he hoped to take the crown for himself (or put Edward Balliol, son of the previous king—John, called *Toom Tabard* because his coat of arms was stripped when he surrendered to the English—on the throne instead).

Of course, the idea of Red Comyn having an illegitimate son, and that son somehow having a claim to the throne of Scotland, is completely made up. But…I mean…isn't that the point of fiction? Plus, I have a serious soft spot for Cam as a hero; he's such a hottie, but he's got a lot of childhood trauma and feelings he needs to parse through. Luckily, he's got a brilliant and compassionate woman to help!

Okay, in my last Author's Note, I talked about the history of Scone Abbey/Palace, and since it's relevant to this book, I'll reiterate. Most of what I wrote about in regards to that structure is completely made up, because the structure King Robert and Queen Elizabeth would've lived in before he built a home in Cardross was destroyed in the 16th century.

Still, it was loads of fun to make up bits about what a royal palace might've looked like, and of course the gardens were my favorite. Characters can get up to all sorts of *interesting* adventures in walled gardens, especially if there are secret doors and whatnot.

<waggles eyebrows>

Next up: fishing! Bet you never expected to read *that* line in an Author's Note. But we've already established that Simone and Mellie grew up fishing, so of course Simone and Cam had to have a scene together, fishing.

AUTHOR'S NOTE ON HISTORICAL ACCURACY

You know what's cool, though? Recreational fishing with a rod—Cam's claim that the value is in just sitting quietly and letting his thoughts wander—wasn't "popular" until later in history.

Oh, fishing poles have been around for thousands of years, but in many cases fishing quickly advanced to nets in order to gather more food (fish) faster. It wasn't until fishing became a sport (like what Cam is doing, when Simone joins him) that we have more records of pole fishing again.

Of course, just because it wasn't written down for a few hundred more years doesn't mean it wasn't happening. It was recreation, as opposed to food-gathering, and there's no reason to believe men and women *weren't* finding ways to relax and enjoy themselves long before someone thought to write a manual on the sport.

Speaking of manuals and stuff being written down, let's talk briefly about Manuscript Culture. This is just a fancy way to talk about the evolution of how we, as humans, share knowledge. First it was oral, then handwritten, then printed, and now it's electronic (like reading novels on your e-reader!).

Cam and Rosa's story takes place at an important point in European history, when books were becoming more accessible to more people. We imagine cold and dismal monasteries with lonely monks hunched over a calligraphed Bible page, but... Well, actually, that image is probably partly accurate.

But! But those monks weren't just copying the Bible, or religious text! In the medieval period, they were also copying books about plants and how to use them, or travel accounts from far-off lands. They were copying allegorical stories and epic poems.

And what's interesting is that it wasn't just monks doing the copying and sharing of written knowledge! In the larger cities, students and booksellers were also involved. In Paris, for instance, the wealthy elite could have their own library hand-copied for a fee.

The old term for this period was the Dark Ages, but it's been discarded because it's really not true. Information was being spread in all sorts of ways, including precious books, among all sorts of people. It wasn't just monks who were educated, as more and more people realized how big the world really was.

Speaking of which, just a quick mention of Algiers, where Rosa's grandfather was from. In the 13th and 14th centuries, there were plenty of merchants and travelers jaunting around the Mediterranean, North Africa, Italy, France, and Spain. Ibn Battuta got started shortly after this book takes place, and left his home in Tangier, Morocco, to travel over 117,000 km in his lifetime (Africa, Asia, India and China)... almost *ten times farther* than the Italian Marco Polo did (who was about a hundred years earlier).

Algiers was called *Jaza'ir Banī Mazghanna*, which means "The Islands of the Sons of Mazghanna". The Mazghanna were a confederation of tribes in North Africa, and the city was spread across the mainland and four islands. If you say the Arabic name "The Islands" aloud (*"al-Jazā'ir"*) you'll get an idea where the modern name "Algiers" comes from.

These cities in North Africa, Egypt and what is now the Middle East were some of the most advanced in the world. Not just in trade and power, but education and travel as well. There were public school systems and universities for both men and women long before such a thing caught on in Europe. In fact, the world's oldest continuously operating university (University of al-Qarawiyyin in Morocco) was founded in 859 *by a woman.*

That's...that's not really relevant at all to this book, except I think it's really cool. Also, I think it gives some background as to why Rosa's grandfather believed so strongly in educating his own daughter and granddaughters. Luckily, his son-in-law agreed, and Rosa was raised with access to an epic library.

Which leads me to my last note: *Lanval*. This is a *lay*, which is a type of narrative rhyming poem, usually with chivalric themes. The oldest surviving lais, including *Lanval*, were written by Marie de France.

Not much is known about Marie, other than hints we get from her famous poems. We don't even know if she was living in France when she wrote them, but since they were written in a French dialect and because of, you know, her name being *"de France"* and all, she's considered to be the first French female poet.

Her lais, including *Lanval*, were widely known, and I love the idea of the courtly love appealing to Rosa, while the naughty bits appealed to Cam. Okay, there weren't *actual* naughty bits.

In the story, Lanval is passed over for reward by King Arthur and while he's moping, is approached by the handmaidens of a fairy who wants him to become her "close friend" (winkwink), and will give him a bunch of awesome riches as long as he doesn't tell anyone about her. Queen Guinevere is impressed by Lanval's wealth, and comes on to him. When he turns her down, she tells Arthur Lanval tried to proposition *her*. Lanval says No Way, I Have A Hottie, and then in the climactic trial scene (spoiler alert!), his gorgeous fairy lover shows up to exonerate him.

Quite romantic, quite lovely, and yes, there's descriptions of naked beauty that teenaged Cam would like.

I owe a debt to Dr. Judith Shoaf at the University of Florida, who not only translated *Lanval* into English, complete with rhyming couplets, but who made it available to the public. Read the text I quoted from **here**.

AUTHOR'S NOTE ON HISTORICAL ACCURACY

Whew, this has been a long Author's Note. But you read all the way to the end (I hope you learned something!) and you deserve a reward.

I bet you're reeeeeally curious about what Isabel, Brigit and Avaline are doing hanging out with Charlotte Bruce, aren't you? Is it possible, as Court and Rosa have suspected, that there are *more* teams of Angels working for the Queen?

If you're ready to find out, you should check out **The Pirate's Angel**. Fans of Charlotte's twin brother from *The Bruce's Angel* are going to be thrilled to discover Tav is back, and you've been reading so much about Lady Isabel of Strathbogie, you're probably ready to meet her in person!

Keep reading to find out more about **The Pirate's Angel**!

But first, I want to extend a personal invitation to join my reader group on Facebook. This is a fun, supportive community where we chat about romance novels, history, cute critters, and crafts. If you'd like a behind-the-scenes look into my stories, and want to help name some of my characters (Gillepatric was named thanks to a contest I ran in my Cohort!), then please do come hang out with us in Caroline's Cohort!

And now for Tav and Isabel…

THE PIRATE'S ANGEL

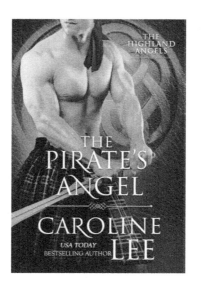

The Black Banner has been the scourge of the Western Isles for as long as there have been stories of fierce and bloodthirsty pirates.
But sometimes, a lady is desperate.

Tavish MacLeod is the latest in a long line to wear the black kilt, but life has gotten simpler since his twin sister became Scotland's spy-mistress. Sure, he's pillaging and burning less often, but thanks to his royal connections, he and his crew are handed all the juiciest opportunities to help Scotland's interests at sea. A royal privateer, so to speak.

Which will come in handy, since this latest mission isn't a mission at all.

Lady Isabel de Strathbogie is one of the Queen's Angels, an elite group of spies masquerading as ladies-in-waiting. She loves her place at court, secure in her knowledge of her skills and her place...until disaster strikes. When her young son is kidnapped along with one of the royal princesses, Isabel's desperation rivals the Queen's.
No one can know of this danger to the royal succession, which means Isabel is on her own for this mission... And she'll do anything to save her child, even if it means partnering with an uncouth barbarian in pirate garb. But no matter how he makes her pulse pound and her heart long for something long missing, she cannot allow Tavish MacLeod's allure to distract her.

Her ability to deny the yearning she feels in his arms might be her key to her son's life, and the very fate of Scotland itself. Is she strong enough?

Find out in ***The Pirate's Angel!***

OTHER BOOKS BY CAROLINE LEE

Want the scoop on new books? Join Caroline's Cohort, an exclusive reader group! Or sign up for my mailing list by texting "Caroline" to 42828 to get started!

The Highland Angels
The Bruce's Angel
The Highlander's Angel
The Laird's Angel
The Thief's Angel

Steamy Scottish Historicals:
The Sinclair Hound
The MacKenzie Regent
The Sutherland Devil
The MacLeod Pirate

Sensual Historical Westerns:
Black Aces (3 books)
Sunset Valley (3 books)
Everland Ever After (10 books)

The Sweet Cheyenne Quartet (6 books)

Sweet Contemporary Westerns
Quinn Valley Ranch (5 books)
River's End Ranch (13 books)

Click **here** to find a complete list of Caroline's books.

*Sign up for Caroline's Newsletter to receive exclusive content and freebies, as well as first dibs on her books! Or if newsletters aren't your thing, follow her on **Bookbub** for a quick, concise new release alert every time she publishes a book!*

Made in the USA
Coppell, TX
23 September 2021